7PM

6 Tales of Sex, Murder, and Revenge

CHRIS HEINICKE

Table of Contents

*To my dear wife, Glenda—whose love, support, and
belief in me helped make this novel possible.*

BRITTANY

CHAPTER 1

I REMEMBER THE first time I slit someone's throat, a merciful action following the process of slicing off his scrotum and making him swallow his own testicles. But he deserved it, and I mean, really fucking deserved it. It was the first kill of many, but still the one I enjoyed the most.

Ever since my junkie mum first brought him into the house not long after my fourteenth birthday, Russell decided my body existed solely for his own perverted amusement. It didn't surprise me, though. The first time he set his beady little grey eyes on me, I shivered as he absorbed every inch of me in one sweeping gaze. The way he smirked, I may as well have been naked.

Before then, I already hated my mother for so many reasons. The selfish bitch could never find it in herself to spare a single dollar for me to go on any school excursions, swimming lessons, or even for food on some days. But she always had money for drugs. She always had time for whoever wanted to put their dick in her, but my presence always served as an inconvenience. It all made sense the day Grandma told me the only reason I existed was her daughter couldn't stay sober enough to leave the house and get an abortion.

I wished Grandma were still alive. Before she died, I spent most of the first ten years of my life with her. An excellent cook, generous with her cuddles, and always telling me great stories, Grandma seemed able to do anything, the lone exception being able to help her own daughter beat her addictions.

At first, I felt anger at Grandma for dying, therefore forcing me to live with my mother full time again. The truth was, I missed her and didn't know how my life could go on without her. I never knew my real father, but I had been told he travelled from city to city playing in whatever pub or club would have him. Even with the amount of time and energy spent trying to find a clue to his existence and whereabouts, I couldn't find the smallest detail about him, not even a name.

So, for the years after, I kept my mother's house going, stealing money from her purse when I could so I could buy food. Most days she looked at me as if I were a stranger, and I looked at her with a mixture of pity and hate. But she was my mother, and I would take care of her for as long as needed.

Every week a new man frequented our house. Some were kind enough to throw me some money to allow them some alone time with my mum while others wouldn't even acknowledge my existence. But, one day, it all changed forever when 'HE' came to our house for the first time and stayed until he was taken away in a body bag.

The dark times began the first time he walked into the bathroom without knocking and saw me in the shower. I'll never forget the way he exposed his rotten teeth as he looked up and down at my barely formed breasts and the area between my legs he would soon invade uninvited. Even though I quickly grabbed a towel tc cover myself, the damage had already been done.

Just two nights had passed when a peaceful night's slumber became interrupted with a spider-like movement of calloused hands trickling along my legs all the way up to my most intimate place. My body tightened as the offending fat finger was shoved in and out, unable to move while my mind failed to wake my body from shutdown mode. All I could do was cry all night, even hours after he ceased his perverted actions. I avoided the wet patch on the sheets he created from rubbing his cock while he fingered me, waiting until morning to show my mother what he did.

When your own mother refuses to protect you from the ugliness of the world, a child with no one else in his or her life needs to learn to be strong or find some other coping mechanism. Russell was too big to fight off, even with my height of nearly six foot at just fourteen. He stood a few inches taller than I did, and about three times wider. Just two nights after the first time he molested me, he stole something from me I could never get back, the one thing I wished to share with a special guy one day.

I screamed and cried as he put his weight on me and thrust himself in and out, over and over and over. When he finished with me, I curled into a ball and cried hysterically, my mother not once coming to check on me. Feeling dirty and sore in nearly every part of my body, I prayed for death to take me away from this before the sun rose again.

But the reaper never came, nor did he the next night or the night after. Every night was the same. When my period finally came, I felt relieved I wasn't carrying some unwanted devil spawn inside me, at least—and I hoped the raping would stop for a few days.

I could never have been more wrong. He simply

turned me over and took me up the ass, a much more painful experience.

I had so few friends at school, but I soon learned to use my assets to get the type of attention I attempted to use to numb myself from what Russel was doing to me. I had a pretty face, full of innocence and framed with long and silky dark brown hair. My legs went from the ground all the way up to my little round ass, the length of my legs the main contributor to my height.

It wasn't hard to get the boys my age to have sex with me. I never received a lot of enjoyment from the experiences, but at least, I was able to fuck people my own age. Some good-looking types, some not so great, but at least, I was able to choose with them. Within months, I had slept with every boy in my class but two, the gay boy, David, and the quiet, shy boy, Billy.

I knew Billy liked me. In fact, he seemed to be the only friend I had left after going into full-on slut mode. He actually asked me how I was, wanted to know things about me, and what I wanted to do once school finished, and we were to make our way in the world. I had never known anyone sweeter, apart from Grandma, and not once did he pass judgement on me. We hung out a lot and would visit a new café every week. He was smart and funny, and never attempted to get into my pants.

"One day, Billy, I hope you find a sweet girl who deserves you," I once said to him. It couldn't be me—the dirty slut who had a secret home life she couldn't tell anyone about. But as fucked up as it was, I didn't want to get family services involved and find myself in foster care, locked away in a house thousands of miles away with annoying families. Or another pervert wanting me to call him Dad.

So I stayed and let Russell tear my soul away piece by piece and continued my nymphomaniac lifestyle with the boys my age, as well as some a year or two below and above my age. Sex meant nothing to me. I endured it from one creep and used it to try to feel some sort of love from others, even if just for a few minutes. Numb inside, the only thing keeping me going was the need to get good grades, score a scholarship, and get the hell out of this shithole town.

The day came when I graduated high school and waited impatiently for a letter of acceptance to university. Billy called to say he had been accepted into some type of scientific course, not surprising considering how smart he was. I told him to come over and wait with me for the postman to come.

Not less than five minutes later, he arrived, and we sat and talked on the front porch for an hour until the letter arrived. Billy looked over my shoulder as my nerves took over, and I fumbled through the process. To this day, I still remember the moment I read the words, 'your application has been successful.' The tears flowed fast and free, and Billy wrapped me in his arms for a moment, reassuring me I had one real friend in this world. I looked into his eyes, catching a glimmer of something I never saw before. I nodded at him. His head moved closer to mine, and without putting any thought into it, I closed my eyes and waited for his mouth to reach mine.

"What the fuck's going on here?" Russell's feet thumped through the house, his gruff voice slurring probably due to the effects of another booze-fuelled morning.

Billy relaxed his embrace and stared back at Russell, "Karla's going to college, away from this God-awful place."

Russell stared directly into my eyes, his gaze visually raping me. He dropped the beer bottle and stomped towards Billy. I could just tell this wasn't going to end nicely. "She's not going anywhere while I'm in charge of this house."

Slowly backing away, Billy didn't stand a chance. The punches flew like a hurricane from Russell's beer-filled temper, hitting his target twice in the face and kicking him in the ribs repeatedly as the teenager hit the ground. I jumped on Russell's back and started smacking him with my free hand, my efforts in vain, as he flipped me over his head.

Landing in a pile next to Billy, I stared at this beast hovering above us. Was there anything this perverted prick wouldn't do to hurt someone?

"I'm going to kill your boyfriend here if he ever speaks to me again." Russell's nostrils flared. I've seen him angry before but nothing like this day.

"Just leave him alone, Russell. I'll stay. I'll stay and do whatever you want me to if you promise not to hurt Billy anymore." Tears moistened my cheeks. I knew what I had signed up for if I didn't do something drastic.

"Don't do it, he'll destroy you. Run away, run away now, and don't ever come back to this place," Billy struggled to smile through his injuries.

"I warned you not to speak," Russell said and pulled out a gun. "Say your prayers, little boy," he said as he lined up his target.

"Russell," I yelled, taking my singlet top off, "let him go, and we'll go inside."

He turned to face me, licking his lips at the sight of me in my lacy bra and denim shorts. I didn't need to see Billy's face to know of his disappointment. But I knew Russell would kill him if I didn't distract him.

"You better be off my lawn before I finish fucking your girlfriend, boy," Russell yelled. He grabbed my ass, and I felt my whole body tense up. Mind you, hardly a day went by when he didn't invade my body by some method. His hand travelled to the front of my shorts while we walked, pulling down my zipper and undoing the button with one hand.

I stopped walking and turned to him. "Why don't you go lie on the bed and get ready for me." My hand slid into his jeans, and I cupped his cock and balls in my hand. "I've got a surprise for you."

He peeled away from me and slid his shirt over his head, and then turned back to me. "You better hurry up, girl."

I smiled back and took my shorts off while he watched. I unclipped my bra and saw his leering eyes wash over my small breasts, and then he walked away to the bedroom. I could hear my mother snoring from somewhere, probably from the spare room where she liked to shoot up. I took some long deep breaths and searched through the kitchen drawers for what I needed.

"Where the fuck are you, girl?" I heard the monster's voice.

A few seconds later, I went into the bedroom he shared with my mother and saw him lying on the bed wearing only his underwear. I walked over to him, exaggerating each step taken, wearing only a white lace G-string. "Russell, let's try something new." I showed him the lengths of rope.

"What the fuck do you think you're gonna do with them?"

"Wouldn't you like me to be in charge for once? I thought I could tie you up and ride you." To emphasise my point, I pulled my panties down, letting him see me completely nude. This was my one chance.

"Oh, fuck, you've never done this for me before, why today?"

I couldn't blame him for his suspicion. Even though

after the first couple of months I stopped struggling, I never initiated a sex act previously. "Please, take your undies off, Russell."

His creepy smile took over his face, and I almost pitied him as I saw how foul his remaining teeth were. I looked at his exposed cock, the instrument of evil having ruined my life for so many years, and probably the cause of my fucked up mind.

"Russell, I need you to lie flat on your back and stretch out your arms and legs."

My heart raced as he did what I asked. I started with his hands, tying a knot around each wrist and then around the legs of the bed, as learned from my Grandmother, who taught me things I didn't get to learn in the local youth club. He chuckled away, and I felt his eyes on my body the whole time.

I had to keep it together. I would only get one chance at this.

"Fuck, baby girl, I don't think I've ever felt so hard."

I grabbed his erection in one hand. "Nice, Russell." I pumped it a couple of times and then released it. "You're not quite ready for me yet." I looked at his feet.

Russell sniggered as I tied a rope around each ankle, and then tied the other end of each to the other bed legs. Looking like a starfish, I knew he was ready for me.

"Well, come on, get on board. I've never had you on top before."

With good reason, I think to myself. I climbed on top of the bed and inched closer to him, moving like a cat. I parked myself a few inches from the horrid erect thing that haunted me for years and grabbed his balls with one hand, massaging them gently.

"Just fucking get on top, you bitch," Russell almost yelled.

"I need to cut something first." I leaned all the way to the right, reaching under the mattress and fumbled until my fingers located the treasure they searched for...

Russell's eyes lit up, and for the first time ever, I could actually see fear in them. My right fist holding a switchblade I had hidden beneath the mattress a few weeks ago, I sliced at what my left hand was gripping.

He screamed as his scrotum became separated from him, the fluids soaking the sheet beneath him.

There was no way my mother could sleep through this ruckus. I needed to be quick. My left hand wiggled inside the detached hairy sack, and my fingers found his testicles. I closed my fist around one, and with a bit of effort, I pulled it free. I repeated the process for the other testicle, and I held both in front of his face.

Russell couldn't put any words together. I couldn't even imagine the agony he was enduring, but I could tell by the fact I was getting wet that at least one of us was enjoying it. I placed his two misplaced testicles near his mouth. "I want you to eat them, Russell."

He cried, but managed to spit out a couple of words. "Fuck you."

"If you don't eat them, I'll cut your cock off."

"You fucking sick—" His opened mouth gave me all the time I needed to place his own balls into it. I almost felt sick as he involuntarily took a swallow and coughed as the unwanted morsels travelled down his throat.

I didn't want to risk him vomiting on me, so I got off the bed and put my knife to his neck. I then pushed with all my strength until the whole blade went in. His blood poured out like water through a whale's spout. I slid the knife across, and the wound grew to a couple of inches long before my mother entered the room.

"Oh, my God," she yelled. I smiled back at her.

"I don't want to hurt you, Mum," I said to her as I

withdrew the knife from the bleeding throat of Russell. I could only assume he was dead by then as I watched my mother charge towards me.

I held my knife ready in case I had to defend myself. Running the few feet to get to me, her drug-fuelled body was put down as the noise of a few shots from a cop's pistol hit her in the back.

She fell face first. It was then I saw the handsome cop for the first time. He was telling me to put the knife down, and I obeyed without hesitation, my whole body shaking.

I began to cry as the officer put his gun back in his holster and picked up a blanket, placing it on my shoulders. Covering myself, I could only imagine what would happen next. I had been caught red-handed at a murder scene with the murder weapon in my hand.

"It's going to be okay, Brittany," he told me.

I whimpered, "My name's Karla."

"Not anymore," he placed the knife in my dead mother's hand, and then slung me over his shoulder and carried me outside to the police car parked in the driveway.

Chapter 2

THE LAST THING I remembered was being placed in the back of Ed's police car and given a can of cola to drink. I had no idea how long I had been asleep, but when I woke, I found myself in a bed wearing a pair of silk pyjamas. Aside from the bed, the only furniture in the room was a built-in wardrobe and an oval mirror hanging on the wall. I crawled out of bed noticing the window to my left and went to have a look to see what was outside.

An old white stone building ran parallel about twenty feet away from the one I was in, with healthy green lawn separating them. I couldn't see a person in sight, nor hear a single sound, and with no clock in the room or my mobile phone in possession, I could only take a guess what the time might be.

Where the fuck was I, and who dressed me for bed when I was passed out? My body didn't feel violated, so I was thankful for the fact no one took advantage of me.

A knock on the door ripped my mind from its thoughts. "Who is it?" I called out.

"Ed, the policeman who took you away."

I sighed. "Come in."

The dark haired cop smiled at me as he opened the door, and I couldn't decide if he looked more handsome in his police uniform or the singlet top and shorts. The glistening glow of sweat on his face and arms gave me the impression he'd been on a run.

"Where have you taken me?" I asked him, looking at his muscular thighs. My eyes moved up and centred on the area I felt guilty for glancing at.

"This is your new home—well, for the duration of your training, anyway," he said while taking a few steps towards me.

"Training?"

He took a seat on my bed and patted a spot next to him. Like an obedient puppy, I obeyed his visual command and walked right up to him, placing my ass so close to him, we almost touched. He must have been about ten years older than I was, but the way he made my body tingle, I didn't care.

"You're a killer, Brittany. You should use your natural killing instincts and work for us."

"Why do you call me Brittany?"

"It's your name from now on. As far as the authorities are concerned, Karla Young was kidnapped after her mother and step-dad were killed in drug-related multiple homicides. You start your new life today."

"What if I don't want to be a killer?"

"You already are. The way you murdered your step-dad shows premeditation and a lust for blood. You're the rare type who fits our mould." He looked me up and down. "And you're hotter than wasabi-laced chili."

I looked down and blushed. I didn't care how sweaty he was or how grubby I felt. My pussy begged for him to fill me.

"You need to shower and change into some fresh

clothes. Looking at you, it might be tricky to find clothes that fit your height until we can get to a shop. Come with me." He stood reaching for my hand.

I accepted. Getting to my feet, disappointment soon hit the moment he released his grip. As I followed, my eyes absorbed the tight ass of his, and I fantasised of the idea of holding two handfuls of his delicious flesh in my fingers as he lay on top of me, pumping my body hard on the bed in my room.

What the hell was I thinking? I had killed a man only a day before and saw my mother shot dead, and now I found myself thinking about having sex with a much older man who I barely knew. But looking inside myself, I felt neither guilt nor remorse.

I had slipped from the leash of the monster my life had been. No more rape, no more heroin needles on the bathroom floor, and no more of the school where I willingly wore the label of a class slut with no friends.

But I had something better than popularity. I had Billy, the one person in the world who didn't hang out with me because he wanted something from me. I sure as hell hoped he was okay.

We walked down a long corridor, past many closed doors and the cement cold on my feet. For such a vast place, I found it weird we had yet to see another person. Exiting the building, we travelled a short distance of low-cut lawn leading to another building.

Stopping at a closed door, Ed smiled at me and opened it. "I hope you're not shy." Hearing the sound of water running, I peered inside. I saw a male and a female showering side by side in a communal bathroom, as naked as the day they were born. I guessed their ages to be around mine—give or take a couple of years. As their eyes turned to me, I could see the two of them smiling.

"This is Faith and Oliver, the latter being the one with that big fucking snake between his legs," Ed said.

Seeing what he meant, I thought to myself there was no way Oliver would put the whole of his huge cock in me. Just the thought of it made my pelvis ache. When I looked back at Ed, he had already taken his shirt off and prepared to pull his shorts down. A voice told me I shouldn't be peeking, but if he was getting his cock out, I'm not missing out on seeing it.

"Don't be shy, girl. We do this every day. There are no secrets at boot camp," Oliver said, looking me up and down.

Ed was fully naked and showering next to the well-hung boy, and I could not help but admire the physical greatness of both of the male specimens near me. Faith showered without paying attention to any of them, and I would guess she had seen this every day for some time. Only slightly shorter than me, her curves were more pronounced than mine, and I couldn't help but wish for tits like hers

"Are you going to stare at our bodies all morning, or are you going to have a wash?" Faith asked. I started thinking she wasn't happy about not being the only female in the room any longer.

I turned my back to them and lifted my silk top up and over my head, tossing it to a nearby shelf. My shorts were next, and I proceeded to stand under a shower head fully naked, turning the taps to get the right temperature.

Ed stood next to me, took a quick look at my body before going back to washing himself. I managed to resist my desire of going over to rub soap on his tattooed and muscled body. I wished for some alone time in the shower to relieve myself of the frustration.

"So what's happening today?" Oliver asked.

"We teach the new chick the basics," Ed answered, taking a few steps toward Oliver. "You better go get ready," he said grabbing Oliver's face and pulling it to his own, giving him a kiss on the mouth.

The bar of soap slipped from my hands. Two fantastic looking male specimens—I was left thinking they were gay. Just my luck. Oliver turned his taps off and walked away to grab a towel while Ed smirked in my direction, reading my face. Looking at my shock, Faith cut the water flow from her showerhead and walked in my direction, smacking Ed on the ass while walking past him.

"No reason for you to miss out," she said. Getting closer to me, I couldn't help but admire how beautiful her body was.

So perfect.

"Don't be shy, Brittany," Faith smiled at me from less than a foot away. Her face moved toward mine, eyes closed and her mouth opening. My heart rate accelerated while goose bumps took up temporary residence on my skin as our lips touched. Her mouth soft as mine, our tongues soon made contact and frolicked in a crazed wrestling match.

"I'll leave you ladies in peace." I heard Ed's voice in the background as a pair of smooth skinned hands travelled down the sides of my body to the cheeks of my ass, pulling me in close to the person whom they belonged to.

Her breasts touched my mine, and even under the flowing water, I could feel my wetness grow as our pelvises touched. "Relax," Faith whispered while pulling her face away from mine, and then lowered it gradually until her mouth was positioned between my legs. I spread them wide in order to receive her more than competent tongue to give me the pleasure that no male had ever been able to deliver previously.

******

AN HOUR LATER, I heard a knock on my door, and a blonde woman, who I guessed to look about ten years older than me, stood in the doorway. The black T-shirt and matching yoga pants fit her snug, and I assumed it must be time for some type of exercise, and hoped for more of a clue as to what the hell was going on.

Most people in my situation would probably find themselves concerned with what was happening, but how many have come from a situation as I have? The stranger at my door breaks the ice. "I'm Emily, and I'll be training you in hand to hand combat. Follow me, Brittany."

Before I could answer, she turned her back. Dressed in the clothes I changed into after the memorable shower I had with Faith, I followed closely behind. "So what exactly is this place, Emily? Why me?"

"I'm not in charge, Brit, but I can tell you this facility is designed to train you into a deadly weapon. I'm what is known as a Praying Mantassassin. You've heard what the Praying Mantis does?"

"Basic high school biology, they fuck their mate, and then bite their head off and eat them."

"Yes, the basic concept of what we do here, minus the eating part. We're hired by everyone from government agencies to pissed-off spouses, anyone who can afford our services to take out someone they want to have taken out. We don't ask questions why, we don't veer from the way they want us to do the kill, and we most certainly don't ask them their personal details. You could say we offer a prostitution service with a very unhappy ending."

Unable to find any suitable words, I wondered what the hell I should say? This wasn't anything I ever wished for, but the thought of it did strike up a degree of excitement. I knew by the joy I felt at killing Russell, I could totally do it. "Sounds like fun."

Emily stopped dead in her tracks and pointed a finger in my face. "You don't get to say it's fun until you've done your first kill. You might have killed your stepdad, but many targets will be much better opponents, hence why we often kill after sex when people are most vulnerable and relaxed."

"So I have to fuck old men, too?"

"If the target is an old man, yes. Your target might even be a woman, but from what I have heard about your shower incident this morning, I can't see you having a problem with that." I noticed her smirk while saying the last sentence.

I don't do well hiding the blushing of my cheeks.

"It's okay. We're a little bisexual here, even the stud muffin, Ed. It opens up the possible jobs you can be hired for if you are inclined that way. Hope those shoes fit you well."

The sneakers were a size nine and a nice fit while the denim shorts were so small, they should be referred to as denim undies rather than shorts. And the singlet top only sat a couple of inches below my boobs. I've never been shy of showing this much skin. I just hoped I could do the training they expected me to do dressed like this.

******

EMILY AND I arrived at the exercise grounds, a flat area of short green lawn already occupied by Faith and Oliver and a tall, bald-headed man who looked like he could crack coconuts on his forehead. "Who the fuck is that?" I asked.

"Stop your quivering... girl. That man is the one who will be the difference between life and death, so listen to him, watch him, and for fuck's sake, don't piss him off."

I kept my mouth closed for the remainder of the walk. The air chilling my exposed skin, I looked at Faith and Oliver alternating between sets of push-ups and ab crunches. I knew the cool air wouldn't affect me for long.

"On the ground now," the man yelled as soon as got in line with the other two.

I almost smacked the ground when getting on all fours, and I could hear Faith chuckle next to me. All the signs pointed to it being one shit day.

"Brit, why haven't you started? That's an extra twenty push-ups. Get going NOW!"

I had always hated push-ups and never been any good at them, and with my build, I was never sure I would ever be any good. I spread my fingers as I got into position and my lowered my body. The pain soon travelled along the nerves of my spindly arms at the same time I was thrusting against gravity to get my ass high in the air.

"One. Thirty-nine to go. Come on, princess. Get moving." The man's voice boomed through the air, and all I wanted to do was to get up and slap him.

Lowering myself again, I repeated the process. Like a fire burning beneath my skin, I agonised through the second push-up and wondered how the hell I could find another thirty-eight left in me.

But I pushed on, and upon the instructor yelling out five, I could see four people with eyes directly on me. Squeezing my eyes shut, I centred my thoughts on the minute strength remaining inside me, and my brain commanding the aches in my body to leave and allow me to continue unimpeded until I reached my quota.

Hearing the voices of Faith and Oliver and Emily cheer, I allowed myself to collapse after the last push up. A wave of relief washed over me, only to be cut short when the booming voice cut through the excitement. "Another twenty."

I wanted to cry but letting him get the better of me wasn't something I would allow. As sure as I was that the pain would cripple me later that day, I decided to just do as he commanded and gain his respect as well as everyone else there. Of course, it would only happen if my jelly arms could push through.

"The rest of you get on the ground and give me twenty, even you Em," the man said, the one referred to as the drill sergeant.

The other three faced the challenge and knocked it over within the same couple of minutes it took me to do the next single push-up. As sweat flowed from my brow into my eye, the salty liquid stung and blurred my vision while my muscles burned.

"Nineteen to go, princess. Move it."

I pressed on through my pain, one by one, I gained on the target, and I can't contemplate how I was able to do this with my sapped energy. Something within pushed me to keep going, like a fire continuing to receive fresh fuel to burn. I didn't know how many I had left to complete, but a voice of authority kept me updated.

"Five."

I can do this. My arms now shook as I exerted any pressure upon them, but I had exceeded my personal expectations by so much already. I faced adversity before, I had overcome many worse life experiences, and so what were a few more push-ups?

"Four."

Through my peripherals, I became aware of the others standing around me. One by one, they chanted my name until their voices gathered in unison, giving me the type of boost normally reserved for sporting teams with official cheer squads. I'd never been high before, but that moment gave me some kind of incredible natural high.

"Three."

I no longer felt like I was inside my own body. I felt like I evolved into a motherfucking superhero able to put my body through anything with not a single barrier in sight.

"Two, one, none."

I don't remember those last three, but when DS yelled none, I allowed my body to sink to the ground, and then I smiled at what I achieved. Faith was the first to come over, putting an arm around me and kissing the top of my head.

"Get back to your spots," DS yelled.

Those words made everyone move, but before leaving me, Faith whispered in my ear, "I'm gonna spoil you tonight."

I didn't know if I'd have the energy to do anything but lay back and let her give me oral pleasure like she did in the shower. I rolled over onto my back.

"Five laps, princess." DS pointed to the nearby sports oval.

"You've got to be kidding me."

"I don't joke around. Now get up and run around that oval," he said looking down at me, as I remained laying.

"This will hurt tomorrow, and I'll blame you," I held back the tears.

"I'm counting on it."

******

AFTER THE FIRST day of exercising and learning hand-to-hand combat, I could barely lift my utensils to my mouth during dinner at the mess hall. I thought if I had to do that every day, I couldn't fathom how I could survive a week.

"It gets easier," Oliver said from across the table.

"Yes, it does. I've been here a month and already in the swing of how things work. Tomorrow, we should be at the shooting range if the routine is consistent," Faith said.

She's so beautiful. I'd never found myself attracted to someone of the same sex before, but the way she satisfied me opened a whole new world no man had ever shown me before.

"I'm so tired. I'm going to bed early tonight." I looked into the eyes of Faith sitting next to me and hoped she caught my meaning.

"I'll call into your room before I go crash. Massage your muscles so you are ready for tomorrow. Those pistols can be heavy if your body's tired." Faith stood and took her dirty plates away.

Oliver leaned in close. "Don't get too close to her. Sure, have your fun, but don't get too attached to anyone here. We're to be trained as killers, and we need to have emotions like DS."

"Okay, I'll take that into consideration," I said.

"I'd love to come by your room one night, help you relax."

I didn't know how to answer him, so just nodded. All I wanted was to lie on my bed with Faith's tongue between my legs again. Why don't guys ever want to do that for us? We're expected to put their cocks in our mouths and make them come, but why are they never keen to return the favour? "Maybe you should," I said, giving him a wink.

I cleared my plates and thought about my informal invitation to the well-hung boy. I decided should I ever find myself in bed with him I'd need a decent tube of lube.

I pondered the path ahead for me while walking back to my room, knowing I would be trained how to take lives in various ways. I questioned if I could do it again.

The night air cool, I concluded the short journey to my room with a spring in my step as my eyes caught the heavenly outline of Faith's body standing outside the accommodation building. I ran to her, admiring her form in the little shorts and singlet top.

"I thought you were never coming," she said to me, looking me up and down.

I said nothing. Instead, I grabbed her face in my hands and kissed her until I almost ran out of breath. I never thought I'd fall in lust with a chick, but the feel of soft feminine skin against my own and those sweet lips and big tits took me on a sexual journey like none I had ever experienced prior to my stay at this place.

"You keep that up, Faith and I might be coming before you know it."

"Hmm, all ready to go, and it's not even seven p.m. You better try and return the favour, though."

I ran my hand from her face down to the front of her shorts, forcing it inside her panties and sliding my middle finger between her legs. She was moist already, and as she reached for the moistness between my legs, we heard a voice nearby.

"Girls, take it to your room."

We turned to see the perpetrator, my eyes lighting up when I saw it was Ed. "You should come and join us, officer." I smiled at him.

"As much as I'd like to, I have to go do something. Just make sure you get a good sleep. You're learning weapons tomorrow."

"Will you be there?" I asked.

He looked me up and down. "I'll be interested to see what you're capable of."

With that comment, he turned and disappeared into the night. I looked back in Faith's eyes. "Like he said, let's take it to our room."

******

WEAPONS TRAINING WOULD have to have been my favourite part of the training, and my love for using knives only grew. I learned to shoot well in a short time too, holding a big piece of steel and putting holes in targets shaped as men came easily to me as I imagined them having Russell's head, or even some of the boys I fucked in high school. Of course, DS stood over us telling us a better way to grip a pistol or thrust a blade, but over time, a feeling inside of me grew of him holding a special affection for me, which he did his best to hide.

Faith and I grew closer, and I felt like I'd fallen in love for the first time ever. Some nights we slept in her room, some nights mine, and on the odd occasion, we slept under a blanket beneath the starry skies. Oliver continued to hit on us on an individual basis, but many nights he reportedly received a visit from Emily, who quietly told me he was the owner of the biggest cock she had ever had inside her. After several weeks, I had almost forgotten what having sex with a man was like, and I didn't miss it.

"You know you'll have to go back to having sex with men when we're on assignments," Faith told me one night as we lay beneath a blanket near the edge of the property we were living on. An electrified fence with spiralled barbed wire at the top kept anyone in and everyone out, not as if I had any idea where we were anyway. And why would I have wanted to leave? For the first time ever in my life, I felt safe, satisfied sexually on a regular basis, hanging out with some cool people and learning to kill and getting super fit in the process.

Life was good.

"What about tomorrow? How will you go when we have our test assignment?" Faith asked me. She leaned above me, her breasts against mine as she stroked my hair.

"I'll be okay. I'll think of you when I fuck the person they send me, and when it comes to the killing, I'll think of Russell."

"I love you, Brittany." She kissed me and almost consumed my lips in the process. When she withdrew, a tear abseiled her face, and it felt like a dagger point pressing against me about to pierce my skin.

I ran a hand through her hair and smiled. "I love you, too."

Sitting up straight, her voice now cowered into a whisper, "Let's run away together, just you and me. We know how to defend ourselves now, how to kill with our bare hands if we have to. We can go away, far away and go see the world. You... and me."

I wanted to cry, but I had to be strong. The romance of the idea to run away and travel had appeal, but the day I killed Russell gave me a taste for blood. "We have a job to do. Let's do it for a while at least, save some money, and then think about what you said."

"I'm scared, Brit." The tears flowed freely. I sat up

and hugged her tight, and remained holding her while she cried and cried. I had no idea how much time passed, but eventually, we lay down again with her head on my chest, and at some stage, we fell asleep.

******

"RISE AND SHINE, sluts," a female voice screamed at us.

I opened my eyes and the sun's light smacked me and caused me to blink. I had never seen this woman before, this bald headed voluptuous woman, who couldn't even be five foot tall at a guess. Not many women can rock the bald look, but this woman was immaculate.

No point trying to cover up. The blanket only covered us from the waist down as we slept and pretty much everyone we had met at the compound had seen us naked anyway. We grabbed our clothes and put them on as quickly as naughty schoolgirls trying to dress when they heard their parents open the front door of the house.

"Come with me," she said as we put our last items of clothing on. For such a short woman, she carried herself with speedy legs.

"Where are we going?" Faith asked.

The woman stopped dead in her tracks, spinning on her heel to face us. "You should know not to ask questions."

The remainder of the walk to our destination remained silent apart from the sounds of nature, and when we ceased our journey, we saw a white picket fence surrounding a quaint looking country cottage in the middle of a green paddock. Why had we never seen this little place before?

"Your final test before your first assignment. I'll be doing a demonstration, hope you enjoy." For the first time since we had met her, she smiled. Opening the front door, we followed her to a room on the left of the hallway. Wigs of many colours sat upon mannequin heads on a dresser while numerous dresses hung on rails stretching from wall to wall.

"Oh, my God," Faith said, taking in the sights of dozens of high heeled shoes supported on racks.

The woman headed straight for a black bob wig, placing it on her head, opening a drawer and putting on a pair of opal blue contact lenses. Guiding us down the hallway, she sent us to a narrow room, shutting the door behind us and locking it. With barely any room to turn around, we couldn't help but look into the bedroom through the two-way mirror taking up nearly the whole wall. A man looking to be in his forties laid on a king sized bed wearing nothing but a pair of silk boxer shorts.

"I feel kind of like a voyeur watching this." Faith smiled while watching the man lay on the bed. All I could think about was Russell's hairy frame and his sneer that used to make my skin crawl. It's obvious this man on the bed would meet a similar fate as the woman entered the room wearing a red silk dress hugging her every curve.

The man pointed to a pile of notes on a bedside table.

"How do you suppose he got here?" I asked Faith.

Shrugging her shoulders, she kept her eyes glued to the scene playing out in front of us, as the woman crawled over the end of the bed and reached for the man's only item of clothing. Pulling them down off his hips, she glided them over his legs and feet before throwing them over her shoulder. The man's excitement showed as she lifted her own lone item of clothing over her head, her natural gigantic breasts bouncing while leaning over him and guiding his stiff cock inside her. Upon his successful entry, the woman began to bounce up and down while straddling him.

"Those things will hit her in the eye if she bounces any harder." Faith giggled.

I could barely believe it as they got straight into it without any sort of foreplay or the use of a condom. Unless she knew him already...

The flexibility of the woman was astonishing. She bent backwards to reach something on the floor under the bed, and at the same time, I could see from the look on the man's face he must have been close to coming. Within a few seconds, the woman returned upright to her straddling position, and I could see the smile on her face as the man relaxed and folded his arms behind his head. His smile soon changed to panic as he noticed what she held in her left hand.

The knife struck once, then twice and then repeatedly through the man's chest, blood squirting and pouring out in all directions. He didn't have a hope.

"Oh, my God," Faith said as the face of the man turned our way, his dead eyes seeming to stare straight into our own. "He can see us."

"No, he can't, he's dead, and on that side, this window looks like a giant mirror."

The woman dismounted the bed, rolling the bed coverings to conceal the dead man from view. Disregarding the blood splatters on her own naked form, she left the room and a few seconds later, opened the door to our narrow room. "See how easy that was?"

"Yes." I smiled at her. I noticed a smear of blood on her breast and wiped it with a finger.

"Kinky." She smiled back at me. "I like that. I'll be back soon. I kind of need a wash."

Leaving us alone, she made sure to lock us in again. Faith stood in close, and I could see those tears of hers again. "I can't do this, babe."

"But haven't you done this before?"

"I lied. I've never actually even seen a dead body for that matter. I have to leave, and I want you to come with me."

******

I SAT OUTSIDE as Faith met with one of the upper ranked members of The Praying Mantassassins inside the small office. In all the time we had spent there, neither of us had ever met anyone higher up than the drill sergeant and Ed, but we were sure those at the top of the ranks had seen our training captured on video cameras situated around the training grounds.

Faith was adamant about leaving, even after I begged her for the best part of two hours. I needed to stay and continue, despite my love for her. Seeing that man who thought he was experiencing a service provided by a high-priced escort killed post-coatis raised so much excitement inside me, adrenaline wise and sexually. Maybe I was sick, but after watching what that woman had done made me realise I wasn't the only one.

Ten minutes since Faith had entered the meeting, DS ran from the office to speak to me. "Faith will be leaving immediately and can't come out and say goodbye. But she wants you to have this." He opened a closed fist and presented me with her silver necklace with a capital F pendant hanging from it.

"Can you give something to her for me?" I asked DS. I unclasped my bracelet, the only thing I possessed once belonging to my late grandmother. I didn't want him to catch sight of my tears, but with his eyes directly on mine, it couldn't be helped.

He nodded while accepting the piece of jewellery and deep down I knew I would probably never see her again.

******

THE FIRST NIGHT without Faith was the loneliest of my life. I missed the feel of her body on mine, and her friendship, the best friend I've had since Billy. Oh, Billy, who I still thought about from time to time. I always hoped wherever he happened to be and whatever he was doing, I hoped he was okay. If only I could have reached out to him, to let him know I was doing fine. Now.

There had been no further word on the test assignment, or even news of postponing it for a later time. Grabbing the F-shaped pendant on my necklace, I stared at it for a few minutes and put it to my lips.

I removed all my clothes and climbed into bed, alone for the first night in weeks. The quiet of the night sounds most rambunctious when you're all alone and confused and embarking on an uncertain path. My room became almost a stranger to me, a place where I no longer belonged.

A soft knocking on my door shook me from my thoughts. "Who is it?"

"Oliver. Checking to see if you're okay."

Taking a deep sigh, I wondered what the hell he wanted. Maybe I needed sex with a man again before I started work in the field. With no locks on our doors, I was able to yell out, "Come in."

As he opened the door, I couldn't remember if I first noticed the smirk on his face or the bulge in his skin-tight jeans. There was no denying his hotness, and as he closed the door behind him, I sat up in bed and allowed the covers to fall, exposing my upper body to his hungry eyes.

"You look like you've been waiting for me," he said taking a few steps towards me.

"You wish. Let's face it—we've seen each other naked nearly every day in the showers."

"Yes, but we haven't been alone." He lifted his shirt over his head, exposing his washboard abs

"Fuck it, we know where this is headed." I rolled the covers from me completely and opened my legs a little.

"Looks good enough to eat," he said staring at my recently waxed pussy, the result of an impulse treatment recently requested from the beauty therapist who paid weekly visits. I don't know if I got it to remind me of my little girl self before puberty and Russell, or because of how delightful it made me feel.

I could judge how hard he was already from the outline in his jeans, and I ached for him inside me. "Hurry up and get that big fucking python in me."

"Wow, so eloquent." He stood a couple of feet from me and quickly removed his shoes and socks and unzipped his jeans. It soon became apparent he was going commando, as his stiff member soon made an appearance. I touched myself to get some moistness before his imminent invasion.

"There are condoms in the drawer," I said pointing to the bedside dresser.

******

I WAS UNABLE to take his whole length inside of me, but he filled me nicely and had great prowess. Quite often guys with big dicks think all they have to do is push it in and out to please a woman, but Oliver sure put in a performance. He fell asleep rapidly after the act was completed, and as I looked over him, I could see his pile of clothes next to the bed. Something shiny caught my eye, reflecting the soft light of the salt lamp.

Curiosity nagged and got the better of me. Carefully climbing out of bed, I crawled around to his side of the bed to take a close look at the shiny metal object in his rear jeans pocket. Pulling it from the pile of clothes, a familiar circular item made my skin crawl. My grandmother's bracelet.

"Oh, shit," I said out loud.

Oliver stirred and turned around to face me standing near his side of the bed. "Lost something?"

I held it in front of me. "Where the fuck did you get this?"

"My practical assignment—the first one, at least."

I felt bile rising in my throat, still fully naked and vulnerable. My mouth opened, but words failed to form.

"She was great if you know what I mean, but you were even better." He pulled a pistol from under my pillow and aimed it at me. I had no idea how it came to be under my pillow or where it even came from. "Remember what the instructors say, this isn't personal." He pulled the trigger.

"You think I would keep a loaded gun in my bed?" I said as the empty cartridge caused the gun to make a clicking sound.

Oliver dropped it and lunged at me, in hopes he could catch me before I found a weapon to use on him. I swivelled on the spot and readied my fists for his recovery. I'd never sparred with him in training, so I felt completely unsure if I could take him or not.

"At least you put up a fight, unlike your girlfriend." His facial expression changed to match his taunting words.

Who the fuck chats during a fight? I swung a punch at his face, expecting him to block it as he met it with a deflecting arm. This gave me just enough time to raise my leg and kick him square in his exposed groin.

He screamed as the bridge of my foot smashed his flaccid cock and balls, and it was just the advantage I needed to punch him in the throat. Hearing him struggle for air as he fell in a heap on the ground, I knew what I had to do then.

I opened a drawer on my desk to see my babies lying together in a row, my knife collection—each one sharper than the next and waiting to lose their virginity. Picking the one I favoured most for its natural balance and grip, I heard Oliver moving behind me.

"You really gonna kill a fellow student?" he asked. Now on his feet, he leaned on the bedside dresser for support.

I nodded. "This is for Faith." I leapt a couple of feet towards him and slashed at his body.

Blood squirted from his wrists like busted fire hydrants, his desperate attempt to block the attack in stopping the knife from cutting his body. The escape of blood would possibly kill him without my intervention, but that wouldn't mesh too well with my current rage levels. "Did you fuck her before you killed her?"

He nodded, pressing his bleeding wrists against his chest.

"You're going to die, Oliver."

I could see tears forming on his face. I felt unable to feel sadness for him, for what I was about to do was revenge against him for killing my first love. Is this how it will be every time I kill someone? I felt no hesitation, no fear, and no pity for the man in front of me.

"Thanks for the great sex, Oliver." I slashed at his throat in a smooth arc, my sharp blade meeting little resistance as it sliced through his jugular vein, his blood showering me as it escaped the deep cut. "But I'm a Praying Mantassassin now."

Staring at Oliver's dying, naked body, I almost didn't hear the noise of the door opening behind me. I stood dead still, and thought this was it, the cavalry had arrived, and they won't be happy I killed their poster boy.

"You owe me fifty dollars, Bjorn," I heard Emily's voice.

"Oh, shit. Well, a bet's a bet, I guess. Can't believe I've gotta clean this fucking mess, though." As I turned, I saw the man called Bjorn for the first time. His flawless olive skin gave him the European look to match his accent, and his smirk, a sign of his approval of my nude physical presence.

"We need to get you a new room, girl, right after you take a shower. Congratulations, you passed your practical test. Now you're ready for real assignments," Emily said with a half-smile forming on her face.

But there was something I needed to ask. "Faith?"

"Sorry, girl. Like young Olly here, she too failed her practical. He apparently fucked her, killed her and threw her body in the ocean. It should wash up in a day or two. You're the lucky one of three who made it through this intake."

I swallowed hard, but a time like this called for looking strong. "Yay me."

CHAPTER 3

IN THE THREE years that had passed since I first became an official Praying Mantassassin, I had killed forty-four people, ranging from politicians, cheating husbands, lawyers, key witnesses before they could give testimony, and even a couple of women. Each mission had been a success, and Ed kept track of every investigation just to ensure the police weren't on my trail.

I was good.

I spent a lot of time at the compound helping to train and to observe. Quite often, new recruits were older than I was, but usually, they were more than happy to learn from someone as proficient with knives as me. Whenever I saw a new group of three or four hopefuls, I was reminded of the time Oliver, Faith, and I were completely unaware of the process deciding who became an official Praying Mantassassin. There are occasions when even the lone graduate doesn't make it past the first few missions without getting themselves killed or captured. Nevertheless, the captured ones soon meet their demise before they can offer any information about our operation.

For the first time in nearly four years, I found myself back in my hometown, ready to be picked up from my roach infested motel for a date with the one boy I realised I truly loved. It had been a long time, and I never had the chance to say goodbye, leaving me often wondering if he knew what had become of me.

I checked myself one last time in the grubby mirror, my makeup only lightly applied to enhance my delicate facial features. The sleeveless and low back white summer dress hung on me as if it had been tailor-made while my push-up bra exaggerated my naturally small bust. I breathed in and out a few times, with each one longer than the previous. I filled a cup of water.

"You'll be okay," I said aloud as I stared back at the woman who was just a girl when she left this town. My hand trembled as I raised the cup to my mouth, and I spilled a little down my chin as I took harsh gulps.

I decided to dispense with high heels, feeling more natural walking out of the motel room in my near flat Gucci loafers. The money's good when you do what I do, and a girl has to treat herself with brand name clothing and shoes at the very least.

Without sounding boastful, the looks I attracted didn't surprise me. My hair hung straight, and the blonde streaks made me think about the possibility of going completely blonde one day. At least unlike the days when I was a young girl living in this town, I can stand here and not feel like bait for dirty old fuckers like Russell. If I needed to, I could take anyone down.

A few nervous minutes later, I saw an old red station wagon stop at the kerb in front of me. I could make out a male face on the driver's side of the car, and it only took a few seconds for the driver's identity to establish itself as he exited the car.

"Billy," I yelled, as he looked my way and smiled.

Gone were the glasses, pimples, and an awkward stance. He had become a man and a big juicy piece of highly fuckable man flesh. The years had been kind to him in the looks department, but as he ran up and hugged me, I could see he still possessed his sweet boy nature.

"Karla, you look even more beautiful than you did in school," he held me tight, and I could have happily stayed in this embrace for hours.

"You haven't turned out too bad yourself. So you taking me somewhere nice or what?"

"Well, of course." He ran to the passenger side and opened the door for me. I couldn't help but smile, always the gentleman.

"You still driving your mum's car, I see."

"Yeah, I know. The job at the cinema doesn't pay so well."

I regretted my words immediately. Poor Billy could have gone to college anywhere, but with his mother's ailing health, he found himself stuck taking his part-time after school job into a full-time one so he could remain here to take care of her. Words failed me.

"But I get to see the films before anybody else does. Being a manager does have its perks." His words rescued the awkward situation mine had caused.

The drive to the restaurant was a quick one, given the size of my hometown and lack of places to eat. Hungry Duck is the pick of the places to dine in my hometown, and although not a five-star eatery by any standard, I remembered they cooked a decent steak. The young woman serving at the counter looked me in the eyes. "Karla?"

"Yes, Monica. It's me. And tonight I am on a date with the best-looking boy from school."

While she was at work, she couldn't use words like slut, so instead, she led us to an intimate table for two by the window. Billy pulled out a chair for me before taking one opposite. "You're a real gentleman. I feel unworthy."

"Don't ever say that about yourself, Karla. You're the one girl worthy of everything. I wanted to save you myself that day, but the great thing was your mum finally standing up for you. Shame she went after that cop and got herself shot."

I nodded at Billy's version of what he believed happened the day I killed Russell. Would he have still held me in such high regard if he knew what had actually happened? Part of me felt he would love me more if he knew how I finally stood up to the beast while the other part felt the truth would have scared him to know what I had been capable of doing. I never told him about the rapes or abuse. Instead, I told Billy that Russell beat my mother and I up.

"Why did you never ask me out?" I asked him out of the blue.

Billy smiled. "I was shy, and you were way out of my league. And as a friend, I could keep you close and never lose you. I loved you back then, more than you could have known, but I loved you so much I couldn't risk being the type of boy who would let you down like a boyfriend."

I reached across the table and grabbed his hand. "Billy, did you ever think it was the other way around? I was hardly a good girl back then."

He smiled but didn't say anything. How could he when he knew how promiscuous I was? I searched for some way to change the subject. "What else have you been doing since school? Any ladies on the scene?"

"My mother's been sick, so I've been working and looking after her, nothing much else really. No time for sports, holidays, or even a girlfriend. But she's my mother, and I can't leave her to fend for herself. And I don't have the money to pay for her to go into care."

A tear fell from my eye. "Well, Billy, I'll make this the date of your life."

Smiling, he picked my hand up off the table and brought it to his lips. My skin tingled. His grip both firm and gentle at the same time, it sent a shiver down my hand all the way up my spine. "Just seeing your face again made this the best date of my life."

"So, have you ever had a girl?" a direct question, but one I felt I already knew the answer to.

He bowed his head. "No, I haven't Karla. I've been waiting for you. I know it sounds crazy, but I haven't thought of any other girl as I have you. I had to see you one more time to make sure I felt the same, and seeing you now confirms it."

I felt so bad for him. Having feelings for anyone never seemed to work for me in my line of work. What the hell could I do with him after the date? It had been risky enough to ask to leave the compound for a non-mission objective, and even after three years, blindfolds were still used so I didn't know the way to get there. How could it have been possible to do this on a regular basis?

"I'm sorry. I have no right to put that on you, Karla."

I smiled back at him, and before I could say anything, a waiter stood next to our table. He took our order and as he left, gave me a departing smile. Billy didn't say anything but poured another glass of wine for each of us.

The food was delicious, as expected, and after three courses, the two of us felt rather full but not uncomfortable. Billy asked me many questions about my new life, and each time I lied to him, I felt my soul decay a fraction at a time. I told him the same series of backstory lies I had told to dozens of people.

Billy asked for the bill for the meal, and although I requested we go Dutch, he insisted on being the traditional male and paying for the whole meal. The poor guy would take a year to earn what I earned in a typical mission.

We walked hand in hand back to his car, and it took everything I had inside to prevent myself from insisting he put me on the bonnet of the car and fuck me there and then. Luckily, he had other ideas.

"I've reserved a whole cinema just for you and me to watch any film you like." His eyes lit up as he told me his plans.

"You know my favourite film, Billy," I stopped in my tracks and pulled him towards me. "Just kiss me already."

He may have looked different, tall, buff, and cuter than a panda bear hugging a baby panda, but he was still nervous when it came to female contact. His lips touched mine, and one of his hands cupped the back of my head as I pressed my lips firmer to his, and within a minute, my tongue located his. My body tingled as the kiss lingered for what seemed like minutes, and I felt myself begin to get wet.

I pulled away, and while slightly out of breath, I suggested we go see this film before it got too late.

******

"HEY, YOU LOOK kind of familiar." A rough male voice pierced the euphoria Billy and I shared while we walked hand in hand to the cinema.

A bar across the road from where we parked was often frequented by the redneck contingent of the town.

I recognised the owner of the voice, one of Russell's old friends. And then I noticed another face from my past as the man's passenger exited the car. No matter how strong I had become since the day I killed Russell, seeing these two friends of his brought back memories of when I was much younger. Memories of three dirty perverts asking me to dance in my underwear for their amusement.

"Are you okay?" Billy asked.

I turned away from the two men near the pickup truck. "I will be as soon as we hit the cinema."

"Isn't that you, Karla? You're looking all woman now. You need a man to fix your needs," the second man said.

"Hey," Billy yelled.

"Just let it go, Billy." I grabbed his hand tighter and led him away.

Walking away to the cinema, the chuckles of Russell's friends faded as we reached the building.

******

I OFTEN WONDERED if I was born during the wrong era, as a film released around ten years before I was even born began to play on the screen in front of us.

The cinema had been in desperate need of renovations for some time. The seats felt like the springs hadn't been fixed or replaced since my grandmother took me there as a child. Billy draped his arm over my shoulder, and in response, my hand made a grab for his thigh. I didn't wish to wait any longer in the deserted cinema.

My hand travelled higher, making its way to the inside of his thigh. Sliding my hand further, my hand reached the bulge in the front of his pants. Billy's erection was hard as a rock, and my hunger for the confined beast inside urged me to set it free from its confines.

Keeping my hand in place, I peeled away from my seat, stood in front of him gripping his stiffness with a heightened craving, and leaned close to him. My free hand searched for his, and upon locating it, I move it to my thigh. Looking him in the eye, I hadn't wanted someone so bad since Faith. His hand trembled while journeying higher, almost skating along my recently waxed legs until his fingers made contact with my panties.

"Pull them down," I whispered.

He stared into my pleading eyes, and his other hand joined the one pressed against the part of me pining to feel him inside. In a move I didn't think him capable of doing back in our school days, I felt my panties pulled down to my ankles. He rubbed me gently, his finger increasing the wetness. I knew he was inexperienced, but that also excited me in a way knowing I would be the one he lost his virginity to. I unzipped his jeans and put my hand down the front of his undies, freeing his exposed cock with my massaging fingertips. I pulled his jeans and undies to his ankles and then climbed on top of his lap. My knees on either side of him, I lowered myself and used a hand to guide him inside me. I heard him groan as his full length entered. I'd had much larger cocks inside me, but at least, I could take Billy and feel full without the pain caused by excessive size.

Arching myself back, I began moaning while bouncing up and down. I knew it wouldn't take long for him to come, being his first time. I didn't care. It was all about Billy and giving him what should have been his to take for the first time. I wiped them all from my mind, the perverted deceased Russell, the schoolboys who all used me, the fellow assassin classmate Oliver, and lastly, all those men and couple of women I had fucked before they died all in the name of paid work. I really wanted to come, but I had never been able to for a man before, and Billy deserved to be the first to take me there.

It felt so good. For that moment in time, Billy ruled as my sex king.

I swore to myself I'd try to find a way to see him from time to time and coach him to be the best fuck ever. The spiritual connection existed between us, so I surmised the sensual connection would get there. And caught up in the moment with Billy, there was nothing else mattering in the world.

"Oh, my God!" Billy yelled out, and I felt him quivering as he came and shot his load inside me. When he stopped shaking, we sat with me still on top of him. I love young guys for the reason they can stay hard for a while after they've come. I wanted to remain at that moment forever, no red tape or questionable assassin careers to keep us apart. No past, no future, just the moment.

But it can't be. A tear escaped my eye, and I prayed Billy didn't spot it. "Please hold me, Billy, and don't let go."

"When you left, I always told myself that if you ever came back, I would hold you and never let you go. And now you're here. I'm the luckiest man in the world, and I want to be with you till I take my last breath."

"Billy..." How could I let him down gently? There was no way I could do this without hurting him.

"Karla, come back to my place. Please." His puppy dog eyes spoke louder than his words.

I told myself I could do this, stay the night at his place. As it stood, the night was young, and I could have happily continued that one night to remember. "One condition, Billy. You best be ready for rounds two and three, possibly more."

"I'm prepared to put in a whole nine innings."

I giggled and dismounted his lap. We dressed and prepared to face the rest of the night with an unmatched enthusiasm for any previous experience we'd had before. I sure hoped he could match my energy levels.

******

THE JOURNEY TOOK only a few minutes, and before we knew it, Billy had his mother's car parked in her driveway. I hoped she wasn't home, or the sex marathon could have become awkward quickly.

"No, Mum's not home tonight in case you're wondering. She always liked you, so when I said we're going on a date tonight, she got a friend to pick her up and give me a night off. She wanted to be gone in case things went very well."

I leant over, kissed him on the lips, and giggled. "Well, we better get inside then and make the most of it." I didn't give him a chance to do the old-fashioned gentleman gesture of opening the door for me. Instead, I slid along the seat, opened my door, and stepped outside, just to be welcomed by a fist to the side of my head. Unprepared for the attack, I crashed on my side into the cement driveway and saw two men looking down on me. It was the same two men again. How the hell did they know we would be here?

"How about giving us some of your sugar?" the taller one said.

The darkness gave me little chance of making out their features, but his stupid comment allowed me enough time to get to my feet and see the knife in his hand. I thought to myself he better make sure he gets me first, or else I know I can take him if I can get hold of that blade.

"Karla, no," Billy yelled out as I saw him charge for the knife-wielding thug.

"Billy, don't. I got this." I rolled over, put my hands to the ground, and aimed my leg at the taller man. The bridge of my foot slammed into his ankle, and I made sure to avoid his body as it crashed to the ground. One of the first things I took on board when learning to fight at the compound was that the biggest person could tumble like a house of cards if you hit a weak spot.

I saw the blade fall from his grip as he collided with the earth and wasted no time in claiming it from him. "Don't fucking move."

"Karla?" Billy's voice pierced the night sky.

I glanced at him as the second thug made a grab for him from behind and held a knife against Billy's neck. "Put the knife down or your boyfriend gets it," the second thug said.

I stared straight through him. I couldn't allow Billy to get hurt so I contemplated my options. "What's to say you won't kill him if I let your friend go?" I hadn't felt fear for some time, and even at that moment, it wasn't for my own safety.

"Stupid bitch, you shouldn't have fought back. You were supposed to just take it like you did from Russell." The shorter thug smiled.

Those words set off a trigger in Billy. He leaned forward and readied his elbow to smack his captor in the face. I heard the taller thug chuckle as his friend held his grip around Billy and snapped his arm in a rapid arc. Seconds ticked as I saw Billy's eyes bulge as he was released, toppling forward to the ground.

"Billy!" I screamed. I looked at the blade in my grip and the redneck fucker I knocked to the ground, and then I lunged at his throat. As I made contact, I swiped with my weapon hand, and the adrenaline fuelled me through the resistance his meaty neck attempted to put up against me.

Not wasting any time, I somersaulted back through the air and landed on my feet in a crouching tiger pose. Hatred for the murdering stranger in front of me thrust my body as I took a short run at him.

He readied himself but wasn't by any means prepared for a fight with a trained killer. His fists rose in hopes that I would make a straightforward assault at his upper torso. He was unprepared as, within a split second, I dived beneath his swinging fist and the hand gripping his knife and then hit the ground between his feet. His open stance allowed me room to slide underneath, reach up with my willowy arm, and strike him with an open palm between his legs, crushing his manhood in the process, and sending him to his knees as I moved my legs back out from under him.

He coughed and groaned. Getting to my feet, I saw the back of his head and looked at the razor-sharp knife in my other hand. There was no time for taunting, so I plunged my blade at the base of his skull and pushed it all the way in up to the weapons handle.

Some say the sound of a person gurgling on their own blood is one of blood-curdling horror, but right then, hearing this prick choking on the blood pumped from his own internal organs played like a symphony fit for the lords and ladies of death, of which I felt I belonged to at that moment.

Nevertheless, the sonnet concluded prematurely as he fell face down on the driveway. This moment hit me as to what had happened to my first male true love. I rushed over to him, slumped on his side in a pool of his own blood. Putting his head in my lap, I looked at those loving eyes as he had for me for so many years, and all they did was stare back at me as a pair of pale unattended windows.

"No...no...NO!" I screamed, the howling began, and the tears flowed with nothing to slow them down. "Billy, don't leave me now. I've only just got you back."

Some say fate is cruel, but I likened fate to the nastiest piece of shit some motherfucker from the depths of hell liked to slap me in the face with as soon as I felt just a speck of happiness. Why did I push him away all those years ago at school? Why did we play it safe just in case it ruined everything? Because as I stared at the recently deceased love of my life, I couldn't help but think life was nothing but a shit sandwich with no end crust in sight.

How the hell could I explain this to Billy's mum? Or the authorities? I couldn't leave it to chance. I needed to make that call and try to get away from this awful town. This is too big and messy for Ed to fix.

I looked at the sweet face in my lap for the last time ever, and gently placed his head on the ground and wiped my eyes. Getting to my feet, I waded through the night air with the weight of the world trying to impede my movements. My handbag remained exactly where I left it, and I retrieved my phone and made the call to Bjorn to clean this mess up.

He used as few words as necessary and told me to go wait inside the house out of sight. If the police arrived, I wasn't to show myself to them nor leave the house unless I had no other option. I was to shower in the dark as quick as possible to wash the blood off and try to find anything of Billy's to wear, including a baseball cap. My clothes were to go in a plastic bag to be destroyed later.

I understood all this, even if it was the first time I

had required his help. I took a minute to look at the carnage near Billy's car and felt compelled to rifle through the dead man's pockets. I found a wallet, a set of keys, and a plastic bag, which on further inspection contained half a dozen joints. I ignored my no drugs policy, opened the bag, and stuck the end of one of the joints in my mouth. I dug further in one of the dead man's pockets and located a cigarette lighter, and lit the other end inhaling deeply as I heard the dried green leaves burn.

The smoke burned my throat, and I couldn't help but end up in a coughing fit, waiting for it to subside before I walked to the house, and then finished the joint before I entered. I floated through the house as my head spun and I spoke aloud, "I will find you again one day, Billy and Faith, either in the afterlife or a next life. And when I find you both, I won't ever let you go." The tears flowed again. "I promise."

JACK

CHAPTER 1

THERE WAS ONCE a time when I gave a shit. When my life had a compass, a purpose, and there was only one woman I ever truly loved. But this is not a love story; this is the story of how I came to be the empty shell people know me as now.

I SERVED MY time in the armed forces, joining up the day after I finished school, and quickly transferring to the Marines when I showed extreme fitness, strength and survival skills. I rose swiftly through the ranks, served two tours in Afghanistan and came back home and was honourably discharged.

But the world became a different place for me after Afghanistan. An ocean of faces in my city appeared through my eyes as an inhospitable tsunami, and the sounds of gunshots would have me looking through my bedroom window for hours in search of the perpetrator of such noise.

My one bedroom apartment, clean, spacious, and affordable on my gym manager's salary, didn't prevent the darkness of night; it served only to remind me of how lonely my life had become. I lived in one of the biggest cities in the world, constantly surrounded by people. But through my eyes, each one of the eight and a half million faces in my city seemed to cement my place as an outsider.

It hadn't always been the case. Melinda used to be the beacon of light pulling me to safety from the bleak storms of my life. I used to wonder what she saw in me, a grumpy, paranoid, stone-faced ex-soldier with diminutive humour and little experience in romance. But she rescued me at a time when my soul needed a life raft to save it from the river threatening to smash me into the rocks.

I was there when the planes hit, albeit from a safe distance. I saw a man stabbed to death for his shoes, a woman nearly raped in a dark alley and many a person jump from one of the many giant buildings which fill my city's skyline. I've seen the homeless on the streets as I waded through the night, the couples holding hands and glancing at each other like nothing could ever upset their perfect world and the women who walked alone and kept their head low as someone walked their way.

I'm a big guy with a face capable of scaring away would-be muggers. When I walk in their direction, do these lone women fear I'm the type of man who would take them and do the worst acts ever? I used to worry about what people saw when they looked at me, but one day, I helped a lady recover her stolen handbag, and in return, she gave me the best year of my life.

******

"YOU NEVER COOK dinner. Should I be worried?" Melinda asked me as she unlocked and came through the door to our apartment, smelling the roast I had in the oven.

"I just thought it was about time I gave it a try." I smiled as she slid over to me, leaning in for a kiss while I stirred the gravy on the stove.

"Well, I think I could get used to this, coming home from the office and inhaling the scent of meat cooking in the oven while looking at the hottest hunk of man meat standing to greet me in his shorts and tight fitting shirt."

I always thought she was way too kind. Keeping in shape since leaving the forces had been a struggle, but I managed to fit in a run and a little bit of weight training amongst my time managing the gym. But fitness is important to me, and with a woman a few years younger with such an appetite for sex as Melinda, I wanted to be around and able to continue to make her happy. I wondered what I did to deserve her, a beautiful, vivacious and high-flying businesswoman. Most people thank me for saving them from a mugger, or retrieving stolen items, but Melinda wanted me in her life. I tried not to over analyse the situation and instead, just attempted to enjoy it. I'm not a shallow man. I don't sleep with just anyone. There is so much more to this woman than a beautiful face and body and incredible libido.

I loved her mind and the passion she showed for all living things, her true beauty.

"Please take a seat and wait for your meal to be served, Miss." I winked at her.

She smiled back at me, and I truly hoped for the night to go the way I had envisioned it. With everything set in place, I had invested a lot of time in getting it all right, desiring above everything for the result I aimed for.

"As long as the food is as hot as you, I'll wait as long as it takes."

I watched as she kicked off her shoes and walked into the lounge area, fixing herself a glass of red wine. As she took a seat, I watched her slide along the couch and unbutton the top two buttons of her blouse and not caring while her skirt slid up revealing her underwear. I'm a tough and disciplined man, but I swore if she kept wiggling like that and exposing more skin, the temptation would be too high to resist taking her right then in the lounge room.

I finished cooking the three-course meal, calling her into the dining area while placing the raw oysters on our table. We shared a dozen of the freshly caught delicate morsels and a little conversation about our day.

"So what's the occasion, Jackie?" she asked me as the last of the entrée was demolished.

"Don't you remember that day twelve months ago?"

"Of course, I do. I was teasing." We shared a laugh, and I got up to serve the main course. I hoped to hell I hadn't overbaked the chunk of beef or any of the vegetables. I didn't cook very often, but when I did, I treated it with the same passion as everything else, and being a perfectionist doesn't help.

I carved off a little of the meat, sneaking in a taste test, and without sounding conceited, I had no choice but to celebrate its deliciousness.

"Smells wonderful, honey. You should do this more often," Melinda called out.

She was right. I had no excuse but for my own self-doubt. I chuckled at her remark and served the main course of dinner.

******

MAYBE STILL CAUGHT up in the puppy love stage of our relationship, there were still times when I stared into those chocolate coloured eyes as she talked to me, and I could barely hear the words she spoke. With all three courses consumed, we enjoyed our second glass of the bottle of cabernet sauvignon I had saved for the occasion. I don't drink very often, and while two glasses are by no means enough to make me drunk, I began to feel lightheaded with a silly grin plastered on my face.

"I think we need more of that wine. It's making me feel kind of..." she says, bequeathing a knowing wink.

Finally, the time had arrived.

"Let me take a look in the cellar." I stood and departed the dining table, taking slow deep breaths. I kept telling myself this is what I wanted, praying she felt the same. I had walked into gunfights in a land I didn't know with far less trepidation than I felt before taking such a gamble with the woman I loved.

I grabbed the box and returned to Melinda with my hands behind my back. "I couldn't find another bottle suitable, but I found this." I presented the box to her and opened it while getting down on one knee.

"Melinda Reynolds, fate found us and gave us each other, and I don't want to do anything to disappoint fate in return. The only way I can truly show my appreciation to fate is to make sure I have you in my life always. We've shared so much, and you gave me what I thought I would never find, and what I didn't realise I'd been missing until you gave it to me. So please, Melinda, will you be my wife?"

Tears freefell down her face, and I swallowed hard awaiting her answer. Her lips moved, but she seemed unable to say anything. Instead, she nodded and allowed me to slide the ring on her finger, fitting snugly. I got to my feet. She did the same and reached her arms around me as her mouth met mine. My overactive brain almost sighed with relief as I realised this was really happening.

After what seemed to last a minute or two, she released her mouth from mine. "Like there was any chance I would say no."

We both laughed. She grabbed my hand to lead us to the bedroom.

******

WHEN MELINDA AND I made love, it sometimes turned into a two-hour session while at other times, it turned into a five-hour event. But after my successful marriage proposal, we didn't get much sleep at all before my six a.m. alarm pulled me from my sleep. I needed to be at the gym in an hour to coach a fitness circuit class, and I thanked the fact I was super fit to get me through. Melinda stirred, but obviously, her subconscious told her it wasn't her turn to get out of bed.

I showered and dressed in my personal trainer clothes, and checked in on my future wife, all snuggled up in bed with the covers up past her shoulders keeping her naked body warm against the cold morning's menacing chill. I stroked her hair and kissed her cheek, and a tear formed as I took in the most beautiful sight. I felt like the luckiest man alive. The class I teach would go for an hour, and I could get back in time to have breakfast with Melinda before her turn to depart for work.

I jogged to the gym against the biting chill of the crisp morning air, buoyed by a sense of invincibility achieved through the success of asking Melinda to be my wife. The world seemed a magnificent place after all when a man like me could find love. Of course, the demons residing in the dark areas of my mind would still dwell in their place no matter how much good came into my life, but should they try and make an outward push to the outside world, the positivity of my life would assist me in sedating them.

Turning the last corner before the street where the gym is located, I nearly crashed into a man in a black hooded top.

"Sorry about that," I said as I dodged him at the last second. Not looking up, he continued in his direction without a single reaction from my apology. "Asshole," I muttered under my breath.

I continued on my way, unaware of the impact the man with no manners would make on my life.

******

I RETURNED TO my apartment. When I approached the door, I noticed it was left slightly ajar, and this was when I ran in and was presented with the most soul-destroying image I'd ever seen. Inside the bedroom, there was blood everywhere—sprayed on the ceiling and walls, pooled on the bed and pouring from the woman who was to be my wife. I fell to my knees howling and crying until I screamed. Melinda looked as though she had been stabbed dozens of times, and I found myself unable to look at her for long. I felt a sickness like never before and paralysing fear.

"Oh, my God," I heard after the footsteps stopped just short of me. It was the voice of the woman who had moved in next door just a few days earlier. "I'll call the cops."

I nodded, unable to say anything. I stood up and looked over at the mess made of my love, wishing it to be nothing but a bad dream.

But it wasn't. This was as real as shit gets. I couldn't believe I had stood at the top of the world a couple of hours earlier only to be dragged into the depths of hell on the same day. Which led me to ask myself something—how the hell did her killer get in?

"They're on their way, Jack. Come next door and have a coffee while we wait," the lady said to me.

"Coffee? My future wife is lying here dead, and I'm supposed to leave her to have a coffee?"

"Jack, please. I'm just trying to—"

"Help? I'm gonna go find the fucker who did this, so if you want to help, feel free to take up arms, and we'll go hunting together."

"I'm sorry. I'm just going to leave you to deal with this, but my door's always open if you want to talk."

She turned and left. I paced up and down the bedroom with my mind spinning and the tears coming and going. Why did Melinda have to die?

Minutes passed. The sirens wailed louder as the police cars approached the building. I was no stranger to the sounds of emergency vehicles, their presence a constant reminder of the vastness and dangers of our city. Never, though had I imagined they'd be coming for one of us.

The police officers knocked on the door of my apartment, identifying themselves and displaying their badges. I forgot their names as quickly as they introduced themselves, but I was pretty sure one of the uniformed cops said his name was Ed. He didn't say much while the two plain clothed detectives started to question me about my whereabouts during the time of the murder, and whether I had changed anything at the crime scene.

"I swear I didn't do this, detective," I said to the senior of the pair. "I'll come down to the station if you wish."

"For what it's worth, I don't think you did, but if you're willing to submit yourself to a DNA test and fingerprints, then we can rule you out."

I nodded. I had nothing to hide and knew as soon as they entered my name into the databases, they'd see my service record and zero criminal convictions. They had a job to do, and I wanted to do everything I could to help find the person responsible. At that moment, I came to the realisation I wanted to find the person myself.

More police officers entered, and I noticed one of them taking photos while another checked over the body of Melinda. I needed to get out and get some fresh air.

"Are you okay, sir?" Ed asked me.

"No, I'm not. And I don't think I ever will be."

"Sorry, I meant you look sick. I'll come with you." He smiled at me.

We walked to the stairs, taking the trip down to the ground level, not exchanging a word until reaching the pavement outside.

"Hey, I see this shit all the time, and I still don't get used to it. Smoke?"

He holds a packet of Marlboros, and I break my five-year ban of the terrible habit and reach for one and light it up. As I inhale, I welcome the fumes all the way to my lungs, knowing my body will hate me for such a bad decision. But it calmed me for a moment.

"That's some pretty sick shit, what he did to your wife."

I didn't bother to correct him on my marital status. I nodded again, noticing his nervousness at my lack of communication.

Taking a few steps closer to me, he took a long drag on his cigarette and spoke again. "This isn't the first time he's done this. I'm not supposed to tell you this, but there have been five victims in the last month. Each victim was found naked, raped, and stabbed several dozen times. Each one with long dark hair and between the age of twenty and thirty, and very pretty." He took another long puff and continued. "You know we don't like to use the term serial killer with the public. It creates hysteria, vigilante action, copycats, even a sick kind of hero worship. There are actually women who find these creeps a turn on. But I know you're a man who understands the chain of command and due process, so you wouldn't try doing anything you shouldn't."

I coughed and discarded the butt. Why the hell did this psychopath pick my Melinda? I stepped right up to Ed. "You better make sure you find this fucker before I do."

CHAPTER 2

EACH NIGHT, I sat on the roof of my apartment complex, dressed in black to camouflage among the darkness of the city night. I looked down upon this city, waiting for HIM to make himself known to me so I may deal out my own personal brand of justice to him. It had been a week since my love was murdered and facing her family at the funeral was the hardest thing I had ever had to do.

The autopsy results revealed Melinda had been raped prior to receiving the multiple stab wounds, adding to the horror of her death. I've seen war and death and stared at my own demise a number of times during my tour of duty and never flinched. But this terror threatened to strangle the life out of me, and at times, I wished it would finish the job and let me join Melinda in the afterlife.

I couldn't do that, though. I needed to find this monster and save someone else from going through the pain I had endured. If I could save just one woman from a similar fate to Melinda's, maybe I could leave this world having done at least one useful deed.

Seated in a foldout chair, I could switch the view

from night vision to regular through the click of a switch on the side of my binoculars. Energy drink after energy drink wiped the concept of time from the dark recesses of my mind as I persisted in searching for this needle in the haystack that is New York City. I had nothing else to do, and any sleep missed could be made up in the afternoons.

"What are you doing up here?" a female voice asked from behind, almost scaring me enough to jump from my chair and over the edge of the building.

"I'm looking for someone."

"There are eight million people. Do you think you'll find them here?"

"Listen…" I didn't actually know her name.

"Kathy. Look, I think I know what you're doing, and I don't blame you. That's why I brought you one of these." She handed over a mug of steaming coffee. Black, just the way I love it.

"Thanks." I accepted the drink and brought it to my lips, a much better-tasting fluid than the sugar filled cans. "You're welcome to sit with me, but I'm not the best company for anyone at the moment."

"I can't begin to imagine what you're going through. You don't have to talk to me, or tell me anything, but if there's anything I can do…"

"It's okay. I've been in Afghanistan. I've killed people up close, and I've killed them from long range. I've seen people lose their whole head from explosions, and I've had young boys try and put a knife in me. I saw the planes hit the buildings that day in 2001, and I knew from that moment, the world would be spiralling down the toilet before we could ever hope to bring calmness back to it again. We say that we will rebuild and go on like before, but the words are just cosmetic make-up trying to hide a facial scar. Things will never be the same again.”

“But where there’s life, there’s hope. There’s still good in this world, and the police will catch this man. You need some rest.”

“Why do you care?”

“I care about all my neighbours.”

“I want her back.” The tears start to fall, and I looked away, hoping she didn’t catch me. My tiredness diminished my ability to keep my emotions in check.

“I’ve been in love, too. You reach that point where you think you’re on top of the world, and nothing can bring you down. And then one day, it’s taken from you. My story is nowhere near as tragic as yours, but...”

I stared at her, my silence stopping her words, and I noticed her looking away. The next few minutes were filled with an awkward lull, and without looking, I could sense her standing beside me. Why is she here?

“Maybe you and I could get him,” she cut the muted air.

I almost dropped my binoculars. “You? How are you going to help?” I had feared the answer before it left her lips.

“Look at me. I fit the profile of his victims.”

She was right. She was young with dark hair and pretty. But I wasn’t in the habit of putting civilians directly in harm’s way. “I don’t think so, Kathy.”

She sighed. Using her as bait would go against everything I stood for, even though part of me could see her point. “Thanks, but no thanks, Kathy.” I stood and began to collect my gear.

“Look, I’m sorry. Maybe I see you as having the better chance of catching this guy than the police. You don’t have procedures you have to follow or a chain of command. And while he’s still out there, I’m a potential victim.”

I walked up and gave her a hug. "I'll do what I can. I'm just one man watching the city, and I can't be watching twenty-four seven. Please do one thing for me, take this." I hand her a pistol. "If someone attacks you, don't hesitate to—"

"Put him away? What if I freeze in the moment?"

"When your life depends on a split second action, you won't freeze."

******

I BARELY ENJOYED a good night's sleep since Afghanistan, and in the time since Melinda was taken from me, I couldn't remember if I had slept more than two hours at a time. I looked at the clock next to my bed, three fifteen a.m., and I hadn't even been in bed for two hours, let alone slept for that long.

Police sirens screamed through the city streets, and I rolled out of bed to peer through the window as the cars drove past. Praying they're not about to stop at the apartment block I live in, I put on some clothes and ready myself.

I breathed a sigh of relief as they raced past, but being awake and attempting to squeeze in more slumber would be nothing but a waste of time. For over two months now, I had tried to hunt a shadow with nothing to show for it but a bigger case of insomnia and an armed ally in the apartment across the hall.

Every morning, she brought me a large cup of hot coffee, and we talked for a good half hour before she left for work. There was nothing in it but friendship, and I think of that as the reason why we got along so well. And besides, I couldn't even contemplate romance with another person given my emotional state anyway.

Being awake, I decided I may as well go for a run. I

put on my black shorts, hoodie, and a pair of sneakers and made my way to the bone chilling outside world.

It's not a strange sight seeing someone outside jogging so early in the day, although most of the population are behind closed doors. Anything or anyone could pop out and attack me, but part of me wasn't afraid while the other part didn't care what became of my existence anymore.

A flicker of movement up ahead captured my eye to something in a dark alley. Probably a feral animal or homeless bum looking for something heavy to drink.

I followed the sound regardless, turning left to investigate what my instincts told me to heed attention to. The only illumination the area received spilled into it from a streetlight on the street where I had turned in from, and I could see very little up the alley apart from garbage. Smelling like a toilet mixed with rotting food, I held my breath as I stepped into unknown territory.

My eyes scanned the human-free existence in the stinking abandoned area, searching for the source of the quick action alerting me to walk down the alley. The cold and silent air my body discovered unnerved me. This was not unlike the situations I had found myself in while searching through endless tunnels below the surface of Middle Eastern deserts, looking for the elusive masters of terror. Experience taught me to never lower my guard, even when all appeared calm.

But all I could see was a splash of light here and there, piles of litter being the lone visible objects throughout the darkness. Backing away inch by inch, I kept my sight locked ahead ready for something possibly jumping out to make its move. I shuffled backwards, and the back of my shin found something solid. I turned to see the object blocking my leg's movement. Unable to prevent the gasp escaping me as I made out the body lying on the ground next to me, I wondered how I didn't notice it earlier.

It's a woman. Blood surrounded her abdomen as it continued to flow from the numerous stab wounds which claimed her life.

"Gotcha," a nasally voice shrieked from behind as I felt a blunt object hit the back of my head, and my world went black.

CHAPTER 3

"WELL, IT ALL makes sense now." The police officer looked down at me a few minutes after I had woke in a hospitable bed, my hands cuffed to the side rails.

"What the hell is going on?" the words flew from my mouth. "I found a dead woman in an alley, and the next thing I know, something hard hits me in the head. And then I wake up here handcuffed to the bed."

"It was you all along. Killing and raping women, even your own girlfriend, you sick fuck." He punched my jaw as the obscenity came out.

I turned back to face him. "You hit like a child." I never used the term 'hit like a girl.' After serving in the armed forces and seeing how the female officers trained, I wouldn't want to be on the receiving end of one of their punches.

"You won't say that after I hit you again." He pulled his arm back, ready to strike me again when another man entered the room and caught his fist before it could make contact with me.

"Enough, Officer Roberts. He was at the wrong place at the wrong time," the new arrival said.

I recognised his face from the horrible day Melinda

was killed. "Ed?" I asked.

"Griffon, I've authorised your release as soon as the medical staff clears you, but please make sure you don't stray far from home."

"Ed, you can't be serious," Roberts said. "If you let this fucker go, he will kill again."

I opened my mouth but decided not to say what was on my mind. The only person I wanted to kill was my fiancée's murderer, but I couldn't imagine the police agreeing with my intended vigilante urgencies.

"Why do you think he was found at the scene if he did it after eluding the authorities so long? I swear, Roberts, I've heard rookies make more sense than you. Just give me the key to those cuffs."

I almost felt the chill of the staring eyes of Roberts. Were they playing a clichéd good cop, bad cop game? "Thanks, Ed."

"Don't thank me yet, Griffon. We'll be watching you like a hawk," Ed said, accepting the keys from his fellow officer.

I nodded. The serial killer must have been tailing me to have got the jump on me, so if the cops kept an eye on me, then they might just catch their man. The old-fashioned part of me held some faith in the police force.

Roberts stormed from the room, leaving Ed alone with me. "Please, just stay home at night. If news gets out that this killer took someone like you out, a lot of people are going to be scared."

"I don't understand how he got the jump on me. I've been to Afgan—"

"I know all about you. Just leave this guy to us, okay? We have a few leads."

Ed asked me a few questions I didn't know the answers to, apart from the sound of the man's voice. But realistically, I was no help to him. There was something unusual about this cop I couldn't put my finger on, though. He seemed a little too nice, taking a very strong interest in me. After he had left the room, a doctor entered to check me over before letting me leave.

Something seemed amiss. For someone found with a victim, I'd been allowed to just get up and leave. I felt numb from everything going on in my life, physically and emotionally. My only purpose I had in my life seemed to be locating and taking vengeance on this killer, and I didn't even want to think about what I'd do once it was over.

******

I PUSHED THE key in and unlocked my apartment, opening the door cautiously. After the previous night, I couldn't be too sure he wouldn't go back to my apartment to wait for me, possibly finishing me next time.

"Hey, Jack." A familiar voice almost sent me jumping six feet in the air. I'd lost my nerve, and I hated the feeling of not being in control.

"Geez, Kathy, You scared me half to death."

"You need to be more careful out there."

"How did you know what happened?"

She sighed. "The police knocked on my door after they found you unconscious in that alley. They asked me if I knew you were out hunting this killer. I lied to them."

I invited her in to continue the conversation. "Thanks. I don't think it matters anyway. I'm looking for a needle in a haystack. One who can get to me."

Her eyes lit up. "You know what we have to do then."

I remembered our conversation about using herself as bait. It might just work, but I couldn't bear to ponder the consequences if it didn't.

"My answer's the same. He got the drop on me last night so he knows he can take me."

She sighed. It wasn't that she wanted to do this for me, I felt, but her intention to put to rest the silent menace of the city was a feeling echoed by millions. Over three hundred people were murdered the previous year, but the seven deaths by the hand of this serial killer had those people in the know scared beyond belief. Kathy happened to be a brave woman who wanted to do something about it.

"Okay, Kathy, but we do it my way."

She smiled and ran over to give me a hug, and in a moment of vulnerability, I welcomed it and embraced her in the same way.

******

IN THE TWO days since, the killer claimed another victim, once again aged in her mid-twenties, long dark hair and beautiful. Discovered naked with multiple stab wounds on a rooftop downtown. I'd said it before, and I'd say it again, it's a big city, and as much as I wished it, I couldn't be everywhere. I felt sad for the poor woman, and if she had a partner, they must have gone through the same hell I had. Not to mention any family she had. I had only been able to face Melinda's parents once, and it was at the funeral. They were nice enough, but through their tears, I couldn't help but feel their eyes upon me, their minds perhaps placing some degree of blame upon my shoulders.

Darkness filled the sky, and the time came to go fishing for a killer.

Kathy dressed casually as there remained no correlation between what the victims wore and their fates. They were all just going about their everyday business, not necessarily dressed to impress or anything like that.

As she made her way, I prayed this crazed killer hadn't spotted Kathy and me together at any time. The plan was for her to head nowhere in particular, from block to block in one direction to hopefully draw him out. In the city that never sleeps, Kathy aimed to keep to the quieter streets and alleyways. Keeping a distance between her and me, I found it hard as a man being my size to remain inconspicuous.

I would have to be naïve to think Kathy and I could accomplish the mission in one night, or a week, or even in a month. But I weighed up my options. What else did I have to keep me going but a lust for revenge?

"Excuse me, sir," a homeless looking man stepped in front of me.

"Sorry, I'm in a hurry—"

"Sir, I just need a dollar. I'm so hungry."

I looked at his wrinkled features, telling me of a hard life, and one dollar will hardly dent my finances. Pulling my wallet from my pocket, I felt a heavy force from behind smack the middle of my back, the wallet falling from my hand as I regained my balance to face my attacker.

The skinny man who attacked me laughed at me and disappeared among the crowd as he ran away. No way in hell would I let this prick get away with my wallet, so I turned to face the homeless man just to see if he, too had disappeared. By this time, I'd lost sight of Kathy.

I chased the wallet thief across the road, crossing three lanes before having to stop in time to dodge one of the city's world famous yellow cabs from turning me into mincemeat. At this stage, the thief faded from my vision while cutting through a darkened alley. It didn't take me long to catch on to what was happening. I surmised the thief had been put in place as a decoy.

But I would use it to my advantage. I made it to the sidewalk on the other side of the road and resumed running in the direction I had last seen my target head in. The alleyway barely lit, I knew how easily this made the possibility of the man getting a jump on me. But on that night, I was prepared for anything.

I picked the wall on my right, almost sliding along with my shoulder as I shuffled down the darkened alley step by step. Every few seconds, I found a rear door to the shops facing out to a busy city street in the opposite direction to my current location. The cold air would chill the bones of most people, but I was one of those who had never been bothered by cold weather.

The sound of footsteps caught my ear. Throwing caution to the wind, I picked up the pace and headed to the source, who appeared to have been alerted to my quickened pace. This would be the end of it—he had no strategy but to run from my pursuit.

It took all of a few seconds to catch him. Upon capture, he immediately began to plead for his life.

"I don't want to hurt you. Just give me back my wallet," I said to him before gripping one of his scrawny arms.

Smiling through a toothless mouth, the man passed me back my wallet. "All you had to do was ask."

I stared him down. All it took was a second for me to notice a nervous twitch in his left eye, the kind of sign I saw a few times when enemy soldiers were captured and questioned by a translator over in the Middle East. It could only mean one thing.

"Where the fuck is he?" I yelled, grabbing the man's shoulders.

"Who?" he quivered on the spot, unable to hide anything from my menacing form.

I slapped his left cheek. "The one who told you to steal my wallet."

"I don't know what you—"

I slapped his other cheek. "I don't have time for lies."

"Please, you're mista—"

Another slap to his face.

He began to cry, cowering and attempting to fall to the ground. With little time to deal with his crap, I opened my wallet and pulled out a pile of notes. "Here, take the fucking money. I just need to know where the man went who told you to take my wallet."

The speed of his recovery betrayed the fear he displayed prior to the offer of money. He licked his lips as his eyes surveyed the pile of green paper I had passed him while his fingers shook.

"So tell me where he's going." The volume of my voice raised, and I hoped it didn't attract any unwanted attention.

"He's setting a trap for you. Says it's personal. Don't go up there, man."

"This isn't about me. Just tell me where he's going."

******

AS I WALKED through the city, all appeared as a blur. People, lights, cars, and buildings all blended into one crazy entity as I waded through it towards my destination, the Janel Towers on Neill Avenue in The Bronx. I had no idea if anyone saw me, or if they did, whether they took any notice. Maybe as an individual, I was just as much a blur to the rest of the city as the city appeared to me. At that moment in time, I decided, after all my business with the killer ceased, I would be out of New York City, never to return again.

Nearing the apartment, I scanned the rooftop for movement. The blackness of night hid anything I tried to take in of the roof of the twenty-four-floor complex. With nothing else to go by but the information from a man paid to steal from me, I decided to take a chance on him telling the truth. I thought I might never get a better chance again and potentially save lives in the process if it did pan out.

Heading to the entry door, I clenched my fists so tight, I felt like I could punch the building to the ground. I took a deep breath, then entered the building and made a direct route to the elevator. While waiting for the elevator, I wondered why this man was using the rooftop to stage something. He could have picked anywhere in the city. It was as if he knew I had a thing for heights. A little phobia I grew up with that the war couldn't even take from me.

The elevator vacant, I stepped in and pressed a button for the top floor. As usual, when my mind knows my body's leaving the ground, it tingles as the floor beneath me takes me to a higher place, floor numbers ticking over as the lift rises. I closed my eyes, mentally trying to push out the dizziness and searching for the calmness before the storm that would soon erupt when I finally met this menace to the city's women.

The door opened, and I headed straight to the staircase to take me up to the roof. My thoughts shifted to Kathy, wondering if she'd been caught up in all this, and cursing myself if it was too late for her. I could never forgive myself if something happened to her after going against my better judgement. But my focus returned to finding an end to this killer's little reign of terror on the vulnerable, and it would either be him or me who would meet their end on that night.

Taking two steps at a time, I found myself upon the topmost surface of the building. The air silent and attempting to chill my bones, I swear I could have heard a pair of butterfly wings flap through the sky should one have passed.

"Thanks for showing up, Mr Griffon," a voice slithered through the silence.

I turned to face the voice's owner. His face hidden in shadow, the man held Kathy out in front of him with a knife held near her throat. The expression she wore displayed a horror I had never witnessed before.

"Please, let her go, take me instead." I said the words slowly, pointing at my chest when the last three words come out.

"You've got a few inches height on me and at least thirty pounds of muscle. No thanks."

"So why get me to come up here, then?"

"Because if you want to save your friend here, I need you to step over the edge of the roof. I don't need the likes of you chasing me around the city like some sort of Batman wannabe. I'm here to deliver the women of this city from their evil ways, and I still have so much to do."

Peeking at my friend, the nerves set in. "How do I know you won't kill her after I'm gone? What guarantee do I get she'll be fine?"

"There is no guarantee, but the promise that I'll slit her throat right here in front of you if you don't start moving now."

My thoughts dug deep inside me. *So this is how it ends? I become a pile of crushed flesh and bone on a sidewalk with my last thought being of the uncertainty of the fate of a friend. Do I look at the bigger picture and make a dash for the killer, knowing I can end his terror by sacrificing Kathy?*

I looked in her eyes again. No, I would not deliberately allow her to be harmed. "Okay, I'll do it. You win."

"I always win, Griffon. Now please pick up the pace."

"How do you know my name?" I asked and stopped in my tracks.

He took a couple of steps forward, keeping Kathy the same distance ahead of him, still at knifepoint. Observing his face, this menace looked nothing as I expected. A young face, barely out of his teens at my best guess, framed with a dark hoodie. "I'm your biggest fan. I know all about your heroic deeds back in Afghanistan, and I wanted to be like you. But no, I couldn't be. They said I'm not psychologically capable of serving on a military force."

"Can't imagine why," Kathy said.

He ignored her. "So I needed to get your attention. I had to practice so I would know when it was time for your woman, I'd be ready. Turned out I quite enjoyed killing, so I did a few more, and more again after Melinda."

"And the raping was because that's the only way you can get any action with the ladies? You sick, pathetic, loser," I said to him.

"Loser? You're the one about to jump off this fucking building, and this city will still have no idea who I am."

It's all the confirmation I needed to know he wouldn't let Kathy live if I did jump. "You want to be like me? Then come on and jump with me. Kathy will tell the authorities that I'm the killer, and you died protecting her while taking me down. Come on, do it."

His eyes flinched.

"Come on, this is your chance to be a hero." I beat a fist against my chest.

"But I'll be dead," he said. I took close note of his arms and sensed his grip on his hostage weakening. I couldn't make a move yet, though. He could slit her throat in a lot less time than it would take me to rush him from several yards away.

"You don't have any other way out of this. On my way up here, I may or I may not have called the cops. Do you want to be standing here when they storm the rooftop?"

"You're bluffing."

I took a few steps, heading for the roof edge and taking in the night sky. An unusually clear night illuminated many more stars than usual. A beautiful spectacle in what could well have been my last night. My stomach tightened, and my head began to spin as I stepped closer to the brink. I looked to the ground below, lit up from the artificial light from the few streetlights and infrequent traffic. I hated the crashing of limb-weakening waves washing all over me, the hopelessness of a phobia consuming my normally strong inner self.

"Funny how you bluffed your superiors all those years when you flew out on missions. How did you manage to ignore your fear of heights as those chopper blades cut through the air and lifted you higher, and higher, and high..."

"Shut up," I yelled back at my antagonist.

"You want it to stop? Just jump."

I put my toes over the edge of the concrete tower and closed my eyes. The moment had come. I smiled as I thought about the situation and realised I was to be reunited with my love in the next world. So it wouldn't be a bad thing. In fact, I found myself wanting it all to end.

"There has to be another world. We can't go through all this crap that is life to eventually enter a darkened vacuum where not even your soul lives on," I said out loud, spreading my arms and leaning my head back.

"Maybe there is only the darkness. We're about to find out..." the killer said.

"Enough of this shit," I heard Kathy's voice and spun in an abrupt one-eighty degree twist in time to witness her lean back into the killer and propel him backwards into a concrete wall.

I ran towards the pair of them, knowing the man still had a knife in his hand and would likely overpower Kathy and do his worst. As they crashed, I saw him lose his grip on the blade, and I got the feeling she gained the advantage over him as he squeezed his eyes shut. She jabbed an elbow into his stomach, and on her release from his grip, she turned to face him and kicked him in the ribs.

"Keep hitting him," I called out, just a few feet away. I needn't have worried—she had already brought her right fist to his head, well above the short woman's height.

Crashing down, the killer looked beaten. It wasn't about to stop there. I wouldn't let him see the inside of a prison. Kathy stepped away as I leaned down and pulled the man up by his collar to drag him along the roof, the tips of his toes scraping the surface. Swinging his fists against my sides, the killer's hits did nothing to free him from my grasp.

The bite of the cold air intensified as we veered close to the edge, and at this point, he pleaded for his life. His words only bounced off me. When I decided on a course of action, I saw it to completion unless a superhero force prevented me. It was how my natural survival instincts worked, and it got me to the age I am now.

"If you do this, you're nothing but a killer. You're no better than me, Griffon," his body trembled as he spoke.

I pulled him around, still holding him by the collar, his feet now dangling over the air separating him from the ground twenty-four stories below. His full weight now only supported with my right arm, he tried to reach for the rooftop edge with his feet while, at the same time, hitting my arm with his own fists.

"I had it all, and you took it away from me, you son of a bitch," I yelled. I could hear additional sets of footsteps hitting the concrete. I chanced a quick peek and saw two police officers.

"Jack Griffon, you need to release him," one of them called out.

I recognised the face. "Ed, keep out of this. I'm doing the city a favour."

"It's not your job to hand out justice. Bring him back over from the edge, and you can walk away from this."

I turned back to the killer. "They want me to spare your life. Someone in this city actually wants you to see tomorrow. But Melinda won't see tomorrow, and maybe I won't either. But one thing's for sure," he screamed as I released him, "you won't."

It was just like they showed it in the movies when someone fell from a great height. Arms and legs spun everywhere as if the action would grant them the sudden ability to fly, and his body slowly shrank and disappeared from my view. I smiled and turned to face the arresting officers. I didn't care if they opened fire and ended my life right there and then. I achieved my mission—I avenged the murder of the most beautiful person I had ever known. I smiled at the two cops, my last action before the electric darts fired from the men's Tasers hit me, causing me to fall and shake on the ground before the world went dark.

CHAPTER 4

I WOKE UP on a bed in a windowless room, wearing only my cotton boxer shorts. I had no recall of any events occurring between the electric currents passing through my body and the confusion circling through my mind on my first morning spent at the strangest place I would ever know. Getting straight on my feet, I looked through every square foot of the strange room before spotting the camera pointing directly at the bed from the opposite corner of the room.

"So, I'm being watched," I said aloud, and with that being the case, I expected someone to enter the room at any minute. My mind jumped back to my neighbour Kathy, wondering what her opinion of me became after sending that man to his death from the top of an apartment building. She showed her own survival techniques in escaping the grasp of the man who held her as leverage to get me to kill myself, and I wondered how he managed to keep her prisoner for as long as he did.

I would have tried the door myself, but I already knew the steel plated structure would be locked. I speculated if I had been taken to some weird off the grid type prison.

A metallic-sounding click disrupted my thoughts as a key unlocked the door, and I saw two familiar faces— Ed and Kathy standing side by side and smiling at me. Unlike previous encounters, Ed wore civilian clothing and Kathy in a tight fitting crop top and pants that finished just past her knees. I had never noticed how well-endowed she was up top, and I soon cursed myself for thinking that way about her. I opened my mouth.

"You probably have a hundred questions, and I will answer them in due course," Ed said.

"And I'll answer one for you first," Kathy said. Putting her hands in her hair, I nearly fall over as her mass of dark hair left her closely shaved head. I'm not usually a fan of a bald scalp on women, but it gave Kathy a femme fatale type of look. "Sorry, Jack, but I used you to get close to that killer."

Then Ed spoke. "I made the observation of the personal touch he had made when he killed Melinda. In every other case, the victims were found in alleyways and other impersonal dark areas in the city. But your woman was murdered in the bed she shared with you, so from that moment on, I knew it was only a matter of time before he would draw you out somehow or vice versa."

"But he could have killed me when he had the jump on me that night," I said. The news of being used as bait threatened to make my blood boil.

"Sorry about that, but hey, you're still here." Ed flashed a toothpaste commercial smile at me.

"I had your back most of the time, but I couldn't when you snuck out in the early hours of the mornings," Kathy said. "I owe you an introduction at the very least. My real name is Hayley Jenkins, and I'm Ed's stepsister. We work together, based on this compound you now find yourself on. But my specialty is demonstrating the—"

"You're just as bad as he is. You lied to me all this time, and I thought you genuinely cared. And can someone please tell me where the hell I am?" My temper rose by the second.

The pair of them looked at each other, and Ed spoke first. "You've been recruited by the Praying Mantassassin Agency. We are hired to take out targets as requested by our clients, normally after a sexual encounter. We need someone like you to fill a position, and from what we've seen of you, you're the only man for the job."

"You want me to fuck and kill people? I don't think so. I want to go back home," I said.

"You can't. You're wanted for murder in the city of New York," Ed said. "It wouldn't take the police long to find you."

I rushed towards him, the draw of a pistol from the back of his jeans stopping me in my tracks. "Don't push me, Griffon. As much as I like you and see your potential, I will shoot you in the face if I think I need to save my skin."

I stared into his eyes. As pissed off and empty as I felt, my newfound curiosity gave me a new reason to live. I didn't want to die right then, despite what I had felt the night before. Something always kept me going, a hope of a brighter future somewhere one day burnt like a candle inside my heart.

"Jack, please listen to what we have to offer. You don't have to kill anyone. We want you to train recruits in the ways of fighting, weapon usage, and fitness. We want you as our new drill sergeant." Kathy smiled. She walked right up to me, stopping an inch from my chest. I couldn't deny she had great looks and a killer body, or should I say the body of a killer.

Ed took a step closer to me. "It's not nice how I got you into this, but you'll love it. Money, pussy, and power—it's all yours for the taking here. Let's go take a walk."

He opened the door to the room, and the sunlight smacked me in the face like a length of timber as I stepped towards the opening. He and Kathy guided me in the direction of where I needed to travel along the cement path, and I noticed several large buildings along the way to our destination.

"Before anything, you need to clean up. A shower, shave, and a change of clothes, just to get you started," Kathy said.

"Just try and work with us, and if you don't love being here at the end of a week, you can go back home. You're a good man with great skills, and I think you will fit right in," Ed added.

We reached a large concrete building with a few high positioned windows, barely big enough for someone to stick their head out of. His fingers grasping the door knob and giving it a slow turn, Ed smiled and winked at me before giving the door a robust push and holding it open for me to walk in ahead of him.

"I think I'm in the wrong shower block," I said as I saw six totally naked females standing in a line under several showerheads against a white tiled wall. I shouldn't have been looking at them. Turning away, I looked at Kathy and Ed.

"Jack, it's okay. We're not a hippie commune, but we're free with our bodies here, and in no time at all, you won't even notice the nudity," Kathy said. She grabbed hold of my hand. "There are exceptions for when women are having that time of the month to shower in a private cubicle."

I noticed the open shower stall at the other end of the room. Kathy guided me along behind her to another tiled wall parallel to the one with the showerheads. Attached to the wall was a wooden shelf, placed in such a position for placing clothes and supporting towel railings beneath it. The showering women looked in my direction, and a blonde woman with a physique not unlike a fitness trainer smiled at me as she lathered soap over her body.

I turned away from her and looked back in the direction of Kathy standing before me wearing just a smile. I shouldn't have been surprised, but I never planned to see her this way. I couldn't deny the sight of her nude form ignited illicit thoughts

"It's okay, Jack. I want you to look at me. I want you to do those things to me that are racing through your head right now." She bent down and pulled my boxers to my ankles in a single motion. As she stood, she walked to an unused shower and pulled me along with her.

I blocked out everyone else as Kathy lathered soap in her hands, proceeding to every inch of my body apart from my most private areas, which weren't so private anymore in a room occupied by mostly naked people. Her fingers massaged as they worked their magic while cleaning me, momentarily freeing my mind from everything else in the world. She passed me the soap so I could return the favour, her soft skin like silk on my hands. She guided my hands to her generous sized breasts, my hands running over in an almost feather light touch as I washed them—possibly dozens of times more than necessary. Her nipples hardened between my fingertips as I stood behind her with my erection poking her in the back. She backed into me and pulled my hands down between her legs, parting them. My fingers explored the area as she grabbed the seeking hand and guided my finger to the exact spot to rub for maximum enjoyment.

Kathy moaned, spinning herself around and washing me in those areas she had purposely skipped earlier. Her tender digits enriched my stiffness as she intensified her actions with lathering soap in hand. Just when I thought she couldn't excite me further, she pressed herself against me and lathered my ass. Without warning, a small finger entered me and began to rub me in a place never touched before.

"Hey," I stepped away from her, not knowing if I may have actually enjoyed her uninvited intrusion in that split second before her finger was forcibly removed.

"Guess you're not used to that. I'm sorry."

I noticed there were still two females remaining, and a naked Ed in the shower next to us. They stared for a second until I turned away and grabbed Kathy by the hips and pushed her up against the wall. My arms held her in a stable position beneath her upper thighs as I penetrated her craving pussy.

"Oh, yeah," she said as each inch of my hardness slowly filled her. She opened her legs as wide as humanly possible, and I pumped her again and again and again for a few minutes until I could no longer postpone the pinnacle of my excitement from spilling over.

I felt the tension of the events of the last few months wash away, and although the act was purely about sex and not love, it felt like my body must have craved such a release for some time. Kathy smiled again, mouthing the words 'thank you' before grabbing my neck and bringing my mouth in contact with hers for a long, deep kiss.

******

BECOMING A DRILL sergeant came naturally with my military history and ability to project a loud commanding voice from within. Adding the fact that I was the one yelling orders and not the one obeying them, very little physical exertion was required of me. But saying that, a drill sergeant must never ask his recruits to do what he himself is unable to do. I had read over my briefing sheets for how they expect the new group of recruits to be trained, as well as a brief roster on what should be taught on which days.

Looking at the small group of people, I knew I could intimidate them, even if most of them had seen me naked, and vice versa. A talk with Kathy over breakfast informed me that our interlude was far from a rare thing in the shower block. In fact, it's almost a daily occurrence that people have sex in the shower. She told me the reason for the communal shower is to allow people to expend any built up sexual tension to clear us making us ready for the given day's business.

Ed and Kathy joined the six women and one man on the field, and they received the same sneer given to the others.

"All right, you two. Get in line with blondie at the front here who thinks she deserves to be this close to me." I waited for them to do as ordered and smirked before the next words came out. "On the ground and give me twenty."

Kathy winked at me, an obvious sign of her approval of my methods. My face set in stone, I yelled at her, "Another twenty for the cheeky baldheaded short-ass wench."

She obeyed, continuing her moves while the others had well and truly finished theirs. If she truly believed in what she and Ed were cooking up in poaching me to be a drill sergeant, she wouldn't take it personally.

The day consisted of aerobic type exercise, running and an obstacle course. I hadn't spent so much time talking before, let alone yelling, and by sundown, I felt my throat almost burning.

Everyone showered again at the end of it all, but Kathy washed down at the other end away from where I was. The night-time shower much quieter, no one so much as looked at anyone else while we all rushed through the process of getting cleaned up in the most clinical way possible.

Dinner was next, food served at precisely 7PM. I couldn't complain about the food at the PM compound. It compared favourably with what I consumed in the forces in the mess halls. Observing the groups of people, I dug into strips of roast beef and veggies at a table all alone. Ed and Kathy didn't so much as look my way as they sat at a table together while the new recruits all sat together at two tables pushed together.

Metal clanged on the table as a food tray was placed opposite mine. "Mind if I sit here?" the woman I knew only as Blondie asked.

I looked up at her. "Sure, be my guest."

"By the way, my name's Emily, not Blondie."

I stood and shook her hand. "Griffon, Jack Griffon."

"You've sure made an impact on your first day here, fucking Hayley in the shower and working us all like Special Forces recruits."

"Hayley? Oh, yes, I almost forgot after all this time knowing her as Kathy." I frowned.

"We all have many names. She was placed in New York as a friendly neighbour for you as soon as Ed saw that your girlfriend was killed and as bait for the real killer. I bet she made it seem like she gave a shit about you, sympathising about your girlfriend's death. She could have taken the guy out herself, but you wouldn't have known that until right at the end."

I lowered my head. "Yes." The lies piled up as the day progressed, and the distinction between fantasy and reality faded together in the same shades of colour.

"It's okay, Jack. She obviously liked you or else you wouldn't have made it here." She began to eat her meal at the conclusion of her words.

"I guess so. I'm a drill sergeant, so I don't expect to make friends here."

"Which is a good thing." She pointed to the table of recruits. "See those faces? In a few months, only one or two of those will still be here. The training's tough, the job can be fatal, and the bosses want only the best to work for them. You wouldn't believe who I had to kill to make it to where I am, but that's a story for another time."

"What kind of people do you kill?"

"All types. We're paid to transform people into corpses, and we're paid well. I'm the best, the absolute embodiment of the Praying Mantassassin. I flirt, seduce, fuck and kill all with the same emotionless disposition. Men can't resist me," her voice trails off in a husky tone.

"So basically, this place is like Charlie's Angels' sociopathic, nymphomaniac rebellious sister."

She laughed at me, flashing one of those smiles she must use on her assignments. I looked at her and wondered what it was she wanted from me.

"Just try to make the best of things here. You'll be making more money than you could ever dream of as a gym instructor or soldier and with zero risk and hot women throwing themselves at you."

I nodded. This was not the life I had dreamed, but neither was my shell of an existence back in New York after Melinda died. Yes, I decided to go along with their plans for me, but I would always look for the truth to the conspiracy resulting in me ending up at the compound.

I decided to call her bluff. "Why don't we go to my room tonight?" I asked.

"Well, I wasn't that hungry anyway." She put down her cutlery, and getting to her feet, she shrugged her shoulders, waiting for me to lead the way.

CHAPTER 5

EMILY LEFT SOMETIME in the early hours of the morning, after a few crazy hours of gymnast type sex. The new sun told me I needed to face my second day at my new home. Looking at myself in the mirror, I saw the same person on the outside, but the man inside was someone different. In my previous life, having sex in full view of several onlookers would never happen, nor would having sex with a near complete stranger. Yes, it had all been fun and felt good, but I had always been one of those old-fashioned types who wouldn't sleep with women I didn't feel anything for.

But what else did I have? The menace who came into my life took everything from me, which made finding him my new everything. But I found him, and hunted him and ended his miserable existence only to find out I was set up to do all that.

So I resolved to settle in at the compound, looking for diamond moments in a truckload of rubble filled days. Each day would be the same—breakfast, shower, training, lunch, more training, shower and dinner, and maybe sex with someone. And for what? To teach people to kill.

My room was well stocked with sets of green pants, shirts, and caps, a crude version of an army uniform. But when worn, said uniforms earned me the respect of a group of people for a few hours a day. I had a king size bed, a TV with a box for selecting television shows and movies to view, and a couple of dressers. One held drill sergeant clothes, the other, civilian clothes.

And there was also a toilet and a hand basin in a small separate room. I grabbed a set of clothes for the day and headed over to the shower block.

"Hey, wait up, man." A male jogged to catch up with me. I hadn't come across this man on my first day, and looking at his physique as he wore just a pair of briefs, I thought he'd draw all the attention away from me in the showers, which would be fine with me.

I extended a hand. "I'm—"

He accepted and finished my sentence for me. "Jack Griffon. Yes, I have heard about you already. All good things, my friend."

His skin had the shade which would cause envy to those who sunbake for hours and his accent full of smooth European flavour. I doubted he would ever spend a night alone.

"So you were out yesterday, then?"

"Yes indeed. I can't tell you the details, okay? I'll be around for two days, at least. We have a drink tonight?" he asked.

I had never been a big drinker, but one or two couldn't hurt. "Sure. You haven't told me your name, though."

We reached the shower block. "You can call me Bjorn." He opened the door, and I saw another new face. A long-limbed African looking woman, completely naked, was walking to the shower. At that point, I guessed her to be taller than me and her muscle tone more pronounced than my own.

"Her name is Nakato. She is the only woman here I haven't made love to," Bjorn said.

"She's magnificent." I could picture her out in the jungles surviving on hunted prey and protecting her territory with lethal force.

"Stick to the other women. That one will only reject you time and time again. She doesn't talk much to anybody, and they don't talk much to her. She only speaks to the bosses."

"When do we get to meet the bosses?"

He let out a big belly laugh, and as we reached the showers, he removed his briefs, much to the delight of the young female recruits. I stood under the showerhead next to his and concentrated on having a quick wash and getting the hell to the mess hall for breakfast.

But two young women had different ideas. "You can have Bjorn today, and I'll have DS. Tomorrow we swap," the dark haired one said to her friend. "If you guys are okay with that?" DS became my call sign from my very first day at the compound, a quicker way of saying Drill Sergeant. While such an action wouldn't fly in the marines, I found the abbreviation kind of cool.

"Of course." Bjorn smiled as the other one walked up to him, pressing herself into his chest.

At my age, I could have nearly been this girl's father, but the tattoo on her right breast pretty much guaranteed she must be at least eighteen years old. She smiled at me, and if I said the sight of her in all her glory wasn't a wonderful sight, I would have been lying to myself.

******

BJORN AND I sat together at breakfast, the pair of us

having just had sex in the showers with a pair of eighteen-year-old girls. I couldn't help but feel a little dirty about it, although if only early in the day, I could have used a strong drink.

"It's okay, my friend. We're encouraged to be free here and experience as many sexual partners as we can. You know some of those girls won't be around in a matter of time. They just don't know that yet, so we can, at least, be accommodating to their desires."

"They're so young."

"Yes, but they're women. I won't make love to the underage ones. I do have some morals."

"I was always brought up that things like sex were between two loving people, and our bodies weren't meant to be on display to everyone."

"Yes, but you probably had a mother and father who told you that you would go to hell for that, but if I couldn't make love to so many women, I would be in my own hell. If God didn't want us to lust over the female body, then why did he create them to be so beautiful?"

I could have tried to argue, but what would be the point?

"In Europe, we sunbake naked on public beaches, and no one bats an eye. Why be ashamed of what we've been given?"

"I guess this isn't like me. I'm in my mid-thirties, and in the two days I've been here, I've doubled the number of women I've had sex with in total. How can I concentrate on doing my job?"

"You just do it. Have the sex and move on. Of course, you get into the moment and give it your best because your reputation is on the line, but once it's over, just push the emotion away."

I looked him in the eyes, and he smiled back. "You know if you come out to the field today, I'll be making you work as hard as everyone else."

"I would be disappointed if you didn't."

******

AT THE END of my second day at the compound, I met up with Bjorn and Ed in Bjorn's room. He brought out a bottle of Vodka and three shot glasses and put on a playlist of classic rock with the likes of Led Zeppelin, Pink Floyd, and Deep Purple.

"Welcome to music trivia shots. When a new song starts, the first person to correctly guess the song and artist is the winner, and the other two have to drink. Bjorn is the reigning champion," Ed said. He filled all three shot glasses and while one song finished, another began.

"Brain Damage by Pink Floyd," I called out within a few bars. I knew I was right. My Dad played the 'Dark Side of the Moon' album continuously when I was a young boy.

"You're good," Ed said, and he and Bjorn took a shot.

A few more songs played, and I was yet to take a drink while Ed appeared to slur his words. Bjorn held the same expression as he wore before the game started, like a World Series of Poker player. We shared conversations while the songs played, but I made sure to steer away from asking too much about the place I had found myself in. While Bjorn seemed to enjoy a chat, Ed always looked at me as if he were waiting for me to say something wrong so he could pounce on it. I put it down to him being a cop.

"Cornflake Girl by Tori Amos," Ed said as the playlist took a different turn. "What, you thought we only listened to stuff your dad might play?"

I returned the icy stare. "That was my hope."

Bjorn and Ed both stared at me. If these near drunken men thought they could scare me, they were in for a surprise. I picked up the shot glass and poured the liquid down my throat, the dryness burning all the way down to my chest. I've never been good at drinking straight spirits. I felt my face warm up, and the other two laughed at my short-lived discomfort. The next song came on, and then a few more. Being nineties pop songs, I had no clue. The alcohol ran through my body, relaxing my muscles and causing me to smile for no reason whatsoever. With the second bottle of Vodka opened, I pushed all thoughts on waking up in the morning aside.

"So who here thinks Kathy, or whatever her fucking name is, is the best lay here?" I asked. So I let it slip while my inhibitions were rapidly slipping away.

"Well, she's up there for sure, but I'm biased given she's my sister," Ed said.

I spat out my mouthful of Vodka, not caring that it wasn't even my turn to drink again. What the hell did I just hear?

"Okay, sorry about that, Jack. She's my stepsister, so there's nothing wrong with that. But you know who my other favourite lay is?"

Bjorn stood and removed his shirt, signalling Ed to come over, which he does. They pressed their bodies into each other, hands sliding up and down each other's chests while their lips locked. I'm not homophobic by any means, but that didn't mean I felt comfortable watching this right in front of me. Their hands travelled lower and found the zipper to the other's jeans.

I poured another drink and threw it down, and then another. My ass remained on my chair while my eyes didn't wander away from what unfolded in front of me.

As I poured another shot, both men continued kissing, now completely naked and fondling each other.

I thought to myself, *so this is how Ed answers my question. I'm not ready for this. I need to go back to my room.*

"Hey, Jack, won't you join us?" Ed asked, his eyes moving their way down my whole body.

I tell a lie. "I don't feel so good. I'm not much of a drinker." I staggered away from the table, opened the door to the outside world, and then ran back to my room.

I wondered if everyone at the compound wanted to fuck everything in sight. Opening the door to my room, I saw Nakato lying naked on my bed.

"What the hell," I said out loud. To have called the sight of her breathtaking would have been a disservice to her. It was time to add another notch to my belt.

CHAPTER 6

WEEKS PASSED AND the reality of the place hit me day after day. Sometimes, I got with Emily, and some nights were filled with wild African style lovemaking, while the morning shower interludes occurred about twice a week with young recruits. Bjorn gave up on asking me to join him and Ed for late night drinking sessions while Kathy—Hayley or whatever her name was—still hadn't spoken to me since my first day there.

I hadn't stepped foot off the compound since arriving. Apparently, those high above didn't trust me to such a degree yet. The money was good, and I could buy stuff if I placed an order at the office. I didn't bother with trying to personalise my room. The little amount of money I did spend was on bottles of scotch, books, and CDs.

My time at the compound was just like New York, constantly surrounded by people, but still lonely. It suited me. I received constant sexual release without having to form a relationship with someone who could never shine a candle to Melinda.

I woke at five a.m. and made my way to the shower blocks. I finally had a chance to shower alone without the temptations of female flesh surrounding me. I desired to turn my life around, starting with going to bed earlier and rising earlier, going for longer runs and scoping this place out. While far from a prison, I had never been offered the opportunity to leave for a weekend, nor informed the actual location of the compound. I had my theories, given the climate and varieties of native flora, but I estimated we could be anywhere from California to Brazil. However, if I couldn't leave, it didn't matter.

I opened the door to the shower block and saw I wasn't alone. The young dark haired recruit known as Avril lay naked in a pool of blood flowing from a deep cut in her neck.

"Oh crap," I said aloud.

"So it's begun," I heard Ed's voice behind me. "Once one of the recruits is able to figure out what the practical exam consists of, we soon accelerate to the end of the test."

"So they start killing each other?"

"Yes, we only want one of these six to make it to assassin status. We don't interfere nor warn any of the others of the game."

Game? These young people take each other's lives, and Ed calls it a game? I bottled my concerns.

"I know you had sex with Avril a few times, so I hope you didn't get emotionally involved," Ed said.

"Not at all." It was true—it was purely physical. It didn't make me feel better about the dead girl in front of me, though.

"Use the private shower. I'll get Bjorn to make this mess disappear."

******

AS I MADE my way to the exercise yard, I noticed a male body lying face down on the grass, and upon closer inspection, I could see the face of the only male recruit of this intake. Ed was right about how quick things played out. Emily, Kathy, and Bjorn soon joined me on the field, and the three of them placed a bet on which recruit they believed would make it through.

"They say when Francine saw me fuck and kill that man yesterday, she licked her lips," Kathy said. "My money's on her."

"Get on the ground and give me fifty!" I yelled. "All of you... NOW!"

On the training field, I was in charge, so none of them ever challenged my authority there. But if looks could kill, the one gifted to me from Kathy would have been enough to make the compound vacant. I made them train the whole day with the body of the young man lying in front of them. It wasn't our job to solve a murder mystery, but the seed of curiosity had been planted deep within me to see if I could pick the killer from the reactions.

The remainder of the day flew past without incident, and Bjorn carried out his duties removing the body and cleaning the scene of any blood. I had yet to go to the graveyard at the compound, but I had never been one to make many visits to any. Even visits to Melinda's place of burial were minimal.

The next body to be discovered happened just before dinner that night, outside of the meal hall, and when Kathy heard it was Francine, she shook her head and threw her fifty-dollar bill at Ed, as word also escaped on the death of Bjorn's pick.

"This is happening way too fast, my friend. I don't like the smell of it," Bjorn said to me at the dinner table.

"I thought it wasn't our job to interfere or make

judgement," I said.

"You learn quickly, but normally, the deaths happen during acts of a sexual nature. Avril was the only one found naked and maybe she didn't even have any sort of sex."

I sighed. I swore to detach myself from caring about the recruits after I found Avril in the shower. Death catches up with us all in the end, so why should I care if people like this kill each other?

"I'm just here to train, Bjorn."

******

IN THE EARLY hours of the morning, a knock on the door of my room woke me. When I answered, I opened the door to the red-haired recruit, Bridget, naked and covered in blood.

"Don't worry, it's not my blood. I'm the winner, and I'm here to claim my reward," she said. The corners of her mouth curled up while her eyes looked down upon my groin region.

Allowing her in and shutting the door behind her, I pushed her up against the wall. I pulled my silk boxers to my ankles and took her from behind. During the whole process, she moaned until I made her come, something I had never been able to achieve for a woman previously through intercourse alone.

Maybe the sight of blood gave me some newfound super-powered fucking ability.

"Holy shit, DS. That was nothing short of incredible," she said to me as her knees gave way.

I picked her up from the floor and put her back on her feet. "We need to go shower and wash this blood off."

"Sounds good to me. We get nice and clean, so we

can get dirty again.”

Walking into the darkness from the confines of my room, I looked up at the stars as I thought about how small and minute we really are in this universe. Millions of stars and planets exist so far from us, full of mystery, and a potential for life forms to exist somewhere out there. I waited for Bridget to go on ahead of me before shutting the door. I admired her ass as she went on ahead towards the showers and looked up again before chasing after her.

“I can’t believe I killed them all. Are you proud of me, DS?” she asked me as we reached the door of the shower block.

“Of course, I am.”

She smiled and opened the entrance door and ran on ahead of me again. Without any lighting, the block was almost pitch black before one’s eyes could adjust. As I flicked the switch to illuminate the block, I saw Bridget pointing a gun at me.

“What are you doing, girl?” I asked.

“Phase two.”

“So this is how it ends? I train you to kill so you kill me in return?” I took a step towards her.

“It’s not personal. You’re just the first of phase two. I had known everything about this place before I got here, and I played you all. I’m bringing this place down and killing every single one of you. When they hear the gunshot, they’ll find your naked body with this gun in your hand and me crying that you shot yourself.”

“Fine. Do what you must. I’ll even turn to the side so you get me in the side of the head to make it more authentic.” I wasn’t lying.

“That won’t be necessary,” another voice joined the conversation. Before I could look at the newcomer, the sounds of several gunshots echoed from the walls and floor.

Bridget's eyes stared at me in horror as her lifeless form crashed to the ground. I looked from her defunct body to spot the shooter.

"It happens every now and then—an opportunist slips through the cracks to try to take down our organisation. They start with the recruits and try to move on to take us out. Last time, they nearly took my sister out," Ed said.

I looked at him wearing just a pair of undies and didn't even think about what was about to happen next as I walked up to him and grabbed his face in my hands.

"I'm not gay. I'm not even bisexual."

Then I kissed him for what seemed like minutes and ran my hands up and down his waxed chest.

"It's okay, Jack. I'll be gentle with you."

CHAPTER 7

NEARLY FOUR YEARS had passed since I first woke within the confines of the PM compound, and one particular round of would-be recruits stuck in my mind. Although there were only three in that cycle, all three were worthy contenders, and to think only one could make it through really bothered me at the time.

I had been doing my job for nearly a year when I saw the three of them, and a girl by the name of Brittany captured my heart on her very first day. Not in a romantic way, but her feats of courage and determination were of those I had never seen anybody during the previous three cycles I trained.

Despite her skinny frame and glimpses of her soft demeanor, she pushed through round after round of push-ups I would command of her.

Over time, she and the other two potential recruits built up a strong bond, and I worried her gentle nature might see her be the first to perish.

But somehow, Oliver had managed to kill and dump the body of a girl we knew as Faith, and after an act of passion, Brittany managed to take out Oliver, the young man with lightning quick reflexes.

"Hey man, I'm wasted," Bjorn said after knocking on my door. He sniffed the air. "Hey, you stink like Jack Daniels."

I had been asleep for a few hours after downing another bottle of my new favourite drink and had no idea how long Bjorn had knocked before I woke.

"What is it?" I asked, my head still feeling heavy and blurred.

"Brittany's in trouble. Says she and her date were ambushed by a pair of knife-wielding thugs. She's still at the house where her date lives with his mother, and there are three dead bodies."

"Why can't Ed take care of it?"

Bjorn sniffed a few times, and then I spotted the white powder beneath his nose.

"Are you fucking kidding me?" I asked. "You help run an assassin training compound and decide to snort your weight in coke?"

"If you decided not to hang out with us anymore because of one incident of anal sex in the shower, that's not my problem."

It was true. Since the night with Ed, I had kept to myself every night and didn't have sex with anyone since, male or female. I even resorted to showering every morning at five a.m. in the shower cubicle reserved for women on their period just to ensure I no longer faced nudity and temptation in the form of any person of any gender.

"I lost touch of who I was and needed to cleanse myself."

"Looks like you've had enough of that poison to cleanse a village. Get dressed. Chopper leaves in ten minutes."

I grabbed a set of civilian looking clothes and rushed to the showers to try to sober up a little. As the water drenched my tired body, I thought about Brittany and the friendship we had built up in the three years since she graduated to full Praying Mantassassin status. After her training, I was able to put away the fear of her perishing during the training cycle and build up the type of friendship that made me feel like an older brother type.

The water splashed against my face and body, not doing a thing to brighten my mood or help my senses. I needed to get it together. I quickly dried myself and dressed before heading for the helipad, making sure to grab my pistol, too.

"She's pretty shaken up, said she killed the two men, but they killed her boyfriend beforehand. I don't know if she's been drinking or got high on something, but you need to be a vigilante," Ed said before I embarked the chopper.

"You know I fucking hate helicopters, but I'll take care of your girl. You got nothing to worry about."

"Oh, and you know I have to blindfold you before you get in that thing, though?"

Maybe not seeing where I was going would be better for my nervousness from flying or maybe it would add to my anxiety. I didn't care. For the first time in nearly four years, I would be outside of the compound.

"Fine by me," I said.

I almost felt butterflies circling my stomach as I took my seat next to the pilot, the sounds of the rotor slivering the chill of the night air. I fastened the safety belt and allowed Ed to tie the blindfold around my head.

"You can take it off in ten minutes," Ed said.

"No problem. See you when we get back."

******

I HAD NO idea where we were flying, nor the name of the town we descended into. It took a few fuel stops to get us to Brittany's hometown, and given the relatively low number of streetlights and house lights, I dared to guess the town not to have any more than ten thousand people in it.

I sat and hoped the police hadn't already been all over the scene and taken Brittany away.

"We'll land just down there, it's only two streets away from her current location," the pilot said.

I pulled my pistol from the back of my jeans and hoped to hell I wouldn't have to use it. I saw flashing lights in the distance and wondered if they were headed in the direction of Brittany's position. I knew I would have to get her away from her boyfriend's house swiftly. Sure, Ed was a cop, but he couldn't control the whole of the police force in every town and city in the United States.

"What town is this anyway?" I asked.

"You don't need to know. Just get the girl."

Relief washed over me as I disembarked the chopper and took in the directions given to me by the pilot.

I noticed a man walking a dog across the street from the sports oval where we had landed, but he paid me no attention. I guess people often saw helicopters land on their sporting oval in this place.

I hated not knowing where I was, but I had a job to do, and in the short time it took me to reach my destination, I didn't come across any more people. It appeared to be the kind of town where all the action ceased after dark—unless you were in a hotel.

Looking down at the driveway, I saw three dead males and a wide pool of blood surrounding each of them. Time didn't exist for me to take much notice of any of them, the priority being the survivor inside the house. Concealing my held pistol inside my unzipped jacket, I pushed the front door of the house fully open. The faint sound of sirens sang in the distance telling me not to waste a single second.

"Brittany," I said, keeping my voice to a normal volume.

"What the fuck are you doing here?" Brittany stepped into view from a darkened part of the house and into the lightly illuminated dining room.

Before me stood a woman wearing boys' clothes fitting very loosely and with a newly shaved head. Her eyes appeared vacant, but a bloodied knife remained held with a strangling grip.

"I'm here to take you back."

"Why? I fucked up, and there are three dead men out there. If I go back to the compound, I'm dead."

"No you're not, and that's the honest truth. I don't know what happened, and you don't need to tell me, but we have to get going."

"I don't care anymore, DS. Everyone I love dies. I'm poison."

"Why do you think I'm so detached, Brittany?"

"Because you're an asshole."

"You know that's not true. I loved a woman once. We were going to get married, have a baby or two or three, but some psycho nut job put an end to that." I put a finger of my hand not carrying the gun to my chest. "I think about her every fucking day. She didn't deserve to die, and I didn't deserve to lose her. I had it all. I had everything. For a few moments in my life, I actually held the pinnacle of true happiness in my fingers. Nothing else mattered because I had my soulmate."

Brittany stared at me, a tear falling down her cheek.

I continued, "But she's gone, and I'm never going to

see her again. Every time I fuck someone in that damn compound, I think of her, and not a single woman I've been with could even call themselves a freckle on Melinda's precious skin. And afterwards, I would feel so ashamed of being intimate and not caring about the woman I had just fucked. Most nights, I drink myself into a stupor and masturbate watching porn, and then wake up the next day and yell at people so they can be better killers."

I couldn't believe what I was admitting to her, but the time of caring about my self-worth had long passed.

"Brittany, I look at you, a lot. Not in a dirty way, but when I see you, I see a young female version of me. We're broken, Brittany, and no one can ever fix us."

It was my turn to cry, and at that moment, I didn't care. Brittany took a few steps until she made it to where I stood.

Closing her eyes, she pressed her face to mine, and we shared a quick kiss, the most unusual one I had ever had. There was no passion in it... no lust or even romance.

"Thanks, DS."

"We have to get moving. By the way, love the hairstyle."

Smiling back at me, I didn't spot even a tiny bit of joy in her expression. "Apart from Ed, you're the only guy who hasn't tried to fuck me, and I love you for that. I always knew you had some kind of a soft spot for me."

We held hands as we walked back to the chopper, not exchanging any further words until we stood beneath the rotating blades.

Sometimes in our lives, all it takes is a split second to change everything, and as I looked into the young woman's eyes, I knew what I had to do.

Pulling out my gun, I took a couple of steps away

from Brittany. "Get in the chopper, now."

"What is this?" she asked.

"This is me telling you I'm done." The volume of the police sirens increased. I looked at the chopper pilot, who had a pistol drawn and aimed at me. "Don't even think about it or I'll shoot the bitch."

"No, please. You have to come," Brittany yelled.

I aimed the pistol, and fired, knowing how good my aim would be from that distance.

Brittany grabbed her shoulder and screamed while I made a run for it, hearing the noise of returned gunfire echoing in the outside air.

Putting one foot in front of the other, I headed away from the helicopter to find a place to hide temporarily.

I didn't look back, even upon hearing the chopper ascend and leaving the area. As much as he probably wanted to stop me, I dared to think the pilot wouldn't want to be in the vicinity when the police cars and ambulances arrived.

I put my pistol back in my jeans and kept running until I saw a truck parked down the road at a service station. I checked my wallet while waiting for a driver to return.

"What the hell you doing by my truck?" the driver asked upon his return to his vehicle.

"I need to get out of this town, and I have one thousand dollars in cash for anyone who's happy to let me ride with them a few hours."

He looked at the paper notes in my hand. "I can take you as far as Alabama. But remember one thing, I don't want any trouble."

I looked in his eyes and hoped my answer would satisfy him. "I eat trouble for breakfast."

"Well, get in then. It's gonna be a long night."

I opened the door and took a seat, looking ahead at

the darkness in front of us. I hoped we would be heading in the direction I wanted and not coming from the opposite direction. I closed my eyes a few minutes into the journey, and for once, I felt good about life again— before

I slipped into another dream about the better times in my life.

ED & HANNAH

CHAPTER 1

Ed

I REMEMBER THE day I graduated from the police academy, making a pledge to protect and serve the public. I never strayed from said promise, but I did partake in a double life. A life which saw me choose who I would protect and who I would allow being fed to the angels of death—my Praying Mantassassins.

It was a smooth operation. Most of our assassins were female, hired to fuck the targets of our clients, and then kill them. Our organisation didn't care too much about the reasons or motives behind someone wanting someone else to be taken out—we just assess the job and take their money. In a crazy world, people will always want others killed for all numbers of reasons.

Our sole purpose was to cash in on a lucrative market.

My job involved placing myself in several police precincts, getting into databases and pulling up information on clients and targets. In addition, I ran interference when necessary and covered up crime scenes. No one in the force suspected me of anything until *she* came along, walking toward me down the hallway at the precinct with her inviting smile tacked in place and her hand extended to capture mine.

"Hi, I'm Hannah Hall. I recently graduated from the academy and am excited for my first day on the job."

I accepted the warm touch of her hand in mine. "Ed Nelson."

Her eyes stared into mine a little longer than they should have. I couldn't deny her beauty, our first meeting just a precursor to her following me like a puppy. The truth was, I preferred men to women, but if my job involved getting intimate to keep my cover or achieve part of a job, then I didn't have a problem with it.

"So what do we start with today?"

"Well, I operate better after the second cup of coffee, so a white one with two sugars would be fantastic," I said.

"Great," she said, disappearing from view, and I hoped she knew where she was going.

After she had vanished from sight, I made a quick phone call. "Who the hell have you partnered me with?"

"Don't worry. She's just a new recruit, as keen as mustard but not real bright. Information in front of me says she only just passed the theory in her training. Just go about your normal work, and I'll be in touch if anything comes up."

The call ended abruptly, and I stole a curious glance at my personal mobile phone. Nothing required my attention. I smiled and returned my phone to my pocket a few seconds before Hannah reappeared and passed my coffee to me.

"Thanks," I said. I took a sip and nodded my approval to Hannah. "I need to drink this, and then we'll head out."

"Okay," she said. That lingering smile appeared on her face again, and I didn't understand the look given to me, like a sixteen-year-old yet to master the art of disguising their fondness for someone.

The sergeant walked my way. "You two, we have a domestic dispute. You'll probably get there and be told nothing's wrong, but you know the drill. And Ed, try not to punch someone in the face this time."

"Hey, that's not fair. That guy deserved it." I threw the rest of the coffee down my throat and grabbed the keys to my assigned squad car.

"What's he talking about?" Hannah asked.

"You ask a lot of questions. Last domestic dispute I attended, I was partnered with a woman around your age, and we get to this house. The man answers. I can see blood on his fists, and he won't let me in the house. Next thing, this kid comes and stands by his side and says his mummy is crying." Hannah picked up the pace and remained by my side while we walked to our destination. "So I ask the boy where his mummy is and can he go get her, to which the man tells me to fuck off. Now, coming from a home where my dad used to beat me up, I couldn't hold back, so I punched him in the nose."

"I think you should get a medal personally, but the law doesn't work that way."

"No, and that's one of the most frustrating things about the job. Do you have a temper?" Despite her smallish frame, she could have been hiding a well-sculpted figure under that uniform. Sometimes, it's the small, wiry types who really pack a punch.

"I keep it under control. I grew up with three older brothers, so I can handle myself if necessary."

This girl interested me the more she talked. I placed

my sunglasses on my head before we hit the morning sun and headed directly for my usual ride. I always loved being in a squad car, driving the streets and being away from the stuffy confines of the office. But saying that, the days would be long if each day was spent with a rookie.

"So how long you been a cop?" she asked me.

"Twelve years. So are you here to work with me or make me feel like I'm being interviewed on a current affairs show?"

Hannah turned away, and we spent the remainder of the journey in silence. If I offended her, I didn't care, and nor was I going to apologise.

******

HANNAH AND I walked side by side to the house, a rundown slum in a community housing project flagged for an incidence of domestic assault. I nudged my way in front and pressed the button for the doorbell. Heavy metal music played from inside, almost loud enough to cause the windows to shatter. We waited a few minutes before having another go at the doorbell and knocked on the second attempt to get an answer.

"Who the fuck is it?" a male voice boomed from somewhere within the tired looking property.

"It's the police. Please, open the door." A few seconds passed after I yelled, and Hannah looked for my lead.

My hand travelled to my holster. Dramatic quiet pauses that occur after telling occupants the police are at their door are generally a cause for concern. Hannah did as I had done, and I knocked again.

"Come on, Mr Davis. Don't make this worse. Please, open the door." My tone remained calm.

More seconds passed by. I looked at the door in front of me and mentally weighed my options. The door seemed to be constructed of a wooden material, not likely to break my foot. As if reading my mind, Hannah nodded at me.

Using the full force of my legs, I kicked the door, centring the core of my strength near the doorknob. With each strike, the timber of the door creaked a little louder, until the fourth attack. At a point where the chipboard structure split, we took the opportunity to look into the house.

"Motherfucker," a male voice boomed. Without a chance to aim my weapon at the solid mass charging past the broken door directly at me, the man tackled me and brought me down with his superior weight advantage.

My head thumped on the ground. My vision instantly blurred as my eyes watered from the impact. Before I could locate my attacker, I received a punch in the jaw, and my head collided with the ground again.

I hated the feeling of not holding the advantage. All I could do was hope Hannah would step up. The man appeared as a blur. Seeing movement, I waited for the next blow to land.

It never came. Cut by the sound of a roaring bullet, the man fell on top of me, and I felt a fluid splash on my face. The man's body crushed mine underneath as he lost control of his movements, and the weight threatened to shatter every bone in my body.

"What have you done?" a female screamed. Hannah ran over and rolled the dead man off me, giving me much-needed relief from the extreme pressure the dead weight put on my ribs.

I coughed a couple of times and rolled over. "Lucky for girl power, hey, Ed?" Hannah said.

"You killed a man."

"Yes. No big deal. He deserved it."

I looked her in the eyes. "Shooting is a last resort. Can you imagine how much shit we're in for this?"

"Yeah, I saw the whole thing, you fucking whore," the female companion of the dead man yelled. "You're gonna get in so much—"

Hannah fired again hitting the woman in the throat. I stood to look at the dead woman for a few seconds and then back at my new partner. "You're a crazy fucking bitch."

"We couldn't have her blabbing her mouth. Her boyfriend deserved to die, and if she was stupid enough to stick up for him, then so did she."

"Fuck, how do we sort this mess out?"

"We put the gun in her hand, make it look like a murder-suicide. Check the house for drugs and plant them on her if we find any."

"How do we explain the fact she has a police issued Glock in her hands?"

She smiled at me and looked around. I figured everyone else in the neighbourhood must have been at work, as we had yet to see any onlookers. Or maybe people were just shit-scared to come out after what Hannah had done to the couple living at the address of the house.

"Punch me in the face," Hannah said.

"It's crazy, but it may work," I replied. "But be warned, this will hurt."

I swung with my left fist, hitting her cheekbone. I didn't hold back anything, and her head twisted around as my hand connected. Expecting her to fall to the ground, I couldn't help but fill with pride as she absorbed the contact and kept on her feet.

"You hit like a fucking girl, but nice work," she said.

I laughed and got her to set up the crime scene while I made a phone call.

"This better be important, Ed. I'm about to go into a meeting," the voice on the other end of the line said.

"My new partner has killed two people on our first call-out. What the hell do you want me to do with her?"

"Call Bjorn and get her away from the scene with you. Make up an excuse to clear off."

I'm the master of quick thinking. "Sure. Consider it done."

******

"IT'S NOT A good look leaving the crime scene like that," Hannah said, rubbing an ice pack from our first aid kit on her bloodied cheek. I managed to break the skin of her cheek, but I was sure I didn't break anything else in the process.

"Well, you're the one who caused the mess, so don't question my methods. What kind of trigger happy habits do they teach in the academy these days? I've got a good mind to turn you in, you crazy bitch."

"I'm sick of these scumbags, Ed. We've got the guns and the badges and can make a difference to clean this city up. The prisons are almost full, which is why the scumbags that should be locked up aren't locked up."

I shook my head, as much as I wanted to openly agree with her. During my half-hearted police career, I'd killed my fair share of suspects who should have been brought in. Maybe someone higher up in the force knew all my secrets and had partnered me up with this crazy woman to make me face the reality of my true self.

If that were indeed the case, they couldn't have been more wrong. I'd never had a problem with who I was and the sins I'd committed. But what if this woman were something else entirely? She could have been the woman of my dreams if it weren't for the fact I preferred men or my step-sister. Or had she been partnered up with me to dig into my other life?

Either way, I had to play the game. If it were sex she wanted, I'd give it to her, and if she were partnered with me to dig deeper, I'd let her do it until I could find out who'd planted her in my precinct.

And then I'd put a bullet in her pretty little head.

CHAPTER 2

HANNAH

AFTER MY FIRST day working with Ed, I found myself home alone lying on the couch watching TV in a dark room, lit only from the flickering of the screen opposite the couch. It was time to make a phone call to Inspector Devon Morrison, my superior responsible for relocating me from my detective duties to working alongside Ed.

"So what have you got for me?" Devon asked.

I took a deep breath. "We were called to a domestic dispute where I shot two people dead. I had a solution, but after the incident, Ed said he knew someone who could take care of the mess, so we didn't stick around."

"Oh fuck. You killed two people. If any of this shit floats back to the surface, you'll be the one explaining it. Like I said, you have four weeks to find something, or else I'm extracting you and putting you back where you came from."

"Look, Inspector. I know it sounds harsh, but doing what I did today could well be the key to earning this guy's trust. If he's dirty and I play dirty, I could blow this wide open."

"You have a defiance just like your father did, and it got him in such deep shit, he never found his way out. I warned you, if you're wrong about this, you're on your own. But if you're right, you need to be careful."

I nodded. "I understand. I better go."

"Be careful, Hannah."

With that, the call ended, and I pressed the remote control in my hand until I found something at least a little interesting to watch while I peeked at the laptop resting on the arm of the couch. I went to the website which had first brought my attention to this supposed PM organisation, searching for any new posts from the blogger known simply as DS.

Hickey's Pigeons contained blog posts from conspiracy theorists from all around the world. From theories denying Neil Armstrong's walk on the moon to the naming of US cities in code to enable visiting aliens a direct path to the Whitehouse—all manner of crazy stuff was there to read. I used to look at the site for amusement purposes only until one headline caught my attention a few weeks ago.

A man simply calling himself DS posted a story about a place where people, mainly women, were trained in the art of seducing and murdering clients. They were schooled to be assassins-for-hire for people willing to pay big money to have someone killed. Looking at the post stats, no one paid much attention to his story, but one particular case grabbed my mind in a way none of the others had.

'She called herself Kathy and others called her Hayley, but although small and charming enough to entice a priest to enter a bed with her, she was the most vicious woman I had ever known. In fact, she had a

secret room where she would have sex with an unsuspecting male while prospective students watched on, and after the act would kill them while they were recovering from the vigorous activity. I was drinking heavily at the time, but before the cleaner did his job, I saw one of these victims for myself and vaguely remembered him from my days in the service. A few years older than I was, Norris Slater was a sniper engaged in duties in Afghanistan in the early days of the war. I ran from this secret room and said nothing, and then drank myself into one of my worst stupors ever, only finding my opportunity to exit months later. They say they're just ridding the world of filth, but I believe in God and America and the justice system.'

I remember the next day at the precinct I was working in looking up the name he gave, and sure enough, Norris Slater was listed as a missing person. So each day I logged on and tracked DS's posts, and even tried looking up the initials for listed ex-servicemen. Although several matches came back, looking each one of those men up on the databases brought no likely candidates for this man called DS.

The website didn't allow for subscribers to contact posters, so I followed each of his posts carefully for any clues until one caught my eye about a police officer serving to cover up the crimes committed by the assassins. Listed simply as Ed, I spent hours at work searching for every officer named Edward in the United States. This was no small feat, but I eventually found the man I was looking for.

His postings in particular precincts matched unsolved murders or missing person cases in the corresponding towns or cities. Inspector Morrison wasn't so keen on my wanting to chase down a lead from a blog poster on a conspiracy theory website, even with the matching evidence I had shown him. But I had done my homework on him, and in a non-accusing way, questioned him about the word on the street concerning a lady he was seen with who wasn't his wife.

It was a dangerous game I was playing, but I knew there was something in DS's posts which required investigation. But using his position to influence the right people, Morrison found a way to insert me alongside Ed within two weeks.

I put the laptop into sleep mode and tried concentrating on the TV show in front of me while my brain ran around in circles a hundred miles an hour. One tiny slip in this mission could see me kicked from the police force at the very least if things went pear-shaped. Or even worse, the mission could kill me.

I decided maybe a glass of wine might relax me. My unit was an open living plan, so the kitchen was located in plain view only a few feet away from where I sat. Peeling myself from the couch, I directed my path to the pantry in search of a bottle of red. It was only 7PM, but I was already settled in for the night in my long t-shirt, wearing nothing underneath. Many nights were spent sleeping on the couch, the glaring light of the TV my only companion.

I selected a bottle of one of my favourite low-priced cabernet sauvignons and thought about grabbing a glass when I heard a knock on the door. Only new to this place due to my assignment, I wondered who could be visiting me.

The bottle still in my hand, I looked through the peephole and saw a handsome man in a white shirt and jeans, and within a couple of seconds, I recognised him as the man I had been recently partnered up with.

"Hi, Ed. What brings you here?" I smiled as I opened the door.

He looked me up and down, my hair flowing just past my shoulders, free of the constraints I usually placed it in for work.

"Have you eaten yet?" He proffered a brown paper bag, fumes escaping and whetting my appetite. He looked at the bottle in my hand. "I love a good red."

"I'll get plates and glasses." I turned my back on him and fetched the required items from the kitchen. Following a few feet behind me, he detoured to the small dining table.

"I just wanted to come see you, talk about what went down today. I couldn't say it earlier, but I respect the choices you made out there. I've always wanted to do something like that, end the miserable lives of a pair of drug addicted, welfare sucking losers."

"It felt good." I smiled back at him from behind the kitchen counter, pouring two generous glasses of wine and searching desperately for two matching plates. Part of my act involved separating my emotions from this façade I was portraying to this potential corrupt cop.

He emptied the contents of the brown paper bag, revealing a container of rice as well as two other containers. "Lemon chicken—your favourite."

One question cops don't ask each other is how they know something. "You know it." I walked to the table and placed a glass of wine and a plate in front of him.

"Thanks, Hannah," he said, and brought the glass to his lips, taking a long gulp.

I took the seat opposite him and piled the lemon chicken onto my empty plate. I hadn't realised how hungry I felt until I smelled the food he delivered.

"You need to take better care of yourself. I get the impression you wouldn't have eaten if I hadn't come."

"I would have scrounged something up, but thanks for coming over. I'm new here in this neighbourhood."

He looked me up and down again. "Hard to believe you'd be alone."

I did a great job at faking embarrassment and looked down at the floor. Feeling vulnerable wearing just a long shirt, I sensed his eyes on me, as if he had superpowers to know of my nudity beneath the lone garment. After a few seconds, I looked up again and into his eyes. "I'm not one to settle down."

We each emptied our glasses only to refill them again. I felt sure of where the night would go and would bring out another bottle if I had to. He gulped his food, washing it down with the second glass of wine.

"This is a great drop, Hannah. I think I'll need to stock up on some."

"I have more, Ed. Give me a minute." I smiled at him as I dismounted from my chair, allowing my shirt to ride up to my upper thigh.

My mind and body were feeling the early effects of the wine, my steps a little less steady than before the impromptu dinner date. From the corner of my eye, I spotted Ed walking towards me, and I made sure to bend over in full view to him to reach a wine bottle, allowing the shirt to ride up my hips.

"Looks like you forgot to put something on," Ed said. A hand touched my exposed ass, and I sensed him standing close to me.

"You always touch your new partners like this?" I turned my head a little to display a smile full of mischief.

"Only when they show me a beautiful ass such as that. You're not exactly trying to hide it from me."

I stood up straight again and faced him square on. "Don't you think this will make our working together awkward?"

"Maybe," he said. His hands reached out and

travelled to the hem of my shirt, lifting it inch by inch. I felt his eyes staring at my pussy displayed to his leering sight, and I made sure to remember I needed to display no inhibitions while on this assignment. His hands continued their upward journey, and I lifted my arms. The shirt soon became separated from my body and thrown to the floor. I stood completely naked in front of him.

"Well, this isn't fair. You've got all your clothes on." I stepped close to him and did the same with his shirt as he had done to mine. His upper body was a remarkable sight.

I placed my hands on his biceps, gently kneading the strong muscles before sliding my hands down to his chest, running my fingertips across his hardened nipples. I slid my hands down to his abs, the texture of the ridges so tight that I doubted a baseball bat could damage him through his armour of muscular corrugations. My hands failed to find a part of him not firm and travelled down to below his navel. I didn't know if I should do this, have sex with someone I might need to bring down. But my mind was on the bigger picture, knowing I needed to do everything I could to gain his trust. And besides, he was so fucking hot, and the wine amplified my desire to feel every inch of him.

He pulled me against him, and he leant down to kiss me on the lips. With our mouths pressed together, we exchanged the lingering taste of wine on our tongues. I could feel myself getting wet and mentally commanded my hands to travel to the button of his jeans, freeing it before lowering the zipper. In one swift movement, I pulled his jeans and briefs to the floor and then cupped his erection in my hands.

His hands came at me, one scooping below my leg at the knee, the other finding the moist area of my center. A finger gently parted my sensitive lips and soon, explored the very essence of my sex.

I pulled him closer to me, the tip of his cock very near my welcoming entrance, urging him to begin an authorised admittance inside me. I closed my eyes as he thrust himself inside me, my back leaning against the open pantry. Him filling me nicely, I allowed my body and soul full immersion to the moment, forgetting everything else that existed outside of this sexual encounter.

I moaned with every pumping movement, the delight increasing the longer he fucked me. My back arched, and I reached for the upper shelf behind me to stabilise my stance before becoming weakened in ecstasy.

"Sorry, Hannah," Ed said, withdrawing from me and shooting his load onto my belly. I looked down as the warm fluid sprayed me. Then I reached down to pump as much as I could from him before he was totally spent.

I stepped back from him and looked at the mess he had made. "Well, I'm gonna have a rinse, and you've had too much to drink to drive home, so I'll meet you in my bedroom."

"Okay. I have to show you something tomorrow, so we'll need to get up early."

"Sounds like fun," I said and smiled while putting a finger in the puddle he made in my navel. I then brought my finger to my lips and licked it. He looked back at me in shock, which was nowhere near as much as I felt for doing such a dirty thing.

CHAPTER 3

ED

I COULDN'T BELIEVE things had happened so quickly with Hannah. I took a big gamble making an unannounced visit, and I couldn't work out whether she was really easy, highly attracted to me, or just trying to gain my trust.

I had to admit she was great in the bedroom—and the kitchen, even the shower. It was the first time I had been with a woman for a few months, apart from my regular interludes with Hayley. I felt it necessary to get her to feel close to me so she might blow her cover if she was, in fact, trying to work against me.

I woke up to the sound of my alarm at 6AM, Hannah's naked body lying close to me. We had to be at the station at eight, but I had a phone call to make which could change all the plans for the day.

"Oh, geez. It's that time already," Hannah said looking at her clock after my alarm woke her. She smiled at me and felt around between my legs. "Can't we just have another fifteen minutes in bed?"

"I have a lot of stuff to do before work, like calling into my place on the way."

She pushed off the sheet and commenced climbing on top of me. "Something better to do than this?"

My body failed to respond to the excitement she expected of me. I needed one of my pills, the ones left in the bathroom of my temporary apartment. "How about later, Hannah. I'd love to, but I think you wore me out last night."

All of my secrets would be exposed to her soon enough if I received authorisation to bring her in. Including the one about my preferred sexual tastes. I did have a plan for her, and my hope was my superiors could agree with where she would fit in with an upcoming mission. The first moment I saw her, I knew she would be the perfect fit, unlike our African assassin, Nakato.

I quickly threw my clothes on, trying to ignore the show she was putting on for me on her bed, staring at me while touching herself. How the hell could any mortal man keep up with her sexual appetite?

"If you could stop masturbating for a second and listen to me, that'd be great."

"Fine." She covered herself with the sheet.

"How serious are you about ridding the world of a little more scum?"

"I'm extremely serious. You saw how much I enjoyed putting those scumbags down at that house. You think you can get me more of that action?"

"I know I can." I bent down and gave her a kiss on the lips. "I'll call you soon."

******

I MADE SURE she wasn't following as I drove away

from her house and travelled for another ten minutes before finding somewhere suitable to pull over and make a call. It had been quite a few years since I graduated from the academy, but I was lucky enough to keep a youthful look about me and pass as a fresh rookie when the occasion called for it. The next assignment would require me to do exactly that—appear to be the younger officer in the partnership with Hannah in a more active role than I was used to playing.

People with money had a way of finding us, and this next mission would involve a few of us to play our parts in a big conspiracy against a real estate agent in this city. It was quite an elaborate show this woman wanted our organisation to put on, and she'd even requested to be the one to fire the fatal bullet. It wasn't something we normally allowed, but a million dollars convinced our superiors to operate outside of our normal practices.

"Sir, I think this new partner of mine might be able to fill in that last role. She's a natural blonde and a dirty slut and doesn't mind taking out the trash," I said into my burner phone.

"You've only known her a day. How can you be sure you can trust her?"

"She's more than willing to jump into bed with a guy she's only known for a few hours, so I have no doubt she can fulfil the sexual part of the role we need. And I don't have any other female contacts on the force anymore. If she turns on us, I'll shoot her."

There was a long pause in the conversation, but time had taught me not to try to push the man into an answer. Cars drove past on their usual early morning routes as I patiently sat in the carpark outside of a supermarket making the phone call. I quite often watched normal citizens of the towns and cities I was stationed in. I would wonder how boring their lives might be, working for unappreciative bosses who paid them less than their worth, all while I got to act a part of a cop, have sex with many people of both genders, make lots of money and kill people on occasion.

"Okay, Ed, but this is on you to fix if it goes pear shaped."

"Don't I always fix things, boss?"

The last part of the sentence was spoken into a phone with no one listening. I felt no surprise. He knew the answer, but he never vocalised how much of an asset I was. But I had gotten what I wanted from the conversation. Then my phone rang again.

"I cleaned up that mess. What happened to you last night?" Bjorn asked on the other end of the line.

"Slept with a woman who I need for the next mission. And what's it to you? You trying to be my dad?"

"No one knew where you were, Ed. Please, just be careful with this woman. She's a cop, like you."

"I doubt very much she's a cop in the same mould as I am. Just relax. I got this, Bjorn." I cut his call and thumped the seat next to me. He and I had always had a thing going, but I knew he preferred women, unlike me. That had never been a problem for me, though, having not had a relationship since I was a teenager. Even Hayley and I were only there for each other for fun.

I sat for a few more minutes and threw around ideas about how to bring Hannah in, as it was way too early to take her to the compound. I checked my phone for inspiration. I found a name and called the number.

"Emily, I need you to set up the meeting room at the gym. I'll call my sister and get her to bring a man."

"Sounds interesting, Ed. What have you got going on now?"

"A potential member for our 5PM mission. We might have to kill her after the mission, just in case, but

I need to make sure she has the stomach for it. You won't like her—she's as sexy as you are."

"I highly doubt it, Ed. You know how much of a freak I am in bed."

I laughed out loud. "Well, I didn't try everything with her that we did together." My experience with Emily had been quite intriguing, and like she said, she definitely was a freak between the sheets.

"I'll have the room set up. You just arrange who'll be in attendance.

******

"WOW, LOOK AT this line-up. Not so sure I have the energy for this," the man in the business suit said. "But no offence, I'm not into dudes."

I winked back at him. As promised, Emily had set the room up with a queen-sized bed, complete with black satin sheets and pillows with red pillow cases. Hayley wore her blonde bob wig and a white singlet top and short black skirt. Emily stood by the door in business attire. She worked at the gym as the manager and wanted to make sure the whole place was vacated except for a select few I wanted in attendance.

Brittany stood in a corner biting her fingernails, which I put down to the fact I had Hannah with me, dressed in her police uniform. I wore the same outfit I'd had on since first arriving at Hannah's place the night before.

"How about you start with me," Hayley said. She pulled her top over her head and pointed to the bed.

The man did as told, keeping his eyes glued to the pair of breasts barely contained in the lacy white bra supporting them.

Hayley and I had grown up together as teenagers.

Her mother had married my father, and we used to sneak into each other's rooms quite often at night. We were each other's first sexual encounter. I still found her a turn-on, she being the only female I had feelings for like that. It had taken me some time to adjust to her fucking men other than me, but it had become kind of necessary for her job, and at least, when we do get together, things turn out better for me than these other guys.

The man in the room stripped down to his briefs and looked around awkwardly at the rest of us.

"Yes, we're going to watch you," I said to him as his eyes met mine. Reading his expression, I could feel his nervousness, fearing that I'd want to have a go at him. "Don't worry, I'm not into pompous old businessman types."

Hayley looked my way as she straddled the man, and smiled as her bra came off, revealing the best pair of tits I had ever seen. Everyone else in the room stared on as she fished his cock out from his briefs, massaging it before shifting herself on top of him, the actual penetration hidden by the skirt she kept on.

A stiffness grew in my own pants, my mind wishing I was in the man's position as Hayley's tits bounced around when she arched her back and bobbed up and down. I'd been inside countless times, so I knew how much he was enjoying it.

Hannah stood watching on as the only person in the room not knowing the final part of the act. If she were in shock of our voyeuristic entertainment, I couldn't see it on her face. The man screwed his face up and let out a big groan, and Hayley bounced a few more times before dismounting.

He let out a few deep breaths and looked at Brittany. "I'm going to need a few minutes."

Hayley walked from the bed to a cabinet. "You won't need a few minutes," she said and revealed the gun she fetched from the cabinet.

"Hey, what the fuck?" The man sat up before Hayley fired just once, hitting him between the eyes. His lifeless body collapsed on the bed, and Emily rushed over to wrap him up in the sheets.

I looked at Hannah. She turned to me and said, "Well, I guess he didn't see that coming."

"No, he didn't." My eyes took in the rushing and tidying motions of the women in the room as the corpse was wrapped and taken away while Hayley put a new set of sheets and pillows on the bed. I knew the next part to come, and a few minutes later, the room appeared as it had when Hannah and I first entered. "And I bet YOU didn't see this coming," I pointed at the door.

Nakato entered arm in arm with another businessman type, smiling just as the last guy had when first seeing the women in the room. Looking through at Hannah, Nakato nudged the next victim forward and said to Hannah, "Your turn."

CHAPTER 4

HANNAH

WHEN I FIRST took on the assignment, I asked myself how far I could go. Could I cross that line if it came down to it? The line separating black and white swallowed so much of each shade I couldn't see anything but grey, and all I could do was work out which part of the grey I felt comfortable existing in.

But if there was once a line, I sure as hell had crossed it already, and when they brought the man into the office at the gym, I would have to cross it again.

"So, Mr Grange, did you say you had a fantasy about getting it on with a police officer?" the African woman asked the silver haired man she had escorted into the room.

He ran his gaze all over me. "Indeed."

It was time for the show. I pulled the band from my hair and spun my head to allow it to flow freely. Taking a few steps towards him, I undid the buttons one by one, revealing more of my body to him with each unfastening. I pushed my emotions away. If I didn't go through with what was expected of me, the mission and my life could both come to an abrupt end. Embarrassment, guilt, fear, and regret could not ride with me if I were to do this convincingly. Something shiny caught my eye on his finger—a gold wedding band hit by the light from the overhead fluorescent tube. I could use the fact I was doing it for Mrs Grange.

"Mr Grange, get on the bed, coz you're under arrest."

I took off my shoes and undid the button of my pants. Mentally blocking out the rest of the people in the room, I allowed the pants to fall to my ankles and then lowered the shirt from my shoulders. I stood a few feet away from the man wearing only my matching bra and panties. Thinking about having sex with Mr Grange did nothing to turn me on at all, and I had to remind myself it was just an act, like a prostitute.

He ripped his clothes off and sat in the middle of the bed. I didn't know which part of him to look at as I spotted a chest covered with a carpet of grey hair, a car salesman type of expression on his face, and a tiny flaccid cock resting on the mattress where he sat. "Are you gonna restrain me, officer?"

Perfect. I picked up the handcuffs from the discarded belt and smiled as I held them near him.

"Hands in front of you. You're under arrest for extreme handsomeness." As I spat the cheesy line out, I felt thankful the other people in the room were professional enough to not burst out laughing at my obvious lie.

I watched him get hard as he presented his hands, allowing me to secure his wrists in front of him. Giving him a subtle push, he laid back and rested his head on the pillow. It felt like his eyeballs were already having sex with me. I unclasped my bra and threw it to the floor, but his eyes were still staring at my panties. The time came for me to take a deep breath and expose it all.

"Oh, nice," he said to me the moment my last item of clothing left my body. "I like it when the carpet matches the curtains, unlike so many chicks who shave it all off."

I couldn't allow his fascination with my pubic hair to distract me. He thought he was there to screw a high-priced call girl.

Climbing on top of the bed, I grabbed the horrid thing between his legs and rubbed it a few times in a firm grip between outstretched fingers. As hard as he was, I didn't feel the least bit wet and ready for him. I closed my eyes and thought about Ed's sexy body from the night before as I sat up and lowered myself on top of his erection.

He was nowhere near as long as Ed, and when I leaned forward and put my hands on the man's chest, I received two handfuls of course hair, unlike the smooth muscular chest of Ed. Moving up and down, I was careful not to move too much for fear his small penis would fall out and push me out of my autopilot mode of fucking.

In less than a minute, I could hear his breathing accelerate. I opened my eyes and smiled at him as I removed his cock from inside of me and pumped him by hand so his load shot up at his chest.

"Oh, man," he said, his restrained hands not allowing him to grab a sheet to wipe himself. I took my gifted moment to get off the bed and fetched my pistol from my belt. I had to finish the act convincingly and think of the consequences later. I turned to him with gun in hand and pointed it at him.

"Hey, what the fuck?" he said.

"Have you heard about the praying mantis and the

way the female eats their mate post-coitus?"

"No. Why are you doing this?"

I ignored his question. "You don't look appetising, so I'll have to do it this way," I said, looking in his eyes as I fired three quick shots in his face.

"Impressive," Ed said.

******

WHILE THE OTHERS cleaned the mess in the room, I ran for the gymnasium showers. I felt dirty in so many ways. I dreaded to think how long it would take to shower and cleanse myself of all that I had done. Alone in a giant shower cubicle, I sat beneath the flowing water, my legs wrapped up against my chest. Surrounded by pale ceramic tiles, I allowed the tears to flow freely.

My father had been my inspiration for entering the police force, and if he knew what I had done in the last two days, I don't think I could have looked him in the eyes again. I wanted to howl and scream, but I couldn't risk the type of attention those actions could bring.

I needed to get my shit together. Any of them could enter at any time, and if I were supposed to be some type of femme fatale, I couldn't be found in such a hopeless emotional state. And if I did everything right, I could blow this whole Praying Mantassassin conspiracy wide open and put the last four deaths behind me.

"Hey, are you okay?" A female voice came from the other side of the locked door of the shower cubicle.

"Yes, I'm fine, thanks."

"You've been in there for nearly half an hour. My brother's wondering what the hell is up."

"Just making sure there's no blood on me, Hayley." It was a poor lie, but the best I could come up with.

"Well, try to wind things up quickly. Ed says you and him need to be somewhere."

I climbed to my feet and turned the water flow off. Grabbing the dry towel from its rail, I went about the business of drying every part of my body before putting the clothes back on that I had worn to the gym. What the hell else could Ed want to expose me to on this day?

******

"YOU DID GOOD in there, Hannah. Real good. Some of the new recruits hesitate and make a mess of it. Occasionally, one will back out of the sex or murder, but sometimes, we get someone like you. Did you feel anything about shooting that man?" Ed asked.

"I felt good. I saw that wedding ring and thought to myself 'you dirty prick.' Any man who cheats on his wife deserves nothing less."

"Wow, sexy and unforgiving. You have it all, girl." He smacked me on the ass and walked to the driver's side of the car.

I climbed in around the other side of his patrol car. I snuck a peek at my cell phone and saw no messages waiting for me. Morrison knew not to contact me until I gave him a new number each day when I purchased a new burner phone. There had been no opportunity so far, and I had to make sure if I did get one on any given day, no one would find it or be able to contact it, apart from Morrison.

My father had warned me about the loneliness and isolation one went through while undercover, and everything he ever told me only proved to be an understatement. He'd said he had balls of steel and a photographic memory, both being the most important tools of any undercover cop. Well, I didn't have balls—

just good old fashioned courage like past powerful women in history.

"I'd be lying if I said I wasn't a little embarrassed having sex in front of everyone in the room. I was thinking of you when I was with that creep."

"Well, that's normal—the initial embarrassment and thinking of me when you're with another guy."

I smiled at him. "Why, you cheeky man." I wasn't falling for him at all, but his sexual prowess had me itching for more "So where are we going now?"

"To meet a man. A sleazy piece of filth whose help will be needed for our next mission. I don't like the guy, but in this line of work, you'll meet a lot of people you don't like. Some of them you get to kill, but some you have to side with for the mission to be a success."

I resisted the urge to ask too many questions, but to not ask any could also shine a light of suspicion onto yourself. "Have you ever killed someone on a mission who you shouldn't have?"

He looked at me through a pair of eyes hidden by his thick sunglasses. "I can't think of many of us who haven't had to work outside of the mission parameters, but you didn't hear that from me, okay?"

"I understand." Ed seemed like a decent person, despite his homicidal tendencies. But I was on a different mission, which would possibly mean having to bring him down. At that moment, I began to wonder if I was actually cut out for undercover work.

But I was already in too deep, and to back out now could mean an end to not only my police career, but my life, too.

CHAPTER 5

ED

I SAT ACROSS the table from the pompous sleazy form of Roger gritting my teeth. "So you're willing to do all this to your best friend in order to have a shot at getting with his wife?" It had been a ten-minute meeting, the majority of the conversation coming from me as I went through the details of his part of the mission.

"Have you seen this fucking goddess?" Roger asked.

"No, I've never met her." It wasn't a lie. Talissa hadn't been an active member for some years, so I hadn't met her. I had seen photos of her, making Roger's summation accurate, if I were into curvy brunettes. "Of course, now we've had this meeting, if you go outside of what I've requested you to do, the consequences won't be pleasant. We need to get this guy to cheat on his wife, and the chat program is the key to it. You'll have a week to familiarise yourself with it, and the names of those users inside of it. You can't write anything down, no evidence whatsoever. Commit it all to memory, and feel free to have some fun. Your friend will suffer the week from hell, and you have to support him to a point. And no speaking to Kate about any of this. She asked for your involvement, but to converse with her about anything is a risk she doesn't want to take."

"So what will happen to Terry?"

Hannah looked at me as I answered, "Hopefully, he'll just lose his job and his wife—and doesn't take things too hard and kill himself. You can't worry about stuff like that now. You've signed up for this gig, and it's up to you how you live with your sins after the act."

"Hey, if it means anything to you, I don't have a conscience. Thanks for this opportunity." He stood from his chair and extended his hand to me.

I stared at him. "Just stick to the plan."

Hannah and I walked from the diner to the car in silence. During our meeting with Roger, she'd remained silent, not being privy to much of the details of the upcoming mission. There would still be a few days to go over her part, and from what I had already seen, I knew she had the capabilities.

"Wow, that man hasn't heard about the bro code," Hannah said as we buckled up.

"You meet all types in this line of work, and many of them are not nice people. What Roger doesn't realise is he won't be riding off into the sunset with the wife of his best friend."

Hannah nodded. She knew not to ask me to clarify what that meant. For the remainder of our journey, we engaged in small talk, our conversation centering more on TV shows and cooking. It had been a hell of a day for her, but I had full confidence she was ready for the job. Plus, I had some video footage of her in case she tried to turn me in.

We pulled up out front of her place, the same

location where I started my day. "Are you going to come in?" Hannah asked.

I thought this would happen. I sighed and looked her in the eye. "We can't keep fucking. What if it gets back to our superiors?"

"Are you serious? I'd be more concerned about that other thing, you know, killing people and stuff."

"That's easier to hide. But if we stay intimate, people will notice our chemistry. You're a hottie. You can get anyone."

"Yeah, I am, aren't I?" She opened the door and left, and I needed to get onto my next investigation.

******

"ISN'T THIS ALL types of illegal?" the young man behind the computer asked.

I pulled out a stack of twenty dollar bills. "Would this make you feel any better about breaking into the police databanks?"

"A few more of those and I might well forget what the word illegal even means."

It felt too easy. I could have gone in offering much more money, but taking into account the man's age and the fact he lived with his mum and dad, I knew I could start low. I presented another stack of paper to him, and he smiled, tapping away at his keyboard.

My gut was still telling me something didn't entirely add up. Hannah seemed too good to be true.

"I want to know everything about her. Her family, who she hung out with at the academy and who she's worked with and for."

"Wow, she's kinda hot," the hacker said. His fingers raced along those keys as he opened several tabs in the internet browser. "So why can't you look up this stuff yourself? You're the one who works for the police."

"At the time we busted you, you had all of the old records downloaded to your computer. I led my superiors to believe that I erased all of your machine's records and the illegally gained information held on your hard drives. The stuff you have could bring so many of this nation's fine officers into deep shit, but I wanted you to keep all that for a reason."

"So what's this enchantress done?"

"You don't get to ask questions. Is there anything else you have on her?"

The man stood. "No, that's it. Knock yourself out."

I took the offered seat and clicked on each of the tabs on the top of the browser window until one caught my eye. I checked the date of the file note detailing a promotion to a Miss Hannah Hall and the name of her commanding officer.

"Okay, I have you now, Hannah." I pulled out a USB stick from my pocket and plugged it into a port on the hacker's machine. "I need you to zoom and crop this so you can only see the two people having sex in this video. And the quality needs to be clear enough that I can make out their faces."

"Oh wow. Sure thing, officer. Mind if a make…"

"A copy? Knock yourself out." I stood and walked away from the computer, grabbing my phone to make a call. "Boss, it's me… I don't care if it's a bad time… That new partner of mine is a fucking detective, not a recruit, and I need to get a hold of her superior, Devon Morrison."

My boss told me to end the call and wait for his return call.

"Holy shit! She's smoking hot," the hacker said.

"You can't share this with anyone until I say. Then you can go crazy with it. Make it go viral for all I care."

"No probs, man. Who's the lucky dude in the video with her?"

"It's probably better for you not to know. How long will this take?"

"I'm guessing about ten minutes, even less if you leave me alone."

I nodded at him and took a walk outside, and my phone rang a minute later.

******

THE HACKER TRANSFERRED a zoomed and cropped video to my phone of Hannah's sexual encounter with the man she killed. It took the young man a couple of minutes to calm down after he saw how it ended—the man in the video getting his brains blown out. A few more twenty dollar bills helped to encourage him to get back on track with the job I had requested.

After I had driven for ten minutes, I found a quiet place to pull over to make a call. On the third ring, I heard a voice on the other end.

"Internal Affairs, Inspector Morrison speaking."

"As in Devon Morrison?" I asked.

"Who is this?"

"You best let me ask the questions. My name is Constable Edward Nelson of the NYPD, and I've been partnered with a detective you might know. Does the name Hannah Hall ring any bells?"

"I've never heard of her."

"Don't lie to me... Inspector. You may have deleted the files, but that doesn't make Hall a new recruit. She's a detective who worked under you before you transferred to IA."

"Who the hell do you think..."

"I've got evidence of her doing something very bad."

"Arrest her then. Why should I give a shit?"

"Are you in front of a computer now?"

"Yes, I'm still at the office. Why?"

"Well, check your email. There's a very interesting attachment in one addressed from a Harry Bollocks. Don't worry, it's virus free, but riveting viewing."

"Harry Bollocks? Is this some sort of joke?"

"Open the fucking email before I send it on."

The line went quiet for a few minutes until he got to the part where Hannah made her kill.

"What the fuck is going on, Ed?"

"You wouldn't recognise the man, but he is a loyal member of the Lambigino mob family, so if they were to get a hold of this footage, what do you think happens to your girl? And the man who ordered her to do the hit?" I asked.

"You son of a bitch. What the hell do you want from this?"

"You excommunicate Hannah and allow me to use her for a job. When I'm done with her, you get her back. You try to contact her, I send this video to the Lambigino Family and attach your name. They might not get you straight away, or even a month or year later. But when they do, they won't come for you first. Do we understand each other?"

"I could trace your number and find you and make you disappear."

"Yes, you could. But if anything happens to me, this video goes viral. I've taken all insurances to make sure what I want to happen does happen. And then everyone gets to go on with their lives."

I ended the call and opened the phone and snapped the sim card in two. I used my baton to smash the phone to pieces and decided it was time to head to PM headquarters.

******

I SAT IN the office of Praying Mantassassins headquarters, talking into an intercom to a person known to me only as Mr M. I had never met him in person, nor seen a picture of him or known anything about him apart from being one of two people who owned and ran the PM organisation.

"Hannah has been acting under the supervision of an Inspector Morrison, who I now have wrapped around my finger. We'll get the mission done and kill Hannah in the process—after she's served her purpose. The video footage will be released after her death, which will be passed off as a revenge killing performed by the Lambigino Family. I'll be stationed far away and let the precinct fight it out with the mob."

"You're a callous man, Ed. Remind me not to ever piss you off in case you find a way to locate me. What about Morrison?"

"His life will depend on whether he unleashes the dogs on me or not. All I have to do is drop his name to the mob and his family starts dropping like flies, and he'll be left for last."

"Nice work, but one last thing, Ed. Don't ever bring another fucking cop into our missions again."

CHAPTER 6

HANNAH

I PACED UP and down the short hallway. I'd tried five times to get hold of Morrison, all to no avail. Instead of speaking to my superior, I was told by his receptionist that he was in a meeting. I decided to give it one more go.

"Sorry, Miss Hall. Inspector Morrison has finished for the day."

"Can you give me his personal mobile number?"

"No, you know I can't do that."

"This is fucking urgent. I'm on an undercover mission, and I need to report something of major concern. Get me the Inspector now."

"Miss Hall, do not try to make demands of me. Goodbye."

"SHIT!" I threw my burner phone against the kitchen floor, watching pieces break off from the main part of the body of the phone. I knew something had to be up, my inability to communicate with him worried me. Had he been compromised? Morrison was my only link at the moment and the only person I could trust. Was it possible Ed had gotten to him somehow?

I had to stay strong. I couldn't let my paranoid mind get the better of me and blow this whole operation. And besides, I was so far deep with the PM organisation that if I were to back out now, I could be in the deepest of stinking shit piles on both sides. I decided to go for a walk and visit a place I hadn't seen for years.

******

KNEELING INSIDE THE old confession box threw so many childhood memories back to me. Back then, I'd asked the Catholic father to forgive me for things like lying to my parents, not doing my homework, smoking behind the school sheds, which had graduated to getting drunk on weekends while still in high school and my first time fornicating at one such party.

"Forgive me Father for I have sinned."

A deep male voice responded, "Please confess your sins."

"It has been ten years since my last confession. In the last two days, I have fornicated with two men, one of those in full view of a number of onlookers. I have lied to nearly everyone I've met up with, killed two junkies and another man after I performed a sexual act on him. Oh, and I fantasised about performing further sexual acts on one of the men I've been with."

"Young miss, we live in different times, and for most things, I would say you need to pray for penance, but you've killed people, so you need to turn yourself into the police."

"But Father, I am one of the police. I've been working undercover and made sacrifices for the greater good, because what I will soon uncover will save so many lives. When I sleep, I see the dead I have put there, and even when I blink. But now I'm alone, and the realisation of my sins weighs heavily on me. I need someone to tell me that what I'm doing still has merit, and there is a chance for redemption."

"Hannah, you must believe in yourself," a third voice said.

I knew that voice. Opening the door to the booth, I saw my father in the flesh smiling at me. I ran up and wrapped my arms around him. Tears fell, and I couldn't think of anything else to say.

"I never told you about the things I did while undercover all those years, and I can still never tell you or your mother. My hands aren't clean either, but sometimes, I had to take one for the team."

"Did you hear everything I said to the priest? No father wants to hear about their daughter doing slutty things."

"No, I didn't like hearing it. But I knew one day you'd be undercover and having to do foul things. If you don't, you can be killed. In my time, I tried pot numerous times, a bit of coke and even acid. I had sex with prostitutes and even the wife of a high-ranking mob boss. Your mother knew I wasn't faithful, of course. She didn't actually ask me to confirm it, but she just knew. I could outsmart anyone when I worked undercover, but your mother always knew if I wasn't honest with her. You might have your father's cop instinct, but you have your mother's beauty and ability to see through the bullshit. If it ever gets too much, give me a call, and I'll get you out and send you far away. I love you, and nothing will change that."

We embraced and cried on each other's shoulders. I had always been Daddy's girl, and I wondered if there was actually a power in the universe stronger than a man's love for his daughter, and hers for him. Nothing could hurt me in the moment of my embrace with my rock and my soft place to fall.

"I have to ask what made you come here? I didn't even know I was coming here until an hour ago," I said.

"I come here a lot since I've retired, helping to give back to a church which has done so much for this community. And your mother hates it when I sit around the house all day."

We laughed for a few seconds, and we relinquished our embrace. I wanted to sit with my father and talk for hours, but I had to leave soon. The mission would be starting in a few days, and I had to get familiar with the part I had to play.

Chapter 7

Ed

KNOWING YOU'RE IN the presence of a rat is partly satisfying in that you know their true loyalties and partly daunting in that if you let your guard down at any time, they could bite you. I knew of Hannah's Catholic upbringing, so it wasn't hard to find out the exact church she might call into. Of course, it was a long shot, but setting up a spy-cam and microphone didn't take much effort, so the cost withered into oblivion compared with the potential gain.

At work, she hung on me like we were a honeymooning couple. Fellow officers seemed to shush whenever we entered a room together, and if Hannah's aim was to get the precinct to believe we were a romantic item, she seemed to have succeeded.

It didn't matter. In fact, it could give me the perfect alibi for when I had to kill her. I would just have to use someone else's weapon.

The small group gathered to listen to the recording I made of Hannah at the church and the women each had their own reaction. Hayley wanted to kill her ASAP, Brittany punched the wall while Emily kept her poker face.

"I fucking knew it. She was trying too hard to get our trust." Brittany pulled a joint from her pocket.

"Geez, bitch, no smoking that shit in here," Hayley said to her. "Let me go to her place and put a bullet in that pretty face of hers."

I walked over to Hayley and pulled her in close to me. "Calm down, my lovely sister. Things will be just fine." I kissed her on the lips, and I just wished I could take her there and then.

"Can you please stop referring to each other as siblings before you make out? It's fucking sick," Emily said. "I'm off to get more acquainted with our temporary member."

"Hey, don't do anything stupid," I said to her as she opened the door to leave.

"Don't worry, Ed. You know I'm good at this shit. I just feel like a bit of a dinner at the hairy V, see if she's good enough to return the favour." Emily smiles as she exits.

"Damn, she's incorrigible," Hayley said and pulled me in for a longer kiss.

"Looks like it's just me and my pot and a vibrator tonight," Brittany said. Hayley and I turned away from each other to watch her leave.

******

HAYLEY AND I made sure we made it to her room at the compound before we fucked each other's brains out. No other woman ever compared to her in bed, or on a table or out in a field, or anywhere we had sex. I guess that's why I got bored of sex with other women. I still liked it, but getting with another man gave me no chance to compare them to Hayley. I never loved another man. I just used them for sex.

"Do you ever think we could just leave all this behind for a while and just go out and see the world together?" Hayley asked me as her generous sized breasts sat upon my chest.

"What else could we do? We're killers, Hayley. It's what we do and love."

"Yes, but we're not sociopaths. We have more than enough money between us to just go. The bosses know us and trust us enough to let us leave for a while. We don't have to come back if we don't want to, either. I love you, Ed. I just want to see every country in the world with you and fuck each other in every single one."

We locked lips again in a kiss threatening to lead to another round of lovemaking. While our tongues danced, I allowed the ideas she presented to sink in and explored the extremities of my brain and heart. Every man and woman have a weakness for someone, whether it be the opposite sex or the same gender. Hunger so ravenous it can consume the person who possesses it and causes them to be blind to everything else surrounding them. She was my Achilles heel, my mirror to the other half of my soul and the most satisfying object I could ever desire. When I was with her, I always swore to myself never to fuck another man or woman again. But given my work, I knew I was just lying to myself.

So why not? Why couldn't we do just one more job and free ourselves of the conformities of our lives and missions at PMHQ? I smiled. A smile so big it filled my whole body and mind with a fresh wave of enthusiasm for a potential new life. Sometimes, the destiny of one's life can change in a split second from the utterance of one idea.

As I rolled over, I grabbed Hayley's thighs and spread them apart. I thrust myself inside her, lowering my body, and then whispered in her ear, "Just this one last job, and we go. You and I... far from here."

She cried and spread her legs wider again and grabbed my ass. "Fuck me like it's the last time we'll do it."

CHAPTER 8

HANNAH

I WAS EXPECTING a quiet night by myself watching a romantic comedy on the TV with a glass of wine and some chocolate, so a knock on the door completely threw me. Who the hell would be visiting me at such a late hour? Maybe it was Ed. He was bad for me and technically, the enemy, setting me up to do some really bad things. But part of me wanted to feel him again—one last time.

Another knock tore me from my forbidden fantasy. Given my mission, I was always cautious answering the door. I grabbed my pistol and walked on the balls of my feet looking through the peephole. A familiar blonde figure stood on the other side of my door, and as I opened it, Emily smiled and gave me a hug and a peck on the cheek.

"So what brings you here?" I asked.

"I just think we should hang out, get to know each other a bit, seeing as we'll be working with each other."

"Okay, I'm drinking red wine. Care for a glass?"

"Just give me a long straw, and I'll drink from the bottle."

A smirk crept onto her face. I got her a glass from the cupboard and filled it to near the top.

"Ah, someone who shares my belief that a glass is made to be filled properly. You're my type of girl, Hannah." Emily walked to the couch and leaned on the right end.

I sat on the other side, and just two feet of lounge space separated us. She kicked off her shoes and put her legs up, almost touching my thigh with her feet. I watched her take a long sip of her drink.

"Nice drop," she said. "So is this what you do every night?"

"Pretty much, unless I have an early start."

She looked down at my legs. "You keep yourself in great shape."

"I exercise when I can. It can be hard with my hours."

"You like being a cop? Must be conflicting doing what we do when you're supposed to be on the side of the law." She didn't mince words.

"I think the type of people your organisation kill deserve it. Cheating husbands, corrupt politicians. Ed's told me a fair bit of the types of people who hire you."

"You looked like you really got off killing that gangster at the gym. A great performance, indeed."

Her eyes stared straight through me. I feared if I even just had a loud thought, it would give me away.

"Did you say *gangster*?"

"Yes. That piece of shit married man was part of the Lambigino family. Not high up on the food chain, but part of it regardless. No offence, but with a new recruit, we set them up with a gangster and hold video evidence just in case they decide to run or get a conscience again."

I hoped my face didn't give me away. "Looks like I better play by the rules then." I drained the rest of my glass and watched Emily do the same to hers. "I'm having another glass. I'm guessing you won't since you have to drive."

I walked to the kitchen and kept my nerves under wrap as I refilled my glass. Glancing to my left, I noticed Emily walking towards me. She showed me an empty glass, placing it next to the one I had just filled.

"I thought you might do a fellow girl a favour and let her stay over," she said, flashing a smile. There had been times I had been hit on by a woman before, so I guessed that was Emily's play. Another test perhaps?

"Sure, plenty of room here." I smiled back and filled her glass to the top again.

"Wine does crazy things to me." Emily took a big gulp from the freshly filled glass. Putting it down, she took a step closer to me. "That's why I don't drink it often." She bit her lip and looked me up and down again.

I drained my glass of the crimson fluid, and the effects of the third glass began to take effect. My mind proceeded to float through the wine-fuelled cloud while my facial muscles involuntarily plastered what felt like a silly looking smile on my face. I decided the best plan might be to call her bluff, so I took a step even closer to her.

"That's why I drink it very often."

Our faces were just a few inches apart. As my eyes soaked in her features, I understood how men could so easily become lured into having sex with her, and how big a part her seductive personality would play in the mission I would help her with. I began to wonder what would happen if I took the initiative. Leaning forward, my lips found hers, and we shared the taste of fermented grapes as she reciprocated my advance. Her soft mouth tasted so sweet, and I couldn't resist the temptation to wrestle her tongue with mine. I had never kissed another girl like that, not even during my crazy nights at the bar when I was training. Men would offer to buy drinks for any pairs of girls who would French kiss in full view at the bar, but having a lesbian aunt, it didn't seem right that while her love for another woman was kept quiet, these girls were kissing for exhibition's sake for free booze.

Emily was different. As dangerous as her persona made her look, she was beautiful. My hands reached for the buttons on her blouse, and as I unfastened the last of them, I opened it up and saw a pair of breasts supported by a lacy white bra, a pair I felt immediate envy of.

"Wow, you're a feisty one. I like it," she said. Pulling the shirt off her shoulders, she eyed my legs, and I wondered if she knew I was completely naked under the oversized t-shirt I wore.

I didn't give her the chance to find out straight away, pulling her into me and locking lips with her again. My hands located her bra straps, fingers releasing the clasp and setting her perfect boobs free. At this point, I knew there would be no going back.

I shook with nervous energy as my hands slid to her front and clasped her breasts, nipples poking out between my fingers. Her own hands reached around to my front, starting just above my knees, gliding upwards to the peak of my thighs.

Her mouth left mine and whispered into my ear, "No panties. Nice."

I put my hands on her thighs and discovered through touch the buttons near her left hip. With the flick of my fingers, I soon had the buttons unsecured and her skirt on the floor.

"I see we wear matching underwear."

I lifted my shirt over my head and stood completely naked in front of her. Grabbing her hand, I guided her to my bedroom and took a few deep breaths before entering uncharted territory.

"Get on the bed." Emily pointed. "I'm gonna lick you like a five-year-old boy licks a bowl of ice cream."

I climbed on top of the covers and leaned back, nervously opening my legs to the blonde woman climbing on top of me, gradually lowering her face to my waiting pussy. I put a finger there first to feel my extreme excitement, and I felt wet enough to accept the invasion of a twelve-inch cock without pain. Her tongue circled and flicked around the area surrounding my most sensitive body part, the part most crying out for attention. She moved her head slightly and allowed her tongue to slide inside me. She pushed her tongue in as far as she could, and then forward to the spongy front wall inside me. I clenched my fists, each of them squeezing a handful of bed covering as I arched my back.

She withdrew her tongue and moved her lips to circle my clit. I didn't know how much more I could take before exploding, and as her tongue applied pressure onto my most vulnerable body part, I opened my mouth and let out a scream, and my body vibrated. My mind floated to a land far away from where I was while my body shook as wave after wave of satisfaction washed over me.

"You're welcome," Emily said as I clenched my legs together and slowed my breathing.

"Holy shit," I said. I wanted to say more, but I felt like I just finished a running race.

"Maybe next time you can return the favour.

Anyway, we need sleep."

"Why can't men do that?"

"They don't own a vagina so they understand very little about the opposite gender's sexual needs. Most men I know slap their tongue around like a dog eating from its bowl, but one man I know, and who you might get to know soon, is an exception."

These people seemed like batshit crazy sociopaths, but they sure knew how to have sex. I waited another minute to calm down from my euphoria before climbing under the covers to get some much-needed rest.

******

THE ALARM ON my phone tore me from a dreamless night's sleep. Pressing the buttons on my phone in a half dazed stupor, the effects of a few glasses of wine the night before made my head spin. After my fumbling fingers finally shut the noise off, I looked at the sleeping figure of Emily and sighed when thinking about our girl on girl action before we slept. I wasn't upset about having been with another woman, but the fact I got so heavily involved with another of the Praying Mantassassins in a sexual way filled my head with conflicted thoughts of regaining a normal life after the mission was over.

Maybe it was already time to wind things up. If the mission were to go ahead, there could be another three innocent lives lost. I crawled out of bed, careful not to disturb Emily, and immediately searched in my wardrobe to put some clothes on for the day.

I knew what I had to do while the opportunity presented itself. I promptly dressed and grabbed my pistol and a pair of handcuffs. I aimed the gun at Emily and stepped towards her one foot at a time.

Her eyes flickered and looked at me and then to the weapon in my hand as I made my way to her side of the bed.

"What the fuck?" she asked. As she sat up and stared at me, I kept watching for any sudden movements which could potentially result in danger to myself.

"You're under arrest, Emily. I have enough information on your organisation to put you and your friends away for life."

"If I didn't know any better, I could swear you've already forgotten how good I was to you last night. I don't like feeling unappreciated."

"Hands behind your back, Emily. You can get out of this pretty lightly if you flip on the people you work for."

"You can arrest me and take me in, but I won't flip on any of my friends. And when they find you—"

"Yeah, come on, Emily. Say it out loud what you'll do. I dare you."

"I'll get you for this, bitch," she said.

I restrained her wrists as she sat up straight, smiling at my advantage. "I can't let you people go on killing the way you do. The party stops now."

"I know we were drinking last night, but remember what I said about recording what you did with that man you fucked and killed? I don't hold the video, but I know if something happens to me or if you even think about calling this in the video goes viral."

"I don't care, Emily. I'm quitting the force once I take you all down. I'm not cut out for this double life."

"Well, in that case, we need to take it up to the next level. Why don't you call your father, see how he is?"

I took a few steps and put the barrel of my pistol against her forehead. "You better not have hurt him."

"How could I? I've been here with you since last

night. Just call your father, let him know you're okay."

Keeping my gun trained on her, I picked my phone up off the bedside table and made a call to his phone.

"Hannah, don't do what they say—" My dad started.

"He wants to be brave, but I know you won't let him die," a female voice said on the other end of the line. "Please select Facetime on your phone. There's something you need to see."

I glared at Emily and selected the Facetime option. When I looked at the screen of my phone, I didn't want to believe my eyes.

"Bet you didn't see that coming," Emily said.

The blonde female could be Emily's twin, and looking from the woman on my phone to the one handcuffed on my bed, I assumed they must be twins.

"This is what happens now. You go ahead with the upcoming mission, play your part, and turn a blind eye to who gets killed. The woman who has hired us for the job will get the blame for it all. What becomes of her is none of your concern. If you cooperate, I don't tell the others, and you get to go back to your life," the woman on the other end of the line said.

"You have a twin?" I asked Emily.

"It's still news to me, but it's a fact which serves us well. I don't trust many people, so hearing there was another one of me out there was the best news ever."

"And how do I know—" I had said before Emily intervened.

"That you can trust us? Well, you can't. But for as long as we have your father hostage, you have no choice. And there's something else you need to do for me. Once the mission's over, I need you to take out the target's wife, and if there's any doubt as to why just look up the name Shauna Logan next time you're at the precinct you work at."

"And before I go, here's your father, for what I hope isn't the last time ever," Emily's twin said.

I looked at my father, his face badly bashed and his clothes all ruffled. "I can't let them kill you, Dad," I said and ended the call before he could mount a protest.

"I'll need that burner phone of yours, too. We can't risk you making a trace on it," Emily said.

I was defeated. I had revealed my hand to Emily, and she already had a much better one. I released Emily from the cuffs and allowed her to dress and leave, and as she shut the door, I cried into my pillows.

I couldn't accept defeat, it was not who I was. Maybe Emily would notify Ed, and maybe she wouldn't, but I had no choice but to go along and wait until I could guarantee my father's safety. I showered, dressed, and then had a look at my Praying Mantassassin mission directives.

They had everything planned to the last detail. This man named Terry Cooper had a wife and two children, and I was to be one of four blonde women who would have sex with him. I had a look at his photo. A handsome looking guy, albeit quite a few years older than me, and a successful real estate agent. I read about what they wanted me to do to him, things to humiliate him, turn his wife and kids against him, and then they would kill him in the end anyway.

I would figure this out. Play along with their games, fuck who I had to fuck, lie to everyone and potentially, bring my name to the lowest level ever. I would do whatever I had to do to get my father back, the only man who had ever truly loved me. Yes, I would play their game until Dad was safe, and then I would make these Praying Mantassassin fuckers pay.

TALISSA

CHAPTER 1

SHAUNA LOGAN, AKA TALISSA

ALL I EVER wanted was to be loved, adored, worshipped and satisfied several times a week in bed— or even on the kitchen table.

I craved it. Longed for it, even.

Despaired it would never happen. Not to a woman like me.

Was it wrong to be an old-fashioned romantic, though? Just because I kill people for a living doesn't mean I don't have a heart.

Or dreams.

I mean, what else was I supposed to do but think about my romantic life, or lack thereof, while lying on my back completely naked with a long-stemmed red rose between my teeth. The artist had barely spoken to me since I entered his studio, disrobed, and posed for his sketching skills. Through his eyes, I'm not a sexual being. I'm a beautiful piece of art. But I knew that already.

I'm not your usual Barbie girl beauty, though. I

have a big arse and pale skin, but my breasts are large while my hair is long, black, and silky. Men say they love the curves of my body and the feel of my hair on their bare skin, but for a lot of them, it's the last conversation they have with anyone. Despite being what many may call plus-sized, I have the reflexes of a cat and the stamina of a marathon runner, allowing me a high degree of competence at both killing and having sex.

In the semi-darkened room, lit only by the illumination of the flames of a few scattered candles, the artist's pencil continued to scratch away on the paper on the easel, oblivious to my inner desires. I couldn't wait to see how he'd translated my womanly form to a two-dimensional sketch. While walking through his gallery on my way to his candle-lit studio containing the lounge I was now laying on, I'd spied his many works. I was impressed by the number of beautiful subjects who'd allowed him to sketch them in all their glory.

"Finished, Talissa. Thank you very much for your time," the artist said as I heard him place his pencil on the bottom of the easel.

When I sat up, he didn't even look my way, such was his professionalism. "Can I take a look?" I asked.

"Sure, miss." He glanced at me as I eased myself off the chaise lounge.

I walked toward where he stood by the easel, passing my clothes lying in a crumpled heap on the floor, and stopped next to him. "My God, it's fantastic," I said, viewing the finished piece. I put a hand on his shoulder as I studied the vision of perfection of the A3 artwork.

"I had something great to work with," he said.

"I bet you say that to all the models." I leaned into him as my mouth hunted his.

"We shouldn't do this," he said, and the thought he

might try to pull away flitted through my mind, but I was quicker. And before the words faded, our lips touched, and I pulled his body against mine.

I lifted my mouth away from his for a second. "Do you realise how much of a turn-on it is to be a subject of your artistic talent?"

"It's not supposed to be sexual. It's about capturing the essence of nature's most beautiful creation, and you're one of the best I've ever seen."

I kissed him again, ignoring the stale taste of coffee from the last cup he'd had, and pressed myself as firmly against him as possible, so much so, I could feel his hardness pushing against my naked form. Whatever resistance he might have had about fucking his client seemed to disappear at the thrust and grind of my hips and breasts against him. He began to unbutton his shirt while I unzipped his trousers.

It was all so easy. Almost too easy.

Annoyingly predictable.

Wasn't there any man who could resist a decent set of tits and a naked arse? But maybe I was being unreasonable. I had become a professional at seduction over the years. It was what I was paid to do.

My hand reached inside the underwear beneath his jeans, and I allowed his stiff cock to be free of the restraints of his clothes. I looked down on it, jutting there—pale and ready, and I made a decision that went against the common practice of my profession. As I rubbed his length, my other hand patted gently around the easel, my fingertips searching for a suitable object. A few seconds of blind seeking brought reward. My fingers located the object I craved. Gripping it tight in a fist, I swung it around and stabbed the artist in the neck. I repeated the action.

And again. And again.

Blood squirted from the punctured areas in his throat. I pushed him away from me before I became showered in the blood of the dying man. He fell on his back, his hands shaking as he attempted to cover the wounds in his neck with his fingers.

I had done it again—killed a man because someone with money wanted him dead. I tried to remember what the reason was for this man dying, but for the life of me, I couldn't recollect what it was. Had I become so detached from the precious gift of life that my mind blocked out the fact this man might have had a family who loved him and would cry at his death?

I turned away from him and gathered my clothes, keeping an eye on him while I dressed. It only took a couple of minutes for him to stop moving, and I gathered the artwork he drew of me and departed his studio.

******

"SO YOU KILLED him with one of his own pencils?" a male voice boomed from the speaker.

I was sitting in a windowless office on the Praying Mantassassin compound speaking into an intercom to someone I'd never seen. "Yes, but you know me."

I never favoured a particular weapon. I liked to use whatever I could see near me. In a situation where you find yourself needing to kill someone, you can use almost any object in a lethal way. I've used scissors, electrical cords, cutlery and even a frying pan once, although it took a great number of hits.

"You're a very resourceful young woman, Talissa. We have a very high-risk assignment coming up, and we believe you might be just the woman for this."

My eyes lit up. High risk meant high rewards, and I

was getting closer to my goal of saving enough money for a house of my own. Apart from that, I spent money on my shallow desires to keep up with the latest trends when it came to shoes, handbags, expensive perfumes, and dresses. I was always buying them because to earn the money I earned and not treat myself would do little to keep me from asking why I kept spilling blood for no other reason than monetary gain. When I dropped in on my parents on occasion, they told me I spend too much money on frivolous purchases, but they had no idea how much money I earned. Nor did they know of the secret payments I made to their business's bank account to help keep them afloat, hidden from them thanks to their accountant. Not their fault they thought I worked as a receptionist for a law firm.

"Tell me more."

"You'll be partnered with the new guy. He calls himself Diablo. He's Spanish, incredibly tall and handsome, and an ex-member of the CNI."

It took me a few seconds to think who the CNI was, but I remembered from my theory CNI stood for *Centro Nacional de Inteligencia*. "You think we can trust someone who used to serve in Spain's intelligence agency?"

"Yes. We've already had word he killed two of the highest ranked agents before fleeing his way over here. He wants to serve an organisation who pays and treats their soldiers what they deserve. In fact, if you make your way to the meals room, you can meet him straight away."

What else could I have said but, "Okay, I'm on my way."

I walked with a spring in my step. I always had a thing for European men, and we had never been discouraged from having relationships or sexual encounters with fellow assassins. It was a quiet day in the training yard, just two young women sparring against each other trading blows with boxing gloves and headgear. It seemed so long ago when I, myself, was at that stage.

I smiled, but at the same time, I felt sad for them, knowing eventually one would have to kill the other. They didn't know it yet and wouldn't until it was actually time. The younger of the two was a blonde who looked like she should still be at school, and the older one appeared old enough to be her mother, albeit if she gave birth to her while still a teenager herself.

Looking away, I continued my short walk to my destination. As I opened the door to the meals room, I saw several women hanging off an Adonis-like creature as he walked along the food counter, adding spoonful after spoonful of cooked meat and salads to a growing mountain on his plate.

Perhaps the sound of the door opening drew his attention, but he looked up from the buffet, turned his face toward me, and then his eyes met mine. I ignored the daggers the other women threw at me with their eyes. I felt my knees weaken, and it took every bit of willpower I possessed to stay upright. My heart threatened to beat its way out of my chest as he began to walk my way, his smile growing, and my own mouth forming a smile of its own. I tried to slow down my pulse or risk the chance of making a fool of myself by being tongue-tied.

"Hello there," he said, his dark eyes looking up and down my body, taking in the curves of my figure-hugging attire.

I'd always been a sucker for a handsome man with brooding eyes, and the way this man who called himself 'the Devil' used them was enough for me to surrender my panties to him right there and then in front of everybody. The other women took up a pair of tables a few metres from us. I could practically feel their eyes on me.

"Hey there, mister, did you ask if you can sit with me?" I asked with a cheeky grin. I felt proud that I got myself back together to say something intelligible.

"No, but you're welcome." His sexy accent thick, I could have sat with him and listened to it all day, every day if I didn't have training to conduct and people to fuck and kill.

He sat down on the bench seat near to where I stood, and like a puppy desperate for a pat, I put my ass about a foot away from his, close but not touching.

"Are you comfortable, ma'am?" he asked, his voice a deep husky drawl.

"I like to make the newcomers feel welcome."

"Thank you very much. I would just like a little bit more room to eat." He lifted his cutlery with a decisive movement of his wrists, and the request for more space seemed appropriate given his eating pose gave him a condor-like wingspan.

Who the hell did this guy think he was? Did he think he could treat me like a second-class citizen because he's a man? I turned and saw the group of five women giggling at me. To hell with those bitches. I picked up my plate and cutlery and moved to a table to sit by myself. If that Spanish hunk of man-flesh wanted to play hard to get, I would play harder.

He caught my eye when I looked in his direction, piercing my soul with unspoken words of untamed passion.

Oh shit, I thought as my own passion rose to the call.

I suppressed it with a decisive glance back at my

plate and resisted the urge to look at him again while I ate.

No, he would have to wait.

******

THE NEXT DAY, I walked to the female section of the shower block, only to discover a shirtless Diablo with a sledgehammer, accompanied by a group of men with various tools. The men took a good look at me in my cotton panties and a singlet top, and it reminded me of construction workers in the city whistling at women walking by in short skirts. At least these guys kept their approval to a visual level.

"Good morning, young lady. We're making some changes here," Diablo said. His mouthful of white teeth greeted me with a broad smile, and his gaze rested on my unsupported breasts and my erect nipples, which tented my tiny top.

"Would it save you some time if I just took my top off right here?" I asked.

"That won't be necessary," he said, and his gaze slowly lifted to meet mine. "The changes include a common shower block so you can all wash together without inhibition."

"Wow. Perverted much?"

"Part of your job is having sex, yeah? So it's time you all learned to be comfortable with each other's bodies."

I laughed aloud at him. "You're hilarious." I lifted my top over my head and shook my chest at him. "Here you go, you Spanish perverted fuck, a pair of titties."

"Yes, they're magnificent. I thank you for showing them to me and to all these horny young men here. Oh, and the girl walking this way."

Turning, I spotted the young blonde I saw training in the yard the previous day. I couldn't help but notice the sneer on her face.

"Cover those ridiculous things up, you show off bitch," she said as she reached me.

I grabbed her by the throat, pushing her back until she crashed into the concrete wall behind her. With my other hand, I curled it into a fist and jabbed her in the side, pushing the wind out of her with one punch.

"Learn some fucking respect, you little skank," I said to her as I let go and she slid to the ground. I pointed at Diablo. "And you will wait until I have my shower before you start swinging that hammer. By the way, have you thought about when we ladies are experiencing that time of the month?"

"Yes, lady. There will be a separate cubicle for that scenario."

I opened the door to the block and found a shower cubicle with a fresh towel hanging and ready for me. I didn't really care about showering in the future with everyone else, but I couldn't help but wonder if this new guy had an ulterior motive.

******

I MET UP with the blonde at training, as it was my day to take her and the older woman to the shooting range.

She walked up to me timidly. "I'm so sorry, Talissa. I thought you must have been a new recruit. My name's Emily."

I shook her hand. When it came to students, I never held a grudge. The other woman introduced herself as Helen, a dark-haired beauty who told me she had been Emily's guardian for several years. Looking at them, I made a guess as to who would come out the victor when the time would come.

"You'll do okay if you lose the attitude," I said to Emily.

The walk to the range took five minutes, and I used that time to learn what I could about Emily and Helen. They seemed likeable enough, but when it came to recruits, you made sure not to get close to them. In fact, I'd made it a habit not to get close to anyone in the three years I had been at the compound until they had at least made it through the trials.

Even then, I never fully allowed anyone to know much about my inner self. If I wanted to leave the compound one day, I didn't want any personal friendships or romantic interests to cause me to second-guess my decisions.

I flicked the switch for the lights, and the three of us each picked a lane. The two recruits informed me they had experience in shooting guns. As the targets moved into place, it took little time to see they were both proficient with firearms. All I could do was request they practice shooting a couple of times a week, just to keep their skills up.

"Where did you two learn to shoot?" I asked.

"The commune where I grew up we needed to hunt for food. If we didn't shoot something, it would mean a vegetable only dinner. The thing is, I like meat, so I made sure I killed something," Emily said.

"I did a lot of sentry work, and even though I never had to shoot anyone, I made sniping my craft," Helen said.

I stared into her eyes, and if she were lying, I didn't read anything there. "I'm impressed." I looked at her target one more time, a perfect grouping of bullets in the target's head. The phone in my pocket vibrated, and I scooped it out to see the text message greeting me.

Office now.

I knew it meant either a mission or urgent action needed to be taken on something. "Back to the training ground, ladies. Run a few laps until someone takes over."

I took a deep breath and made my way to the office.

CHAPTER 2

"I NEED YOU to speed things up. We need a young girl for your next mission, so Emily needs to win out."

I've never liked the idea of getting involved in the process of which recruit got through the culling process, but my boss was asking that of me.

"I think we could use both of them, boss. The older one is quite the competent sniper. Maybe there's a spot for her."

It was never a rare occurrence for him to fall silent during a conversation, and in the case of my request, silence could only mean he was at least thinking about my proposal. I didn't care for the life of either the girl or her guardian, but interfering in the trials could never be a good thing.

"This is highly irregular, but I can see merit in it. Can you upload some footage of Helen's shooting skills?"

All training at the firing range was recorded and kept for a month. "Give me five minutes," I said.

I tapped away on the nearby desktop computer and connected to the CCTV network. Finding the relevant section and time recorded was straight forward, so I picked a five-minute section to send to the boss. Any section would have been suitable such was Helen's accuracy.

More silence followed as he watched what I sent him. I peeked through the window, absorbing the calmness of the nearby ocean, and wondered what would happen if a boat were to find us just a mile inland.

"Okay, the lady has potential. It will save us hiring outside help for the sniping part of the mission. Just get her to practice at the long-range targets, and do it tomorrow. We only have a small window for this mission, and we need everyone ready. The mission outline will be arriving by fax. Get Diablo in there with you."

"Yes, sir. Speaking of Diablo, he's making some weird changes here like the shower block."

"I'm well aware, Talissa. I didn't expect you of all people to have a problem with it. He came to me with the idea, to allow you all to know each other well. Now, is there anything else? My time is too precious to debate the sanctity of your body, which you've used as a weapon on dozens of assignments now."

In this line of work, one knew when to push a point and when to let it go. Arguing with an unseen superior would get me nowhere, except possibly an early grave. But I had one concern about communal showering.

"Emily's only sixteen years old. It's not right..."

"Talissa, I don't expect my subordinates to question me on the running of this place. You're great at what you do, but you're not irreplaceable. I'm the boss here, and I don't care for second-guessing. Goodbye."

I remained seated while I waited for the fax to arrive and read the assignment details in full before requesting the other participants to meet me in my room. The sun still hadn't made its daily exit yet by then, and there was no evening meal in our bellies, either. But they were all keen. Diablo was the last to arrive at the meeting, avoiding the smiles Helen threw his way as he sat on the chair that was near my desk.

"Emily, shit is about to get real. You're going to be used as human bait for a real nasty piece of work and there might be people trying to do bad things to you," I said. She looked young but free of innocence.

"Bad things?" Her mouth twisted at my wording choice. "Like stick their cocks in my mouth? Do these lips look like they don't know the taste of a big meaty...?" she looked Diablo's way.

"Fine. Just trying to make sure you know what could happen." I shifted my attention to her guardian. "You need to fit in some long range target practice. We need a competent sniper who can rock a cocktail dress."

She certainly had the figure to carry off a high priced dress. I visualised her in a light blue, spaghetti strap, figure-hugging outfit. Great as a distraction for male eyes, but nowhere to conceal a weapon. Her rifle would need to be left in the location from which she would be covering us.

"Diablo, you will act as my partner. We'll pose as sellers of young flesh to members of high society, and our client prefers young American blondes. We need to get his interest in Emily and flush him away from the rest of the party. He'll most probably have a three or four-person security detail, which won't be a problem for us as Helen will be on sniping detail. If we can avoid it, we don't take anyone out apart from our target and, if need be, his minders.

"So who wants him dead?" Diablo asked.

There were times when we were told and times when we weren't—and times when I was privy to information I couldn't share with my fellow mission operatives. The others didn't need to know this mission was yet another case of furious ex-wife syndrome. We always gave them a good week or two to change their mind, reminding them that although we operated smartly without leaving a trail for the authorities to follow, a decision to have an ex-husband or partner killed shouldn't be rushed into.

"I don't have that information. We just need to make sure this man's head ends up in a box to send to our client. Any concerns you have should be settled with the hundred grand we'll all receive for a successful job done. This is the man we need to take out." I showed them all in turn a picture of the man's face, name, and personal details.

"So do I have to fuck that dirty old man?" Emily asked.

"We'll do everything to avoid that," I answered.

"You don't have to treat me like I'm your child. I know what our jobs here involve. I lost my virginity at fourteen. I've been with boys my age and men old enough to be my dad. And girls too."

"It's okay, Talissa. She's done it all already," Helen said.

I kept a straight face, but part of me wanted to slap Emily for admitting the things I, myself, wanted to engage in when I was her age. I had to focus on the mission at hand.

I showed the others the layout of the three levels of the building where the exchange would take place, a private mansion holding secrets of horrific crimes. I had no doubt we would come across some heavy opposition if we weren't stealthy enough.

Helen studied the diagram, noting the locations of the windows. "I'll need to get to this side of the mansion to get the best view of what's happening inside, and even then, I'll be restricted. Try and arrange your meeting to take place in this room here." She pointed to a large entertaining area. "If the blueprint is correct, there would be a lot of glass along the wall of that room."

"You'll be situated on a jutted edge with a sea wind blowing in your face. You'll also need to counter in a trajectory range as bullets pierce the glass," Diablo said.

"That's not my biggest problem. What I want to know is how do I get a rifle to that spot?" Helen asked. The location she needed to be at was situated within the boundary of the property.

"It will be in pieces and put in a cake box. If you need to lift the lid, it will look like a proper cake is there, but pray they don't try poking or prodding too much," I answered. "Your cocktail dress will be too tight to hide anything."

Diablo looked her way and smirked. At times, I wondered if he thought about anything besides sex.

"So what will I be armed with?" Emily asked.

"Your good looks and young age will be all the weapons you need. And your mind," Diablo said.

"So we spend the next three days studying every square inch of these blueprints, Helen practices her long range shooting, and Emily, you'll be concentrating on hand-to-hand combat and disarming armed men." I looked over my three fellow mission operatives. Diablo, experienced. Helen, resourceful with a gun, and Emily, young and energetic, ready to make her first kill. I had to admit it was a good team.

What could go wrong?

CHAPTER 3

THE PARTY'S OFFICIAL starting time was at 7PM, and we needed to be there half an hour prior. Diablo, Emily, and I travelled in a black SUV left for us at the location that the helicopter had dropped us. Helen travelled alone ahead of us in an identical vehicle. A big part of our mission depended on her working as our backup eyes, which meant she needed to get through the house and set up her position.

Communication between us would be difficult until she could unpack the fake cake box and set up her hands-free kit. On the other end of the communication line, Diablo would be the ears and voice for the pair of us, able to hide a hands-free kit in a hollowed out novelty keychain.

The journey had been long, but Diablo and I managed to avoid conversation of our built up sexual tension. The communal shower proved to serve him well, a lone male among a group of anywhere between six and ten females on a daily basis, the number differing depending on when some of them were deployed on missions. I must have been old fashioned because the idea of having sex in front of other people never appealed to me. I had never needed to do so on a paid mission, so why would I want to fuck this arrogant Spanish prick in front of all my fellow assassins?

Emily had tried to get with him, trying to seduce him a few times in the showers, but thankfully, Diablo displayed a little morality and declined her repeated offers. Helen's offer was a different story—the two of them screwing like a pair of horny teenagers just a few feet from where I showered. But each woman he had sex with, his eyes were on me the whole time.

A voice cracked through the loudspeaker of Diablo's phone. "Wish me luck. I have arrived at the mansion."

"Good luck," I said. Once set up, she would be able to relay information on how many people were located inside the house and where. We hoped to keep the body count down on this mission, but if we had to take everyone out to get our hands on our target, Big Bill, then we were more than prepared to do so.

I always loved driving along the coast. The calming scent of the ocean and the endless shades of blue settled my nerves and made me realise that in a big world, I'm just one single organism sharing the air with a few billion others. And as we passed the sparsely populated area, I could see from the size of the mansions and scope of their properties why this was the case.

"Nearly show time. Are you good back there?" I asked Emily.

"Yeah, I just have to look pretty, which isn't hard."

I mumbled under my breath. She was right, of course, with her silky blonde hair and sleek body, which appeared as though it had developed well before she was due, Emily was simply stunning. From a perverted point of view, I understood why dirty old rich men would pay a lot of money for her. But as much as the girl pissed me off with her attitude, we couldn't fuck this mission up.

I turned off the road when I saw the mailbox with the number 1124 attached. About twenty feet further up the pebbled terracotta driveway, we had a security gate to pass through.

A baritone voice crackled through the speaker box, "Name and nature of business please."

I took a short breath. "Mr and Mrs Bosworth with a package for Mr William Watsburg."

There was a slight pause, and I imagined a faceless man searching through a list looking for our aliases. I resisted the urge to turn and look back at Emily, who might have been nervous about the silent seconds ticking over. But I knew it was just standard procedure.

"Drive on through. Continue up the path until you are directed by the personnel on where to park. Have a nice day."

I pressed with the lightest touch of my foot to accelerate along the driveway. The sight of a three-storey mansion surrounded by an artificial oasis held our attention as we basked in its magnificence. I surmised how lucrative the drug and illegal arms trades must pay in comparison to an assassin's work.

As I glanced at Diablo, I hoped he was ready for whatever we might have to face and that Helen had reached her location. Diablo smiled at me reassuringly, and when I turned back to the path, we saw our first human on the property, staring as we approached, with what looked like a semi-automatic rifle slung over his shoulder.

The black suited man waved us toward him, his eyes invisible to us behind his thick sunglasses. On closer inspection, I estimated him to be even taller than Diablo and just as wide. As we slowed to a near stop, he walked around to my window and pointed in the direction of a vehicle similar to ours, indicating we should park to the right of it.

I didn't see any point in verifying the readiness of my two fellow operatives. Like me, they didn't display an ounce of nervousness. Nerves give you away when you dance in the devil's playground, and the result could well mean a quick death, or worse, a slow and painful one.

A pair of men similarly armed to the one who guided us to where we parked met us outside the car and escorted us to the entrance of the house. Diablo and I walked side by side with Emily out in front of us.

"The Bosworths have arrived, sir," one of the men spoke into a walkie-talkie.

We waited for about half a minute before an older man greeted us and allowed us inside. "Please take the staircase on the left, and when you get to the top, turn around, and take the next flight of stairs to the third floor." He studied Emily and frowned.

"You must look too old," I said to Emily when we were out of earshot of the butler-looking type.

"It's the tits," she said.

As we crossed the floor on the second level between staircases, we received a curious look from a group of men and women drinking glasses of champagne. From my research, parties like this were commonplace at the mansion. Despite public perception, the rich and distinguished were much wilder behind the doors of a party than a bunch of college kids at spring break.

A man we knew from our mission dossier as Charlie Appleton greeted us as we reached the top of the second staircase. "Ah, good evening Mr and Mrs Bosworth, and who's this young lady?"

"Her name is Kandi, and she is as sweet as her name suggests," Diablo said.

Charlie walked up close to Emily and looked her up

and down. He extended his hand to her. "Security, please frisk the two of them. You know how paranoid Bill is."

Another pair of heavily armed men made their way to us, each one selecting one of us to pat down. The guard who frisked me made a point of feeling me through my red silk dress, cupping my breasts and ass with his gorilla sized hands. But anyone who knew anything about the game we played knew the mansion of a rich drug lord wasn't the place to file a complaint of sexual harassment.

"Yeah, she's good," the guard said, giving me one last look, or should I say my breasts. The other guard nodded and allowed us to enter the main entertaining area.

The room only had a number of armed men inside, the majority of the guests yet to arrive and fill up the dance floor. It was decorated like a 1970s discotheque, a mirrored ball hanging in the centre of the wooden floor, a smoke machine near the stage and an oval shaped bar serving every type of cocktail imaginable.

"This place really gets pumping after ten. You should both stick around," Charlie said. He had a hold of Emily's hand. "Big Bill has asked me to check over his potential purchase on his behalf."

The guards in the room walked over to watch the proceedings as he pushed Emily out in front of him. We knew something like this could happen, but it didn't mean I could escape the feeling of disgust that filled me as I waited for what would happen next. The trick, though, was not to allow my true feelings to surface, or else my charade as a salesperson of young female flesh would meet an abrupt end.

"Dear Kandi, I do what is known as quality control for dear old Bill, so I'm going to need a good look at the merchandise, just to make sure he's getting value for his pussy dollar."

Right then, I swore if I had the chance, I would put a bullet in Charlie before we left. All I could do though was watch as Emily removed her singlet top and little denim shorts and to stand in the middle of the room in matching white bra and panties.

"Oh, very nice, but I'm going to need to see a little more." Charlie smirked. A couple of the guards chuckled and added their names to my to-kill list as Emily unclipped her bra and then lowered her panties to the floor.

"See, grade A merchandise, as promised," Diablo said.

"That's some fine looking Kandi," Charlie said. He unzipped the fly of his black pants. "But I need to make sure she can use that luscious looking mouth of hers."

******

EMILY WAS GIVEN a new set of clothes to wear, a matching pink frilly short skirt, and singlet top to put on over her own underwear. It gave her that look of innocence mixed with mischievousness, and likely to be the subject of a sick perverted man's desire. As much as I would have liked to stop things from reaching that point, I knew Emily would most likely have to screw the dirty old goat before killing him.

"Our host will be with you shortly, and on my recommendation, you will be well paid." Charlie smiled at me and touched Emily's chin. "I hope you have access to more merchandise like this."

"I doubt you could afford such luxuries on a henchman's wage," Diablo said.

Charlie closed the space between him and Diablo in

a split second. "You best be careful how you speak to one of Big Bill's associates."

"Oh boys, a girl could nearly drown in this flood of testosterone," a woman in her thirties said as she entered the room.

"Who the fuck are you?" Charlie asked.

"My new associate, Beth Bachman." Bill followed her into the room. The irony of his nickname Big Bill wasn't lost on me. He would have been lucky to hit five feet in height. "And she has some interesting information."

"Someone in this room has been paid a lot of money to kill you, Bill," Beth said, pulling a pistol from her side. She looked at me, taking in every detail of my body. "Well, I doubt you could be concealing anything harmful under that costume."

She took a step toward Diablo and grabbed him between the legs. "Looks like this guy's carrying a big weapon, but he doesn't seem to be armed. And your little girl has been stripped to nothing already. So maybe it's you, Charlie." She turned around to face the sleazy henchman.

We hadn't anticipated a scenario like this as part of the mission. Diablo still hadn't been able to connect his communication device, and from our position, we couldn't see any sign of Helen. We had no idea who this woman was, but she was right about someone paying a lot of money to have Bill killed.

"Bill's my boss, so no Bill, no big paycheck," Charlie said.

Beth studied each of us in turn and then settled her gaze on me. "Come. Let me get you a drink." She reached for my hand and put her pistol away. "That's one sexy dress you have on there, babe," she whispered in my ear.

I hadn't been with another woman for a few months, and Beth cut a stunning figure in her body hugging little black dress. The long slit along the left side of the garment showed the full length of one of her toned legs, her weapon's holster attached above a black lacy garter belt on her upper thigh. But this wasn't the time and place for anything outside of the mission.

"Come here, little girl," I heard Bill call out and could only imagine what he would put Emily through. I had been with much older men for the sake of missions, and nothing felt as disgusting as the touch of a man forty years my senior.

I hoped Emily could block it out as well as I had learned to do. He put his hand on the girl's ass as she reached him and pointed for her to go in a particular direction. Then he proceeded to walk toward us with a briefcase in hand.

"Payment as agreed. And a little bonus for letting me keep her for a week," Bill said.

I knew Emily would soon be leaving with us and not kept as a sex slave for a week like Bill expected. I hoped having her isolated with him might give her the opportunity to kill him before having to do anything unthinkable with him. She would have to do it quietly and slip away without alerting any security personnel.

Diablo made small talk with a couple of the guards. I counted eight in the room, plus Charlie and Beth. We had zero weapons and zero communication with Helen. If things went pear-shaped, we would be done for.

"So, what brings you here?" I leaned in close to Beth as we stood at the bar.

"I was part of the guest list, a first-time attendee of a Big Bill party. They say anything you want, you can get here." She touched my face.

A few new arrivals entered the room, and the bar

area became illuminated in a misty light, changing colours every few seconds. A blonde barmaid appeared behind the bar, entering from another room, dressed in only a black G-string and high heels. I guessed she was hired more for her silicon-enhanced assets than her cocktail making abilities.

"Just a glass of champagne," I requested, and unlike a pair of newly arrived males to the bar, I kept eye contact with her.

"I suddenly feel overdressed," Beth said to me and ordered a scotch on the rocks.

Our drinks were served at the bar, and Beth pointed to a leather lounge. "Let's go take a seat." She grabbed my hand again and led me to the destination she'd pointed out.

"So, do you really believe someone wants to kill your friend?" I asked while we walked.

Upon reaching the lounge, Beth left me with no personal space as she sat right up against my side. "I think lots of people want to kill him, but he asked me to help out tonight with a little security. I think he's paranoid, but with what he pays, I don't let my personal judgements of people interfere." When she spoke, her breath flowed onto me like a breeze of subtle sensuality.

"How do I know that you don't want to kill him?"

She smiled at me. "Let's quit playing games, life is very short, and you just need to live a little." Her hand ran up my leg, slowing her caress as it reached my upper thigh. Maybe she could feel the goose bumps rising through the pores of my skin as her hand came to a stop a mere inch from the underwear I wore to match my dress.

"What are you doing with my wife?" I heard Diablo's voice boom from beside us.

Beth released her hold on me and stood up near

him. "You don't have a wife. I see how you look at this woman here, and it isn't jealousy I see. It's more like an unrequited lust. I would guess you haven't even been with her."

I moved to my feet quick. "Beth, you don't understand."

She turned and visually stabbed me with the look in her eyes. "You better have a good reason for this deception."

"We pretend we're married for business reasons. We believe people take us more seriously that way."

She pulled her pistol out again and poked me in the side with it. "What kind of bullshit is that? So let me guess—the two of you and that young girl are all in on this?"

"I don't know what you mean," I said, forcing a tear to well in my eye. "Please, don't shoot me."

She pushed me away and aimed at Diablo and fired, hitting him in the lower leg. "You obviously haven't heard of me over at the Praying Mantassassin compound."

Oh crap, how the hell could she know that? Diablo grimaced at the pain in his leg but refused to go down. I had to scramble. "What the hell do you mean?"

"Look at you in that red dress. Your reputation precedes you, *Talissa*. The voluptuous temptress who kills her victims with anything she can find. Well, you are as beautiful and tempting as your reputation, but are you as deadly?"

She swung the pistol back in my direction, and before her finger squeezed the trigger, I spread my legs and did the splits in time to dodge the bullet. Sailing above my head, the bullet travelled past its intended target over to the bar area, hitting a party guest who groaned in pain. I lay on my back and propelled my feet at Beth, hitting her in the stomach.

The gun fell from Beth's grip. I rolled in its direction, only to receive an elbow to my stomach from the recovered attacker. I took a split second to look at the other guards in the room, who appeared to withhold from firing any weapons so as not to hit any of the innocent party guests. They all took measured steps towards us, pointing their weapons in the direction of Diablo and me.

"Stop right there," a female voice screamed.

I turned and saw Emily using a young girl as a human shield, holding a large blade near the girl's throat. The little girl couldn't have been any older than five or six at a guess.

Beth looked at me. "You teach your recruits young, don't you?" She turned her focus to Emily. "You think you can use my girl as leverage against me?"

Lying beside me on the floor, Diablo pulled his keys from his pocket. "Take them, Talissa."

"No, we leave together." I pulled them to me. I knew what his plan was, and I opened the dangling charm on the keyring and grabbed the communication device.

"I will slash her throat, you watch me," Emily said. I looked at her face and couldn't see any signs of nervousness.

"Just tell me where Bill is, and we can all go home," Beth said.

I could tell where this was headed and brought my foot to my hand. The guards were closer, and all they needed was the word, and they would open fire on us. I slid my high-heeled shoe from my foot, the stiletto heel was steel tipped, and a hit to the head could render a person unconscious.

At this stage, I noticed the blood-soaked towel in Emily's other hand, and as she unravelled it, a head rolled out and hit the floor. "This is part of him. Do you still want him?" she asked.

I heard a scream behind me and assumed it was the barmaid or a female party guest. I doubted they would be expecting to see the decapitated head of their party host.

"You would have had to get past six guards between his bedroom and here. How are you still alive?" Beth asked.

"They weren't expecting me to be a killer. Anyway, I'm about to kill your little girl since I'm guessing those guards are going to shoot us anyway," Emily said.

Beth stared straight back at her, and I saw my moment to make my move. I stood and swung the shoe through the air, aiming directly at Beth's temple.

They say some people are blessed with incredible peripheral vision, making them great for serving in the armed services or spy agencies. Beth must have been similarly gifted. She lifted a foot and swivelled on the spot, blocking my arm before I could make contact with her. She thrust her other arm against my blocked one, clasped her hands together, and swung downward.

My elbow almost became dislodged. I barely managed to move my body parallel with my injured arm and jut my leg out to kick her before we both crashed into the polished wooden floor. Several pairs of footsteps hurried our way, but I was unable to see much due to my tussle with Beth. A punch connected with my jaw, my head hitting the floor once again from the impact.

From the corner of my eye, I saw Diablo hobble over to the bar and Emily cowering low and dragging the young girl in the same direction. I rolled away from Beth only to see a guard standing over me and aiming his long weapon at me.

"Shoot the bitch," Beth yelled.

The guard smiled at me, his finger pulling back on the trigger. I tensed. No human had the speed to dodge a bullet from three feet away. I closed my eyes ready for my life's light to end with a bang.

The sound of glass breaking made me jerk my eyes open. The guard hovering above me began to fall forward, the expression on his face seeming to go slack as his gun dipped downward. I managed to roll away before the man, who I guessed to be twice my weight, smashed onto the floor, a bullet hole in the back of his head. Without a whisker of hesitation, I snatched the gun from the dead man's hands and did a quick visual hunt for Beth. I caught sight of her jumping up and placing her hands on the top of the bar, pushing herself into a somersault and landing somewhere behind the bar.

Another guard running my way hit the floor and slid a few feet, dead before his body stopped moving. Helen had obviously made it to her sniping point and had now saved me twice in less than a minute.

"Fucking sniper," one of the heavily armed men yelled. He motioned to his men to form two groups, one to take us out while the other group hunted the sniper. I picked a target and put him down as I quickly made my way to where Diablo, Emily, and Beth had gone.

Shots continued to be fired inside the room, all of them seeming to hit walls and furniture but little else as the people managed to dodge the incoming shots. A quick glance at the other side of the bar, I saw Beth and Diablo pointing guns at each other from just a few feet away.

"Stand down, Beth," I yelled, pointing my own gun at her.

"We're in a quandary. Your girl has mine at

knifepoint, and your man and I are about to shoot each other dead. And if I let you three walk away, there's a mini army here ready to take me down. So this is what happens. Your girl lets mine go, I just shoot your man, and then I get shot in return. Or we stand and argue, and we all die."

I heard a bullet whistle past my ear and crash into the wall of hanging glasses nearby. If I stayed in the open, I would soon be dead so I leapfrogged the bar, leaving my newly acquired weapon behind. Diablo smiled and fired a gun he must have picked up from someone, hitting Beth between the eyes.

The girl held hostage by Emily wailed, and her captor let her free to go and embrace her dead mother. I looked at Diablo again, this time noticing his hand barely covering the red mark on his shirt.

"Oh fuck no, Diablo. Are you okay?" I asked.

"I got her, Talissa. I killed the legend," he said, slumping against the wall of the bar

"What do you mean? She was just a hired head of security." I knelt beside him, trying to ignore the way my heart twisted at the beads of sweat blooming on his forehead and the way he already gasped for breath.

"Long have I heard of the legend of the masterful assassin Bethonius. Word is she was the one who took down and killed the Jackal several years ago, but no one could ever verify the fact that either the Jackal or Bethonius actually existed. But I got her."

It was the last time I saw Diablo smile. His breathing soon stopped, and his eyes stared back at Emily and me, like windows to a house void, of its owner's soul.

"Oh shit, Emily. We need to get out of here." I nearly choked on a tear I couldn't let escape as the emptiness of his eyes left me feeling full of regrets.

"What about the girl? We can't leave a witness behind."

"She's just a little girl. We need to clear this room and get Helen and go." I went over to the counter and lifted my head just high enough to see into the room.

Another bullet sailed by and found more glass, shards falling on top of us. "There's still a lot of heat out there."

"I didn't sign up for any of this shit," the barmaid said. Looking at her red-rimmed eyes, I could tell she'd been crying. But it was the faded, fist-size bruise on her cheek that gave me pause.

She didn't appear to be much older than Emily was, even though the legal age to serve alcohol was twenty-one. But being employed by Big Bill, age legalities probably didn't come into the employment equation.

"I'll try and get you out. Stay close, okay?"

She nodded. A movement to my left revealed Beth's daughter trying to snake past me, cheeks wet with tears. One look at her innocent, frightened expression, and I knew I couldn't just leave her with the wolves.

"Hang on to the girl," I instructed the barmaid with a nod at the child. "I'm going to use both of you as hostages." There were a few reasons that Big Bill might have a child in his home, but I was betting Beth, and he had been more than acquaintances. This meant, with her parents dead, the child's life could be worth more than their own.

The barmaid's eyes widened, but she nodded again and clutched the crying girl to her.

"We have to wait for Helen," Emily said. "If it weren't for her, you would have been killed."

"I know, and I'm not in the habit of leaving people behind. I just hope they haven't got to her." I sat and considered my options. We were safe behind the bar, the steel counter surrounding us deflecting the potency of the bullets flying across the room. It would do for a while, but we couldn't hold out forever.

I peeled off Diablo's jacket and passed it to the near naked barmaid as I nodded at the entrance of the bar's counter. "Where does it lead?"

"To a storeroom, with a little vanity room where most of my clothes are," she said.

A no-exit. "I don't think it will be safe there."

I took Diablo's gun from his slack grip and checked his pockets for more clips. Sliding a fresh one into place with a sharp click, I took another quick peek over the counter and fired my new weapon blindly. It started another thunderstorm of lead hitting the sanctuary, and it hit me that our only hope for a clean escape was for Helen to pick them off one by one.

The firing continued as relentless as rain on a tropical coastal town in spring. "Someone needs to do something," Emily said, her face twisting into a determined sneer. She wrenched the weapon from me, leaned against the bar, and took a quick look before she ducked her head back down and began shooting blindly.

It would do us no good if she got herself killed. I fished around near Beth's dead body and grabbed her pistol, giving me a weapon for each hand. I followed the crazy girl in her endeavour, taking in quick glances and shooting blind from both hands. I couldn't risk peeking long enough to count the number of armed men shooting at us, but I made my first round of rapid firing count, noting that I dropped three targets the next time I stole a quick glance at my damage.

Emily's training had served her well. Between the two of us, we were lowering the odds against us. We hadn't claimed victory yet, and just as we thought we might clear the room, I caught sight of two familiar faces just as I looked over the bar counter.

"Is this woman with you?" Charlie asked, holding Helen in a headlock with a gun pressed against her temple.

"Don't you dare fucking hurt her," Emily yelled and aimed directly at him.

"Well, you better put the gun down then, little darling. You ladies have caused me a little more trouble than I had anticipated. You were supposed to just come in and kill that useless old fucker and leave, but no, you had to take a little girl hostage," he pointed at Emily.

"Who the hell are you?" I asked.

"I'm the real Big Bill, and I'm not happy with the mess you've made here. I should make you pay for the damage out of what you made from this mission."

"What the hell is going on?" I asked.

"I paid your organisation big money to kill one of my rivals, King Kansas. With the promise of getting sex with a tender young thing, he happily pretended to be Big Bill. So thanks, Emily, for that fantastic blowjob. The things sixteen-year-olds know these days are astounding. Any chance I can keep you here and get me some of that oral perfection every day?"

"Why didn't you just kill him yourself?" I asked, ignoring his perverted leer directed at our youngest squad member.

"And start a war? The King didn't know he was a rival. He thought I was his friend. But I need his territory, and by making it look like a disgruntled young whore murdered him, I've ensured the blame will be deflected away from me. You are free to leave now, Talissa."

Something bugged me about the situation. His explanation was too easy. And he hadn't moved to let Helen go.

"You know our names and who we would send in." The organization usually didn't disclose those details to a client. "Tell me who the mole is."

He laughed. "Why should I tell you that? I suggest you leave while you still can. Or we can shoot you both where you stand and this lovely sniper, as well."

A sudden sob behind me from the little girl in the barmaid's arms reminded me of Beth and the other part of this whole plan that didn't quite make sense.

I kept my gun trained on Big Bill. "Why was Beth here with her little girl if you knew we were here to do the job? Diablo is dead and so is she, and despite her reputation, we never had a beef with her before tonight."

"Insurance," was all he said, but his gaze flicked to the barmaid and the little girl standing behind me against the wall.

Helen was able to turn her head and look at me, and then it all came together. Stepping back quickly, I pulled the barmaid and the little girl to me but kept my gun trained on Big Bill. "Put your gun down, Emily. Let's cut our losses and go."

Emily glared at me but obeyed. Big Bill or Charlie, or whatever his name was, smiled and released his hostage. I took a step sideways and kept an eye on the men remaining in the room, aware they had lowered their weapons but had not discarded them.

"We're taking the girl and the barmaid with us," I said, keeping them close to me as I switched my target from Bill to them, hoping their status as hostage would keep us safe

Charlie/Bill nodded and kept his eyes locked on me as the five of us huddled together and exited the room. We had to be on the lookout for further armed henchmen on our way to the car, and we had three floors and a front yard to cover before we were safe.

I looked at our real target's face for the last time as the door closed to the entertaining room. The little girl had to be carried by the barmaid in her arms, and no doubt had many questions to ask about her mother. I toyed with the idea of bringing them both back to the compound instead of releasing them as soon as we were clear of the mansion. I could imagine the life that lay ahead of them belonging to a household like Big Bill's. At least, as a hired assassin, I had the choice 'to kill or be killed' in the palm of my hand. I didn't have to live my life according to the desires of a domineering asshole. It pissed me off that Big Bill put us through all this, and with Diablo dead, I'd never have the chance to see if we had something there. Sure, I could have had sex with him in the showers, but I hadn't wanted to start a relationship like that. I'd wanted him badly, but I'd wanted him to want me like the man in my dreams. Not up against a wall with a crowd staring. And now I'd never get the chance to find out if that dream could have been a reality if enough time had passed.

As we passed through the room and into the relative safety of the hallway, I changed my mind. I looked at Charlie/Bill one last time, realization dawning that our paid objective to kill Big Bill remained to be met.

"Go on ahead, Emily. Shoot anything that moves," I said and quickly passed the hostages to her and Helen.

CHAPTER 4

FOUR YEARS PREVIOUSLY...

HARRY AND I were childhood sweethearts, losing our virginity on our prom night, just like every other cliché high school couple does. He was skinny and had acne, and I was teased as being the fat girl in the class, so I guessed that as the leftovers of the graduating year, we were destined to be together. At eighteen, we thought we had it all worked out. We would go to college, get our degrees, get married, and have four or five children. But life rarely works out the way you plan it.

My parents couldn't afford the college tuition, and girls like me didn't get scholarships. Harry didn't want to go off without me by his side, so we settled for retail jobs and living with my parents until we could afford to move out. His parents cut him off and wouldn't speak to him again, which they would come to regret.

It was a sunny afternoon. We had both finished work and, as was our custom, consumed a picnic lunch on a shaded riverbank. We ate as if we had spent a week on a diet of rice and water and lay next to each other, holding hands and cloud gazing while very little happened. Some days, we would just talk and talk while others, we would curl up together and be comfortable in silence, secure in each other's presence. Some said we were a pair of desperados who couldn't find anyone else, but I always felt that fate pushed us together at a young age by making us undesirable to many of the opposite sex.

We didn't care. It was love. And anyone who ever says there's something that can fulfil you as much as finding that person you connect with is a liar. When I was with Harry, nothing else mattered.

"It won't always be like this, Shauna. One day, I'll be a manager and drive a company car and make enough money to support both of us. We'll end up in that house with the white picket fence with little ones bouncing around and making us laugh," he told me.

I smiled, not because I wanted money, the nice house, car, and everything else. I smiled because he wanted to give me all of that. "I love our life, Harry. I mean I would love to live somewhere not with my mum and dad, but I don't need all of that material stuff. All I need is you."

He rolled over and kissed me, lying on top of me. I felt like doing something crazy so I opened my legs a little and grabbed his hand, guiding it up inside my dress until I let it rest where my panties should have been.

"Oh, my God. Shauna!"

"I want you to fuck me right here, right now," I said. His finger travelled inside me, and I wanted him to hurry up and put something else inside me where he would be able to delve deeper.

Harry sat up and looked all around, and when satisfied no one else was within sight, he lowered his work pants and underwear to his knees and crawled back on top of me. I grabbed hold of his cock and pulled it into me, groaning as he filled me with his stiff appendage. It always made me feel like a goddess when he fucked me as if I was the most desirable creature on the planet.

I closed my eyes and forgot about the world as he pumped me slowly at first, speeding up every few thrusts until he reached his climax. Collapsing on top of me, I held his ass cheeks tight and whispered in his ear to stay inside me.

"I wish I could last longer," he said to me, "but you're just so fucking sexy."

"Maybe she needs a real man," we heard a voice say.

We peeled away from each other, and as Harry tried to pull up his pants, I saw his uncle kick him in the stomach. Harry yelled in pain, and I stood up and swung a hand at the man's chest.

"I love a feisty chick, especially one with a nice big trunk like that," he said after catching my hand before it could strike him. He pulled me close to him and lifted my dress, his other hand squeezing my ass like a vice.

"Let her go," Harry stood up and stared at his uncle. "You do something to her, and you'll end up back in jail."

"I fuck little boys like you in prison on a daily basis, so I'll take my chances." He moved his hand between the cheeks of my ass and pushed against the resistance I built up as I squeezed my thighs together. A fingertip touched my pussy, sending a wave of anger through me resulting in him receiving a kneecap in the balls.

Hitting the ground, he pulled a gun out and pointed it at me. "You'll fucking pay, bitch."

I stood there, frozen in shock, my heart hammering at the sight of that barrel pointed at me along with the instinctive fear of what it meant.

"No!" Harry yelled, jumping at him. As he crashed on top of his uncle, I heard the pistol go off.

Harry's uncle stared at me wide-eyed and shook his head. "I...I... didn't mean to shoot him." He waved his arm around, the gun shaking in his hand as he looked at the limp body draped across his chest. I knew him to have been involved in armed holdups and assaults, but murder had been in a category higher than he had been associated with previously.

I ran over and cuddled Harry lifting him to lean in my lap. "Please don't leave me. Not now, Harry." The tears flowed like I had never cried before. My high school love was bleeding out and not responding to me at all, and I couldn't seem to stop the red stain from spreading from where his heart should have been

"Oh fuck. Shauna, I didn't mean to kill him, please—you need to understand."

I glared straight at him. "Put the fucking gun down, you mother fucking prick."

"I can't go back to prison. They'll kill me this time, Shauna. I won't hurt you if you promise not to tell the cops."

"Put the gun down NOW." I felt like someone else had taken over my body as I watched him place the gun next to him and slowly put his hands in the air.

"Step away from it." I watched as he did as I said, wondering what power he thought an eighteen-year-old girl had over him. "From the age of five, my daddy showed me how to fire a gun," I said as I left Harry's lifeless body on the grass and walked over to the displaced revolver. I picked it up, my hands wet with Harry's bright red blood.

"Shauna, you're not a killer."

"You said it yourself—you can't go back to prison." I

aimed the weapon at him, not realising the kick the gun would give as I fired it and missed him by a few feet.

Sweat poured from his brow. "See, you don't have it in you. You can't control that thing." He smirked, walking towards me as I fired again and missed.

I couldn't believe how much the gun moved in my blood-slicked hand each time I fired. He was nearly upon me. The next bullet would have to count.

"You stupid bitch," he said, grabbing hold of my wrist.

I looked him in the eye and spat in his face, and shoved my gun-holding hand towards his face. I don't know where the strength came from, but before I could put much thought into it, I fired once as I placed the pistol under his chin. The back of his head flew upward before his body fell lifeless to the ground.

I had made my first kill, and while waiting for the police to arrive, I couldn't help but worry I would soon be in prison. But the officer in charge took me aside and smiled at me, telling me everything would be okay. He said I would never have to see someone I love die again while watching helplessly.

The next day, I found myself in the compound of the Praying Mantassassins. I lost weight. I learned how to control the heaviest of weapons and how to use my newfound sexiness to make money from killing people who really deserved it.

CHAPTER 5

I REMOVED MY shoes and tiptoed barefoot to the door I had just exited. I stood on the other side of the room containing so much death within its walls. I could have just walked away with the others, but reminiscing about my youth reminded me of why I got into this line of work to begin with. I allowed my mind to clear and then put my emotions aside.

Simply put, Big Bill had to die.

I prepared to step back into the 'room of death' when I saw a flicker of movement from the corner of my eye. I brought one of my hands around, holding the pistol gripped tight between my fingers around in the direction of the movement, and spied a person hiding under a table. I hadn't seen this woman before, and when I looked directly at her face, the beauty of her dark chocolate coloured flawless skin almost froze me in place.

"Please don't shoot me," she said, her voice as smooth as her complexion.

"He's still in there," I said. I kept my other weapon at the ready should anyone come through the door.

"I can help you. I was hired to kill his rival, too. He

lied to me, just as he lied to you. He must pay."

I saw the tiny pistol in her hand, the type only good for close range kills, but it was better than nothing. I turned my attention back to the opened door. We looked at each other, and nodded, dashing into the room and peeling away from each other in opposite directions. We both fired as soon as we saw live targets, watching men fall as we fired round after round barely taking a breath as we spilled further blood. My new African companion sprinted directly at the last man standing, his shit-eating smirk remaining in place even as the woman charging at him placed the barrel of the tiny pistol at his forehead.

"Wow. Two beautiful women both here to kill me. Tell me, aren't you supposed to fuck me before you snuff me out?" he said. "Princess Africa, I'll give you the pleasure of going first. And then you, Miss Red Dress, I'm saving you as the best for last."

"We're well past that, Bill," I said. "I can't leave here without finishing the job I was hired for, to kill William Watsburg."

"You can't just come into a man's house and shoot everyone including the host. If you kill me, there will be consequences, the type you can never survive. Your organisation might be strong, but you can't take on a cartel and the CIA. This is much bigger than you and me, Talissa..."

A shot rang through the room bringing an abrupt halt to Bill's speech as the woman I'd found hiding under the table ended his talking as she pulled the trigger. She turned to me and smiled. A smile short-lived as sirens wailed in the distance.

"Come with me. We have to go," I said.

She followed me as I ran back through the room we were in a few minutes ago and headed for the stairs ahead of me. Her speed was much quicker than my own, and as she made it to the ground floor, I had just made it to the bottom of the first flight of stairs. A number of bodies lay randomly as we made our way to the front door of the house.

The others had made it to our transport. In the clear of the night, I could see flashing red and blue lights approaching up the road running parallel to the ocean. They would be upon us soon. If we were to make our escape down the driveway leading to the road, it had to be now.

"Talissa, we need to get moving," Helen yelled, standing behind the vehicle she'd arrived in separately.

The volume of the sirens intensified, and I had to come up with a plan. "Emily, can you drive?" I asked.

"Of course, I can," she answered, giving me a look like I was stupid.

"You take the barmaid and my new friend here away. I'll take this little girl and Helen. We need to each go a different direction so at least half of us get away."

"Are you sure about this?" Helen asked me.

"Oh, yes. I've never been so sure in my life." I picked up Beth's grief-stricken daughter and put her in the back of Helen's vehicle, and waved Emily and the other two off as they drove away.

"Come on, Talissa. We need to go," Helen yelled as she got to the driver's seat.

I jogged around and sat in the passenger seat. Helen started the car, but before she put it in gear, I aimed my gun at the side of her head.

"Geez, woman. What the fuck are you doing?"

"Someone gave Bill information about all of us and the only way he could have known about us all was with eyes and ears inside. I know it was you or else you would have been shot by his men," I said.

"No way, Talissa. Why would I turn on a group of people who included someone who is like a daughter to me?"

"Because you knew about the Praying Mantassassin recruitment process. You knew that only one of you two could make it through to the next level, so you found a way to get yourself into a gig that would ensure we could skip that process and neither you nor Emily would have to die should you survive."

"That's bullshit, Talissa..." her words died as I pulled the trigger and stopped her chatter. Wasting no time, I grabbed the little girl from the back of the car and ran as fast as I could to hide in the fake oasis at the front of the house.

A few minutes later, the lights were down the driveway, and I made my move when the first car parked about ten feet away from my hiding spot. Scooping the girl in my arms, I left any weapons behind and ran towards a police officer who appeared to be in his forties.

"Help me, help me," I called out. "There were some crazy people shooting each other at the party."

"Lady, please calm down. Did you get a good look at any of them?"

"No, I hid as soon as I could and rescued this poor girl who lost her mother in the crossfire. I was just there as a guest. One minute, I was sipping champagne and the next..." He shone a torch on me, the light forcing me to turn my eyes away.

"We'll need to ask you a lot of questions, miss, but I have to say thanks for saving the life of a little girl."

It was time to step up the act. "There are dead people everywhere. I thought I was going to die." In my line of work, the ability to force tears was a handy trick to have up my sleeve.

A female officer made her way over. She put a blanket around me and embraced me. After a couple of minutes, she spoke to her superior. "Sergeant Hall, want me to put her in the back of my car?"

Chapter 6

"YOU DELIBERATELY CAME close to exposing our organization by nearly getting busted and then killed a fellow Mantassassin on nothing more than gut instinct. By rights, I should have you killed for your conduct, Talissa. But you've been one of the best, which is why we've decided to let you go, instead."

"But, sir…" I pleaded into the intercom, shocked at the announcement. For my insubordination, I did deserve death, and maybe that's what I truly wanted after all the years of causing it to happen to other people. But to be let go? That filled me with icy fear.

"But nothing. You'll be given money. And a new identity to begin a new life. Find a man, settle down, buy a house, and maybe have some kids. Live a normal life. You've more than earned it. Just remember though one day, we might need you back. So keep your skills up and don't get back into that same shape you were in when you arrived here."

"Helen was the mole. I can prove it if you give me a few—"

"You're not listening to me, and I'm starting to get a little unhappy."

Tears welled in my eyes, real ones this time. I knew nothing else anymore except the life of an assassin. The Mantassassins had been my family for so long I'd forgotten what a real family was like.

"Where do I start?" I asked as my heart pounded. "How do I go and live a normal life now after everything I've done and seen? I was just a girl when your man Gary found me."

"Pack up your things. I'll have some information printed for you. I'll put you in contact with a woman who knows her way around and maybe some people you can talk to about work. If you ever see any of the others, don't tell them this, but you've been one of my favourites, and I'll miss you. This is why you don't die— well, not just yet anyway. Have a good life."

The boss ended the chat, and I sat looking out the window for a couple of minutes at the freshly mown lawn outside thinking about all those years of training before making my way to my room. I would have to slip back into society and be a regular woman, not able to fuck and shoot at will. How the hell was I supposed to live like that?

******

"DID YOU KILL her?" Emily asked as I entered my room. She sat on a chair near the table with a pistol in her hand.

I nodded. If the girl wanted to kill me, the answer wouldn't matter. "She was the mole, Emily."

"You know that's not true, and it wasn't your decision to make. To kill her. You should have let her come back here, and then you could have made the accusation. I could kill you, bitch, but they'd only come after me, and it would be a waste. You better pray that I never see you out in the world."

She stared at me as she stood and made her way out of the room, and I was left alone with a few minutes to pack all of my worldly possessions and get ready to be taken away. I thought about Diablo and the love we never made and now would never make. Life is so short, and I swore from that moment on to never make the same mistake.

The dating game was a pain in the ass to play. So many players, guys who would tell you everything you want to hear just to get between your legs, and the ones who tell you they're married within minutes of having sex. I couldn't deny that I had needs, but I wanted more than an hour of fun. And with some guys, I barely even had fun.

After making the mistake of having sex on the night of meeting a new man several times, I decided to stop frequenting the seedy bars and flesh market nightclubs. My new friend suggested a change of scene.

She introduced me to this bar frequented by white-collar types. It looked like a tidy and calm establishment, its clients more inclined to have a relaxing drink rather than a drinking contest, and the music at a level allowing people to converse without yelling.

I sat with my friend by my side on stools near the bar's main counter, wearing my favourite red dress and doing quick visual scans of potentially datable guys as they walked on by. No matter how hot the guy was, I would do things right and not get into bed within hours of meeting. I would make them wait, possibly until the fourth of fifth date.

They would have to seduce my mind before my body. They would need me to know them from the inside out while they got to know a fabrication I had memorised to pass off as my life. I could look at men and surmise whether they were keepers or casual fuckers.

"Excuse me, lady, but I haven't seen you here before," a man in a black suit and tie with a light blue shirt underneath said to me.

I turned and looked at the source of the voice, handsome smiling face looking right at me. He caught my eyes, and I felt glad to have been seated as the smell of his cologne subtly hit my nostrils and made my skin tingle. His eyes stayed level with mine, not lowering to my cleavage or the hem of my skirt sitting squarely with my upper thighs. "Um, I've never been here before." Okay, he had me mentally scattered, and I couldn't think of something else to say.

"Your glass is nearly empty. Would you care for another drink?" He extended his arm. "By the way, my name's Terry."

I accepted his gesture, soft skin on a perfectly manicured hand and his grip firm but not crushing.

"I'm Talissa."

"Wow, that's different. But I like it."

I knew he was worried he said the wrong thing, so I smiled back. "I think it's Italian for danger."

His smile grew. He ordered me another glass of red wine, pronouncing a name of a drop I had never heard of before and a glass of scotch for himself, on the rocks. "I like danger," he said and winked. As our drinks landed on the bar, we each quickly took a sip and our eyes locked onto each others again.

I told myself to settle. My pussy would hate me, but I would not give in to its desires. I hadn't felt this way upon first meeting a man since...

"Would you care for a dance, Talissa?" Terry asked, cutting off my thoughts.

I had to release some energy somehow, and any sexual tension would have to be fully released via battery-operated means later on. It was time to make sure I did things right, no matter how excited I got being with this Terry guy. One can never meet someone and know it will be happily ever after, but I had a great feeling about this guy.

"Sure, I would love to dance."

We danced on and off for the next three hours, and amongst it, I learned about his real estate career and his taste in the finest things in life. The way he looked at me on the dance floor, I felt I would surely be one of those in time. At the end of the night, my friend, who I had all but abandoned, left the establishment with Terry's friend, who seemed a polar opposite to Terry.

"Terry, I want to see you again," I said.

He smiled, and even though he probably wished it was him and not his friend getting lucky that night, he kissed my hand. "Oh, you will see me again. Same place next week, I will be here. Goodnight." He waved down a cab for me and told the driver to make sure I got home safe.

For the next few weeks, we met up every Friday night, talked, danced, and drank, and then finally, we shared a cab, and both went to his place. Our first night together was nothing short of spectacular. We didn't fuck, we went on a sexual journey, followed by another and then another. I woke up in the middle of the night, sat in one of his lounge chairs, and cried. Not sad tears, but the feeling of finding that perfect piece of euphoria.

If this guy truly were the one, I wouldn't let anything happen to him. He wouldn't end up like Harry or Diablo. I didn't think I could ever settle back in a regular life again, but all it took was this one man and a couple of months to make me realise that I could have the dream, to be loved, adored and worshipped, and constantly sexually satisfied as a true goddess deserves to be. There would be no way the Praying Mantassassins would be calling me back to active duty. They just took pity on me for my duty and said what they thought I wanted to hear. But if they did try to bring me back in, I would find a way out of it, even if I had to kill them all.

EMILY

CHAPTER 1

ERICA STEELE, AKA EMILY

I HAVE ABSOLUTELY no recollection of my real parents. My early life consisted of a throng of tattered memories of perverted older men with beards and nude women with long hair in smoky little tents. Those memories come from growing up in a culture of drugs, free love, and crazy people holding no regard for the laws of our country. They just did what they wanted with whomever they wanted without consequences.

One of my earliest remembrances consisted of one of those bearded men lying naked with me on one side of him, and my favourite pretend-mother, Sapphire, on his other. At the time, I didn't understand what they were doing to each other, and I worried he was hurting her when she was making noises as he was putting his 'doodle' in her, as he so eloquently put it.

Growing up amongst nudity and drug taking seemed normal to me. It was as if everyone grew up that way. We all lived in the middle of a forest in tents, living off the land from fruits and vegetables we grew. Many nights were spent around a campfire, singing, and drinking moonshine, and smoking plants that also grew near our isolated existence. A river ran half a mile from our campsite, a source of water we utilised for bathing and swimming. At the age of fourteen, I lost my virginity to a boy of my same age during a warm starry night on the muddy banks of the watery lifeline of our world.

While not a great first experience, I loved the way it made me feel to have a boy inside me. So the boy named Darrell and I did it nearly every day for a week. That is until one of the bearded elders caught us in the act and informed me that having reached the age to have sex, I needed to be sharing my body around with other people too, as part of the accepted practice of our civilisation. Without any exposure to the outside world back then, I had no idea I shouldn't be doing it with anyone at my age, let alone the elders. But whenever I got with one of the older men, something seemed wrong about it, almost as if I was sleeping with my father.

But one day, a woman joined our little commune, and it soon changed everything. Young and beautiful with long flowing dark hair, I took an instant shining to her and hung out with her as often as I could. She was thirty when she joined us, and when we had time alone, she told me I shouldn't be having sex with the older men, that it was wrong, and they were only using me. She also didn't partake when the joints were passed around at the campfire, but when the group sex started, she told me to sit and watch, and she got involved with not just the men, but the women too.

A few weeks passed by, and one day, I was sitting by the riverbank trying to make out with another girl when I overheard two of the male elders chatting.

"If we let her stay, she could tear down everything we've built here."

"Yes, I know. Ever since she arrived here, Erica won't let me fuck her until I have to get rough with her," the other man said. "Some nights, I have a really hard job getting her legs apart."

"Helen has to go if you know what I mean. I think she's trying to brainwash the younger ones into standing up for themselves. I prefer it when Erica happily spreads her legs."

"Yes, she's the hottest bitch here, those breasts and that nice tight—"

"There's plenty more like her. If she needs to go too, we can just go out and seduce more women and girls to our lifestyle. Oh, and you're well within your rights to make little Erica have sex with you. But maybe tell her it's part of the law, and not obeying can mean..."

I turned away and looked in the eyes of Rebecca, who still appeared stunned about me hitting on her. "I'm sorry, Erica. I'm not sure about this," she put her shirt back on.

"Never mind that. I just heard Dennis and Ian talking about Helen and me. I'm worried they might want to kill us."

"Are you sure? I didn't hear anything."

"I don't like sex with the older men."

"But it's how things go here. If we keep them pleased, everything is okay."

I looked in her eyes, and she looked up in the direction from where I heard the two men speak. Maybe she was in on it, too. I had to go find Helen, and quick.

"Erica, where are you going?" she asked.

"Just going back to camp." I walked away from her and headed to the main camp field.

******

I PEEKED INTO every tent, many of them filled with smoke, some with groups of two or three engaged in various sex acts. Helen couldn't be found in any of them.

I scratched my head and wondered where she could be, and as I surveyed the trees blanketing us from the outside world from the corner of my eye, I caught a glimpse of movement. I kept my gaze glued to the location and walked toward it.

Leaves and sticks crunched under my bare feet, but I hardly felt them, my soles having grown accustomed over the years. Our lives were simple and our needs few. No shoes, no underwear, just basic clothes sewn by the old lady, and a constant supply of birth control pills and tampons handed to us from the age of our first period, provided by the old man of the group who made monthly visits to this place he called town.

"Erica, what is it?" Helen's voice startled me as she came out of the shadows before I saw her clearly.

"I heard Ian and Dennis talking about you, saying you had to go because you were a bad influence and maybe me as well if I don't stop trying to resist sex with them. They miss me freely having sex with them, they force me now, and they're not happy about it, blaming you for me not wanting to put out. It feels wrong having sex with those older men. Now it's really starting to hurt because they force me to their beds and then force my legs apart, but what if I'm supposed to be doing what they want, and I'm the bad one?"

Even in the uncertain lighting, I saw her stiffen. "Yes, it is wrong fucking those older men. They're using you because you're young, pretty, and hot. In the real world, they would be put in jail for what they do to you. And you know what I think? I think they probably took you from your family when you were a baby, raising you to be a pot-smoking, free-loving hippy. I can get you out of here.”

My eyes lit up. I always wondered what else was out in the world, but I never thought I would be able to leave—and being forced to have sex made me sad most days.

“Where would we go? How would we survive?” I asked. Part of me also feared change, as well as any action the elders would do to stop us from leaving—or what they would do to get me back.

“You two stupid bitches wouldn’t last a week.”

I turned abruptly and found the bearded Dennis standing behind me, his lips twisted in a creepy smile.

“You followed her here? You’re one hell of a creep,” Helen said. She reached for a satchel on the ground and pulled out a knife.

“Put that thing away, Helen. I know you don’t have the balls to use that.”

Quicker than I could blink, she pulled her arm back and flung the knife through the air. It hit Dennis in the throat. Gasping aloud, I almost fell to my knees as Helen ran over to catch me.

“We need to get to those tents and find where they hide the money, and then we can hit the road and go to a much better place,” she said. She lowered me to the ground to sit as she gathered her satchel and sifted through it.

Each time I looked to my right, I saw Dennis’s eyes staring back at me as if his body was telling me that although his body had died, his soul was watching me, and he would still come for me each day I wasn’t having my period. I put my head in my hands and began to sob.

“Hey, babe, it will all be okay. He was an evil man. Don’t feel sad for him.”

“But I’ve known him all my life, part of me still loves him despite the—” I said cutting my own sentence short. I saw the blood flow out from beneath his body, and thought about the times he used to lead sing-alongs around the campfire as I danced with the other children. But that was before I became one of his many sex toys, and my mind soon switched to the times his hairy sweating body lay on top of mine.

"It's because you don't know any better. If you come with me, I can give you all the answers you seek about your past and where you came from, maybe find your family. Stay here and I'll be back in a few minutes."

I looked in the satchel and found a machete—a massive bladed tool that I thought could double for a weapon if I needed it. My body still shook in fear, but I knew I might have to defend myself.

"I want to help you. I can't let you risk your life for me without trying to help you." Should I have felt bad that I was ready to join up with Helen after only a relatively short time she had been in my life?

She smiled. "I was hoping you would say that. But we need to get going before the others find the body."

******

WE MADE IT back to the main camp area, Helen with a pistol in her hand and me with a machete I had no idea how to use it to full effect. If all I had to do were swing it through the air, I would be fine.

Ian was the first to crawl out of a tent, fully naked and dropping to his knees as soon as he saw Helen with a pistol aimed at him. "Please, Helen. Whatever you're thinking, you don't want to do it."

"Ian, you're charged with the crime of having multiple non-consensual sex acts with a minor," she took a few steps forward and placed the steel barrel in Ian's forehead. "And the punishment is death."

I looked away as the sound of the bullet ripping through the man's head echoed and the screaming started from everywhere around us. I held my weapon high with shaking hands. One of the boys my own age tried to plead with me to put it down, stepping closer and closer to me. Thinking he wanted to talk me down, I swung the machete to my right, slicing his chest open and seeing blood spill in a big pool between his feet.

"Erica," I heard a female voice behind me.

"Rebecca, you don't need to get involved in this," I said. "I'm taking a stand."

Helen looked from side to side for any movement. If everyone decided to rush her at the same time, she might have been able to put two or three of them down, but with over thirty of us living here, we would be overrun.

"Come with us, Rebecca," Helen said. "Come and see the world."

She looked at me and stared, and then back at the boy's and Ian's bodies. Maybe she thought about what she had been expected to do with the male elders, because as she looked back at me, nodded, and pointed to one of the tents. "That's where they keep everything, all the money and the pills and stuff."

"Thanks," Helen said and crawled almost lizard-like into the tent. A short burst of shouting erupted, soon cut out by two quick gunshots. She exited with a young girl in her grasp and a big suitcase.

"I'll need all the men to come out of their tents or else I'll kill this young girl here," she called out.

It took a good minute, but six men crawled from their hiding spots and put their hands up as quickly as they spotted Helen with her gun. Some were clothed, others not.

"In society, what you men do here is known as

statutory rape, and in some cases, rape. In the court of Helen, I find you all guilty."

She lined them up one at a time and shot each of the men through the head. Several others came and watched what she did, crying into their hands and screaming as the majority of the male population of the commune met their demise in a span of just a few seconds. I should have been horrified, but I looked at the line of dead men, thinking of the way they had treated me and smiled. I liked the way my new mentor had the power to take away the whole of a person's existence in a split second. We stood and waited for one of the women to exit her tent.

As I tried to force my pulse to lower, I shook with the machete in my hand ready to use. "Miss Lizzie, you are charged with the crime of doing nothing while men thirty years older than I had their way with me whenever they liked," I said to her.

"Erica, she's one of the nice ones," Rebecca said, touching me on the shoulder.

I didn't pay her any attention apart from lifting her hand away from me and walked over and swung the machete at Miss Lizzie's neck, the blade hitting bone and getting stuck, blood spurting from the wound I had inflicted. I pulled with all my strength to dislodge the weapon as the woman collapsed where she stood in a puddle of her own blood.

"Blades make such a mess. I'll have to teach you how to shoot," Helen said. "I generally use that for chopping firewood or clearing a path through the bush."

"Please, just go and leave the rest of us alone," another woman said, crawling from her tent situated behind me.

More people came outside and looked at us, and in their eyes, I saw fear. I wanted to swing the machete again, but Helen told me it was time to go, to seek another adventure somewhere else.

"There's been enough killing today," the young girl taken hostage by Helen said.

The three of us stared at her for what seemed liked minutes. We then looked at each other, put our weapons away, and started our journey from the commune, never to see it again.

Helen, Rebecca, and I held hands and smiled as our feet tread on new territory.

Chapter 2

WE HAD BEEN on our journey for three weeks, travelling from the state of Pennsylvania to Mississippi by foot and in the back of pick-up trucks. With our newfound wealth acquired from the stash of money stolen from the commune elders, we bought new clothes, and Rebecca and I ate meat for the very first time.

"I don't know how you survived on beans, mushrooms, and vegetables for so long," Helen said the first day we stopped for burgers.

Rebecca and I didn't know any difference. We also discovered these things called shoes, making our long walk much more comfortable for our feet. Even during the coldest months in our tents, all we had was material wrapped around our feet and held in place with string. We had never felt so free, the three of us exploring more of our country with each day we were on the road and making new discoveries, like hot showers, store-bought underwear, and coffee.

Helen had a fair idea who not to travel with, and knowing we had the means to protect ourselves if necessary served as the perfect umbrella of protection for us on our travels. Getting a ride was easy for three beautiful females, but we steered clear of those who asked for sex or blowjobs in return for a lift.

"Why don't we just get a bus? We have the money," I asked Helen after we stopped at a twenty-four-hour diner for breakfast. I'd learned about the world quickly. Before the journey, I hadn't even known what a truck or buses were, having only ever seen the station wagon back at the commune.

"That would be cheating. I'm teaching you girls life skills. I'm introducing you to so many different people and how to decide who you'll ride with and who you won't. The world is a big mysterious place, and no one will ever work it all out. But I've learned a lot in my thirty years, and I want to pass on as much of my knowledge as I can to you both."

"How did you learn how to kill people?" Rebecca asked as we walked side by side behind Helen. Rebecca's question brought the eldest member of our group to stop in her tracks.

"You don't ask me questions like that. It's something I had to learn or else I would have ended up raped by a college jerk. We live in a world ruled by men who crave money, power, and that beautiful object between our legs, and some of those will take what they hunger for by force, as you girls experienced with those men at that hippy commune where you grew up. They were clever in making you think it was your duty. What I will teach you is that females should be taking that power away from them and using our vaginas to get what we want from who we want when we want. We have the power."

I loved listening to her, but I had a burning question. "What if I like girls, too?"

Rebecca looked away.

"Well, we are allowed to have a little fun as well, whether it's with boys or girls," Helen said. "I've been with a woman myself, and the experience was fantastic. It felt weird at first, but kissing another woman's soft lips, feeling the curves of her body with my hands, and having her mouth between my legs was a mind-blowing experience. I think every woman should try it at least once." She smiled at us.

I smiled. It came as a relief to hear I wasn't weird for the feelings I had for Rebecca, but I would have to keep them to myself.

The sun blared down on us, another hot day on the open road with barely a sound to be heard. Rebecca grabbed my hand and held it in hers as we walked. Despite our similar height and build, we looked nothing alike, even dressed in our identical outfits consisting of white crop tops and denim skirts. We were dressed to get attention, which soon arrived in the form of a group of three motorcycle riders.

They stopped in the gravel ahead of us, in full black leathers, dark sunglasses and black half-helmets, the type favoured by a lot of old school bikers.

"Stay back," Helen put her arm out to emphasise her point and walked ahead.

We couldn't fully understand the conversation just up from us, but one of the bikers, in particular, kept looking our way and nodded. There weren't any club colours on the back of their jackets or any patches of any types. With their helmets and eyewear, I couldn't make out their features too well, nor even take a wild guess at their ages, but the smile on Helen's face told me we would get to know a lot about them.

"Girls, you're both eighteen. The leader is their father and seems like a decent man. They're willing to take us on the back of their bikes, but for how long I don't know. This is going to be one hell of a ride," Helen said.

Rebecca and I walked over to the two youngest bikers, picking one each at random to ride with. All three opened their storage compartment and pulled out spare helmets for all three of us.

"Hi, the name's Reece," the rider on the bike I had approached said.

"Reece. I like it," I said.

"My name's Brandon," the other young biker said.

"It's so nice to make your acquaintance," the oldest biker said. "My name's Roscoe."

His big white smile and southern drawl would have been a drawcard for most women his age, and I could tell by Helen's sudden weak in the knees walk that she wasn't immune. I put the full-face helmet on and hopped on the back of Reece's bike and smiled, knowing I was about to embark on a hot new adventure. I put my arms around his waist and pushed my body in snug behind his.

******

I HAD NEVER felt anything as exhilarating in my life before my first day on the back of a bike. I knew what Reece meant when he said nothing came close to the freedom of riding on the open road in the open air and seeing the world on two wheels. He didn't question my answer when I told him I was eighteen. It was only a two-year addition to my real age, and I was early to blossom. His smile had the same panty dropping effect as his father's smile did, as well as his deep south accent.

On that first night, we found a bare patch of land to pull up for the evening, and as Roscoe set up the campfire and cooked us all a plate of beans and eggs, the three of us females looked at each other with the knowledge we would all be getting lucky. Reece's age was the same as my pretend age, whereas Brandon was a year older.

After dinner, Roscoe pulled out a bottle, which had a label calling it Jack Daniels. My first sip of it reminded me of the moonshine we used to drink back at the commune, except much less potent and smoother. The six of us sat around and swapped stories, getting tipsy as the bottle circled between us. The laughter built up until Roscoe declared the hour was getting late and we should all turn in. But I knew turning in would mean a round of hot passionate sex.

"Hey, girl. Let's take a walk," Reece said to me, picking up a blanket and reaching for my hand with his free one.

"Sure, handsome," I said, accepting his warm grip and almost skipping to keep up with him. My body tingled thinking about what I would soon be doing with this hot young guy. We passed a series of boulders and found a patch of grass to put the blanket on that was well out of sight of the others.

"That woman isn't your mother, is she?" he asked.

"No, but she's the closest thing I've ever had to one. I don't know anything about my real parents. I don't know if they died or put me up for adoption or if I was taken from them. The hippy commune is all I've ever known until the last few weeks."

"My mother died a year ago, so the three of us have been riding around the country ever since." He removed his jacket and showed me a tattoo on his shoulder with his mother's name, date of birth and death written beneath a butterfly. "As she was dying, she told us we must spread our wings and be free and never let the ugliness of the world destroy what is beautiful inside of us."

"She sounds like a wonderful woman. I'm so sorry." I rubbed the bare skin exposed from his skin-tight tank. His arms and shoulders were firm.

"Don't be sorry. Seventeen years with a woman like that is much better than a whole life with parents who don't care that you exist, not saying that's the case with yours."

"No offence taken." My other hand touched the side of his face, the stubbled texture exciting me.

"You're so beautiful, Erica. I don't feel like I deserve this night here alone with you."

"Shut the fuck up, biker boy, and kiss me."

His lips raced towards mine and almost devoured mine in his hunger. My tongue left my mouth and invaded his, and it felt like the first time I had truly kissed someone. If it was possible to get off on just a kiss, Reece was the man to do it.

I withdrew for a second, pulling my top over my head, and undoing my skirt, then sitting there in just a bra and panties. The cool night breeze felt like chilled mist on my mostly bare skin, adding to my excitement.

"Well, that hardly seems fair," he said, smirking as he got to his feet and removed his tank top. The faint glow of moonlight highlighted his ripped abs, and I found myself licking my lips as he unzipped his black leather pants and pulled them to the ground. His briefs didn't leave much to the imagination, and I wanted to just rip them off and touch the large package he carried inside them.

I stood up and unclasped my bra. His eyes went down to my breasts, and his hands soon followed. He filled his hands with my well-developed pair, rubbing them gently unlike the boys and men from where I came from.

"That is one fantastic pair of tits," he said, taking his hands off them and pulling me towards him, slamming his lips against mine again and continuing the tongue dance-off we had started a few minutes prior.

One of my hands travelled low, past his navel and down the front of his briefs, grasping the hard cock I found in there and releasing it from its cotton prison. The thing was huge, much larger than anything I had ever had in my hands or mouth or inside me previously. Maybe a sizable man tool was the thing I had been missing on any past sexual experience. I had never come before through any act.

"Oh fuck, Reece. I want that thing inside me. And I want it now."

He pulled away, smiling at me and then crouched down to strip me completely naked. "I'll be gentle with you baby," he said and proceeded to do something no man had ever done with their mouth before. He put his head against my pussy and waited for me to spread my legs a little before he kissed me in a way my body had never been kissed. His tongue found my most sensitive part, circling around and sending my body into a crazed frenzy within minutes as I shook and felt as though my whole body had floated away in waves of ecstasy as I experienced my first ever orgasm.

"Wow, that was freaking incredible," I said. I lay back on the blanket and signalled for him to get closer to me again. "Now I want that huge dick of yours inside me."

******

THE SUNLIGHT WOKE us from a great night of sex and slumber, glaring down on our naked bodies huddled together on top of the blanket. I looked at him and smiled, him returning the favour.

"We should get dressed," he said, looking out in the direction of where we guessed the others to be. I hoped we would be able to find somewhere to shower and get some new clothes. Sitting on the back of a bike in small tops and short skirts was making me cold, and I hoped Helen still had enough money for us to buy some leathers to match the boys.

Once we put our dirty clothes back on, we found the other four, also paired off and looking like they too could do with a coffee.

"Good morning, you two. I'm about to put a pot of coffee on. You look like you could sure use it," Roscoe said.

Not having had coffee for the first sixteen years of my life, I wasn't dependent on it, but the taste had grown on me. Reece gave me a kiss and headed away with his brother to gather some firewood.

"So, how was your night?" Rebecca asked me. I had never seen her grin as much prior to that morning.

"Oh, my God. He was fan-fucking-tastic. He made me come with his mouth and had the biggest—"

"Must be a family thing." She giggled. "Brandon made sex really fun. I thought he was going to really hurt me with that cock of his, but he was so gentle."

"Morning, girls." Helen almost made us jump as she crept up behind us. "You probably don't want to hear it, but I didn't get any last night."

"Why? What happened?" I asked.

"Well, we started kissing. Neither of us had our tops on. Then he told me about how he hadn't been with a woman since his deceased wife got sick. So I said we shouldn't sleep together, and he should wait until he finds a worthy woman before he gets back on the horse,"

Helen said.

"Oh, wow. You are one hell of a woman. So how did you manage to sleep with all that build up?" Rebecca asked.

Helen looked us in the eyes, one after the other. "Ha! Got you both. I fucked his brains out and gave him a night he would never forget." The three of us laughed, and I looked over at the three almost perfect men and wished it would never end.

"But, seriously, life's too short, and you never know when it will be your last day in this world. So if you want something, grab it with both hands, girls," Helen added.

Roscoe checked the saucepan on the fire. The water was boiling so he added a few spoons of instant coffee and then poured it into three cups. "Sorry, I don't have any cream to add, but we'll stop soon for showers and some real café fresh coffee."

The two younger men returned, and Rebecca and I partnered up with them again and shared from their mugs. The hot dark liquid was all right, but if it had been my first experience drinking coffee, I don't think I would have touched it again.

"So how long do you think you three will continue travelling?" Helen asked.

"For as long as the money lasts. I sold up everything after sweet Erin died, and I spent so much time promising my boys a trip around the US of A in their younger years, and barely saw them because of work. So for what it's worth, I'm making up for some of that time now," Roscoe said.

"And we're having the best time ever," Brandon said. He turned to Rebecca and gave her a kiss.

I caught a glimpse of Roscoe's facial reaction, his eyes fixated on his oldest boy and new plaything. It reminded me of something Helen told me the day we left the commune, that each of us must make our own journey and know who to share the road with for a given time.

I didn't want to think of anything but the present, and the present was pretty fucking awesome.

CHAPTER 3

HAPPINESS IS A gift we all want to receive, preserve, and never let go off. But there are times in your life when you can't hold it, and the tighter you try to grasp it, the quicker it falls through the gaps between your fingers. Nothing had to go wrong with our new adventure we found ourselves in, but humanity can't help but crave for chaos in amongst the control.

Is it because we like to sabotage ourselves to seek a new struggle to overcome? Or is it because past crimes have a way of catching up with us?

It had been a week since we first met the three bikers, and each day had been full of riding, sightseeing, and great sex. We made for camp at this one place near Lake Meredith, and a few drinks into the night, we all ended up spending a warm night beneath the stars skinny-dipping.

Rebecca followed me to a spot and stopped close to me. "Let's give the boys something to get excited about." The water was only about knee deep, so she jumped on me and knocked me down and straddled me. She leant down and kissed me, and I returned the favour. Her lips were so soft, and the feeling of her body against mine intensified my excitement. Her breasts nestled against my own, and our pelvises were so close. I didn't stop to comprehend what we were doing, the excitement accelerating inside me.

I could hear cheering from the brothers, stopping us in mid-action and watching as they walked our way. But a different course of action occurred as Brandon approached me, and Reece to Rebecca.

"It's okay, Erica. We're young and not committed," Rebecca said and grabbed Reece's cock in her hand and put it in her mouth.

I froze. He was my boy and seemed too eager to switch girls in a second. I felt Brandon press his body to mine from behind me, his hands travelling to the front of my body and cupping my breasts as I spread my legs and bent forward. I watched Rebecca giving Reece a blowjob while pulling Brandon's hardness into my eager pussy from behind.

He felt every inch as big as his brother had felt as he slowly pushed himself inside. I squealed in delight as his whole length became buried within me, reaching points no man or boy had ever discovered before. I wanted to explode in an orgasm of volcanic proportions, but he had reached his peak well before I reached mine and then withdrew and headed for the land to have another drink.

"What? That's it, Brandon?" I yelled.

"Sorry, babe. I couldn't hold on any longer," he said.

I turned and watched as Reece had Rebecca laid out in inch deep water, pumping her just as he had done to me every night for the last week. How the fuck could I have been so stupid to swap boys for one sex act? I clenched my fists as she moaned, and I wanted to take him away from her and have the younger, but more sexually able of the brothers.

"Fuck this," I said.

Walking away, I headed directly to where Helen kept her stuff. I hadn't seen her and Roscoe for about half an hour, guessing they wanted to keep their acts more private. I didn't know how close other campers might have been to our location, as I strode around naked to get to Helen's satchel. I found it under her clothes and pushed the items inside around until I found what I was looking for.

Brandon sat fully dressed drinking another beer and watching his brother have sex with Rebecca. Catching a glimpse of me as I walked past him, he got to his feet, "Hey, what are you doing?"

I turned and faced him, aiming Helen's pistol at his face. "Don't you take another fucking step closer."

"Please, Erica. Don't do something stupid."

"Too late for that—I did you. Back off, and let me do what I need to do."

Rebecca and Reece saw me coming at them, screaming out at me to please stop. I raised my arm and lined up Reece in my sights. "You think you can just ditch me like this? I bet you wanted Rebecca all along, right? Well, you can have her for every minute of every day in the afterlife."

"No, Erica. You're drunk and too young to understand any of this," I heard Helen's voice behind me.

"I understand everything. I wasn't fucking good enough for you, was I, Reece?" My whole arm shook as my finger began to pull back on the trigger.

"Young lady, think about what you're about to do," Roscoe said.

"I know what I'm about to do. I've seen Helen do it at the commune," I said. Tears fell as I looked at Reece staring back at me with pleading eyes.

"Erica, this isn't a reason to kill anyone," Helen said. "Those men at the commune deserved it, and you and I both know why."

"What are you talking about, Helen?" Roscoe asked.

"You don't need to know. We just need to stop Erica from—" Helen said.

I pulled the trigger all the way, and I saw Reece fall back from impact into the shallow depth he had been standing in. I didn't see where I hit him but felt a body jump on me from behind, knocking me forward onto the ground.

I rolled over and saw Helen with the pistol in her hand. Another voice belonging to Rebecca pierced the air. "Erica, what have you done?"

"She fucking shot my brother," Brandon cried.

"I should have killed you instead," I said. "Why couldn't we just keep things the way they were? Why did you guys decide to fuck it up by thinking you can just swap sex partners? What are we, just toys?"

"I'm sorry, Erica," Brandon said.

I saw Roscoe scoop his youngest son in his arms, "Are you okay, son?"

"She shot me," Reece said, squeezing his eyes shut.

"It's just through his shoulder. He'll be okay," Helen said. She looked at me again. "What the hell came over you?"

For anyone watching us, the sight of the six of us in differing stages of undress, arguing, and fighting might have been amusing. Helen and Roscoe at least had underwear on.

"Helen, you have to send Erica away. She's a loose cannon," Roscoe said.

"I can't send her away by herself. She's only sixteen," Helen said. All attention turned to her on spitting out that comment.

"Oh shit," Roscoe said. "Anything else you're keeping from me? I knew this whole thing was a bad idea."

"The three of you seemed happy to have sex on tap, and after one little fight, you want to fuck this all up?" I said.

"One little fight? You shot one of my boys, you stupid little bitch," Roscoe said.

"Shut up, all of you," Helen yelled. "I'll pack my things and go. Erica, you need to get dressed. You too, Rebecca."

"No, I'm not coming. I'm staying with these guys," she said.

"Rebecca, you're too young," Brandon said. "You girls are jailbait, and I ain't going to prison for you girls."

"I lied about my age too," Rebecca said. "Erica, Helen, I'm really eighteen. I lied about my age to put off having sex with the commune elders."

"Please come with me anyway. You're like a sister to me," I said.

"No, Erica. Our journey together stops now. I love you, but how do I know you won't point a gun at me one day? Or cut me open with a machete? We all knew this was only going to be a temporary thing, but you had to take it all so serious."

"Fuck you," I stormed out of the water, and for the first time, I felt naked and vulnerable. I tripped over, fell to the ground, and began howling.

"Erica, we have to go," Helen said.

I stood up again, found my clothes in a pile, and put them on while Helen retrieved her gear. She looked over at me, the tears still flowing.

"Erica, everything will be okay," she said.

I dropped to my knees, and she came over and

picked me up. I threw my arms around her and pulled her in tight as she patted me on the back as my whole body shook with my sobs.

"It's not fair, Helen. Why does this shit have to happen?"

"Life isn't fair, sweetie. I'm just grateful you didn't kill Reece. He didn't deserve it."

"He ripped my heart out when he fucked Rebecca. Ripped it out and stomped on it again and again. I hate boys. I want to kill them all." I howled again, and Helen continued to hold me until I was ready to walk away with her. I didn't look back at the boys, Roscoe, or Rebecca.

Helen made sure we were out of earshot of our departed companions before she sat me down and spoke again.

"Erica, it's time I told you where I intend to take you. There's a special place not many people know of where you can learn so much. I know you've got what it takes, and it's probably a good thing Rebecca isn't with us anymore."

"But she was like a—"

"Yes, I know, Erica, but you need to learn to not give a shit about people, not anyone. People really suck. They'll use someone like you for your body for as long as you're so ready to give your heart away. You don't need love, and you don't need people. You just need to learn how to use sex to your advantage and how to rid the world of a few people it would be better off without. The place I'm taking us has been highly recommended to me, and we will become highly paid killers."

"I could kill someone right now," I said.

"And you will also learn how to kill your emotions. Emotions will take you down. I know because I'm still learning. This place will make us better people, deadly and better."

"What is this place called?" I asked.

Helen took a deep breath. "It's called the Praying Mantassassins Compound if my sources are correct, and very few people know how to find it."

CHAPTER 4

MY MOOD DAMPENED after we parted ways with the three bikers and Rebecca. Many times, Helen would try to wave us a ride, but I would find a reason not to travel with the people she selected. We barely spoke due to my dark clouded nature.

"Let's get some coffee, Erica. It's gonna be a long day if you won't let us take a ride with anyone," Helen said.

"Sure. Let's stop somewhere. I don't give a fuck. Every town we come across is full of redneck squirrel fuckers who wouldn't know good coffee if they were fucking in it—"

Her hand stung the side of my face as the slap made contact. I didn't see it coming, and she had never treated me as such—ever. I put my backpack down that Helen had bought for me the day after we left Roscoe and his boys. I balled a hand into a fist and swung at her face, hitting fresh air as she swerved her head out of the way.

"Come on, Erica. You want to take your anger out on me, then do it. Try again, you little hippy slut."

I felt as though my blood reached boiling point and swung again, hitting a hand she put up to block my attack. Wasting no time, I swung my other fist at her and struck in the ribs. I stepped back and smiled.

"Weren't expecting that, were you?"

"No," she grabbed her body where I had struck her, "I wasn't."

I put down my guard. I couldn't believe I got the better of her and waved my hands in the air to celebrate. A few seconds later, when her hand was still placed where I made contact with her, I felt worried I had hurt her bad. "I'm so sorry, Helen."

My mind distracted with what I saw, the next punch connected before I even saw it form. The wind spewed out from me as the fist hit me near my navel. I fell to my knees, taking long breaths to normalise my regular breathing again.

"Stupid bitch, letting your guard down like that." Another fist struck me.

My head spun sideways as her other hand crashed into my cheekbone. Her movements were quick as lightning, and I regretted getting into a fight with her as I was sure getting an ass whipping. I prayed she would stop.

"We'll need to work on your hand to hand combat, girl, before we reach the compound or else it could be really embarrassing."

"You...hurt...me..." I said through laboured breaths.

"Yes, and if you came across an actual opponent, they wouldn't stop here. Now let's get some coffee and an ice pack."

I retrieved my backpack and followed behind her.

******

WE SIPPED THE less than satisfactory fluid in the mugs, and I wondered when I would taste decent coffee again. There were only two other customers inside the place apart from us, and they looked as dissatisfied as we were. At least Helen and I were free. The other two diners appeared to be wearing workwear of some sort, meaning they were wage slaves somewhere.

Helen leaned in close and whispered in my ear, "We're getting low on funds. We need to do something."

"I'm not selling my body to any of those freaks," I said. One man sitting on a table opposite looked like he was fifty years old while the other man looked as though he could have possibly swallowed an elephant.

"I'm not talking about that. We're going to take the till."

"What?"

"Stick close to me." She pulled the pistol from her bag and handed it to me. She dug in again and pulled out another. We walked towards the counter, and Helen got the attention of the woman serving behind it and made her come close. "Excuse me, miss?" She pressed the gun into the woman's stomach. "I'll be needing the contents of that cash register there."

"Okay, I don't want no trouble." She pressed a button to release the cash drawer, watching Helen's hands as she emptied it of all the paper notes.

I kept my eye on the other two customers, making sure they didn't notice what Helen was doing. I turned as Helen put the notes in her bag, and a small flurry of motion yanked my attention away as the older diner pointed a gun our way.

"You ladies need to give Gertrude back the shop's money. They can't afford the insurance so if you steal that, they won't be able to get it back," the man said.

"You're going to shoot two women over a stash of paper bills?" Helen asked.

"I will if I have to."

I smiled back at him through my nerves. "Oh, how could you shoot this?" I placed a hand on my hip and kept my other hand with the gun behind my back.

"You think that pussy of yours will keep you safe, girl?" he asked.

"No," I said. I knew I would have to do it right and couldn't miss. I whipped my other hand from behind me and pulled back on the trigger as the gun pointed at him. He fell to the ground, landing on his ass clutching his wound.

"Oh, shit," Helen said. "You got him in the gut, Erica."

"You shouldn't have given me a gun if you didn't want me to use it. We better run, Helen."

The man yelled as he sat in a pool of his own blood his energy too sapped to pick up his dislodged weapon.

"Bitch," he said looking me in the eyes. His stare stayed glued to me, and I found myself unable to tear my eyes away from him.

"He's bleeding out, Erica. You need to put him out of his misery," Helen said.

She was right. It had to be me who did it seeing as I was the cause of the man's pain. I took a few steps closer to him and levelled the gun at his head. "You shouldn't have gotten involved. We just needed the money."

I fired once, hitting him square in the forehead. Even in death, his empty eyes stayed on me, and I wondered if maybe his soul took a long look at me before it flew away to the next world.

"Erica, we have to go," Helen said.

******

WE RAN FOR a good two hours after robbing the diner and killing one of their loyal customers. There were no police sirens within earshot the whole time, but I guessed a town the size of that one would have to call in a patrol vehicle which could have been anywhere within a two hundred mile radius.

"So are we nearly where we need to be?" I asked.

"We're getting closer. If you let us hitch a ride with someone, we'll get there sooner."

"Well, here comes a pickup truck now. And I promise that unless the driver looks like someone who would cook and eat his own family, I'll be happy to go aboard."

"I'll hold you to that," Helen said, hitching her skirt a little higher and sticking her chest out and her thumb up. We found in our travels nearly any man will stop for a hot looking female or two or three. It wasn't necessarily for sex or the expectation of a date that made them stop, but it seemed most men just loved being in the company of hot chicks like us.

The truck slowed for us and stopped a few feet before us, and the driver actually looked like a good-looking guy.

"You can get in the back, I'll get in with him," I said.

"You just be careful, Erica. Oh, and please don't shoot him."

"Hey there, ladies. I can take you about a hundred miles further. Please feel free to jump right on in," the driver said.

I winked at Helen and took the front seat. "So what's your name, little miss?" he asked.

"Felicity." I decided a fake name was needed. "And yours?"

"Mike, but my friends call me Big Mike."

He looked in his mirror and slowly accelerated. I couldn't help but wonder about the 'big' part of his nickname and looked down at his crotch. I didn't notice an overly big bulge in his jeans, so the mystery nestled inside me.

"Thanks for stopping for us. It's getting really hot out there today." I let my short denim skirt ride higher, the bottom of my panties showing themselves to the driver's eyes. I didn't care much for the feel of underwear. After living without them for so many years, it made me feel unnatural. But with the length of my skirt, I would be showing everything without them.

"Gee, girl, how am I gonna keep my eyes on the road when you show so much skin."

"Sorry, Big Mike." I smiled at him.

He put his eyes on the road, and we exchanged some meaningless conversation to the end of the hundred-mile journey he had promised us. We stopped at a crossroads, and he looked my way. "Sorry, young lady, but my house is up there." He pointed to the road going to the right.

"Maybe a detour would be nice."

"There's not much down that way, apart from a few of us farmers. I'd be happy to show you my farm, but I think you're a little young for me."

Helen tapped on the window and shrugged her shoulders.

"I'm kind of tired. Maybe you'd be kind enough to take us both in for the night," I said to him.

He looked me up and down, and I knew he would be only too happy to oblige my request. "Sure, I have plenty of spare rooms."

I wound my window down, Helen now standing on the edge of the road near my window. "Helen, we're staying on a farm tonight."

She gave me a look.

"It'd be good to sleep in a proper bed for a change, don't you think?" I asked.

"Okay, sure." She jumped on the back of the pick-up again, and Mike turned the car down the road to our right. I didn't even feel nervous as he drove us a few miles and then up a long dirt driveway to a large brick home.

"It ain't much, but I like to call it home," Mike said.

"Looks lovely to me," I opened my door and stepped out once we were stopped.

Mike went on ahead, unlocked the door, and then smiled at us. Helen stood next to me and spoke in my ear, "I sure hope you know what you're doing."

******

MIKE LED US to a room that we could sleep in for the night, containing just a double bed and an old crooked wardrobe. Helen and I had previously shared much smaller places to sleep while on our trip, usually on a blanket on a small patch of ground so the one in Mike's room wouldn't be a problem.

"This will be fine," Helen said. "I need to freshen up a little."

I followed Mike to the kitchen. "So you live here by yourself?"

"Yes, it's been in my family for generations, but I haven't been lucky enough to find a lady to settle down with, so I don't know if there'll be another generation to leave it to."

"Really? But you're such a handsome man, and who wouldn't want to live out here in the peace and quiet?"

"You'd be surprised, young lady. How old are you anyway?" He looked me up and down.

"Old enough to know how to do all sorts of things," I bit my bottom lip.

"A girl and her mama hasta eat first. I'll fix us some

supper. Should be ready around 7PM. Feel free to use the bathroom and make yourself at home."

Something niggled at me about his over-generous nature, so I went back to the bedroom where Helen lay sleeping in the bed with just a sheet covering her and her dirty clothes in a neat pile on the floor. I decided the ones I was wearing could do with a wash. I stripped down to nothing and wrapped a towel around me, and then scooped up all of the dirty clothes and searched for a washing machine. On my way to the laundry room, I came across a study with the door wide open, and on the desk sat a computer and monitor with two female photos on it. I took a few steps for a closer look and saw Helen's and my face with a news article.

"Oh, shit," I said under my breath. I walked up to the screen and saw it was a news site, and we were wanted for armed robbery and murder.

I wondered if Mike knew about it and was using tactics to delay our departure to get the police here and collect the reward. I tiptoed out of the study, peeking around the corner first to ensure Mike wasn't approaching.

The coast was clear, and I made it back to the bedroom with the clothes bundled under my arm and shook Helen. "What the hell?" she sat up straight, covering herself with the sheet.

"We're on the news, Helen. Armed robbery and murder. It's all on Mike's computer."

"Oh, shit." She threw the sheet off and gathered the clothes belonging to her from the pile on the bed, scampering to get dressed again.

"He's in the kitchen preparing supper."

We knew the way to the front door involved sneaking past the kitchen and dining room. We would need to either get the timing perfect when he had his back turned or find a way to distract him. I preferred not to have to hurt or even kill him to get away.

"Pack my clothes in your bag, Helen. I'll find a way to divert his attention," I said.

"Oh, Erica, I wish you didn't think you had to sleep with someone to get what we need. You're so much more than that, honey."

"It's okay, Helen. I've learned already how harsh the world is, and we got to use what we have. Give me a minute and I'll be back." I headed to the bathroom and took a quick one-minute shower, lathering myself up with plenty of soap to rid myself of the sweat and smell of wearing dirty clothes.

I wrapped the towel around myself again, not bothering to dry myself off at all, found Helen, and waited for her to follow me. We both took long, careful steps, and once we came to the kitchen, Helen stayed back while I got Mike's attention.

"Supper's still an hour away. Can I help you with something?" he said.

"My clothes are dirty, have you got something I can wear until I can wash and dry them?"

"I've got some long shirts. Can you just stir the pot while I fetch one for you?"

"Of course, I smiled and grabbed the wooden spoon from his hand, standing as close to him as possible in the process. I stood by the stove, leaning over slightly in a way to purposely expose the bottom of my ass cheeks. I caught him having a quick glance from the corner of my eye before he left. I saw him as he walked past a spare room where Helen stayed hidden behind the door until he disappeared from view.

She came running out and caught up with me, and I ran to the front door of the house. Pulling it open, I didn't expect to see the policeman standing there with a pistol in hand.

"Oh shit," I said. "There's a man in the house who tried to rape me."

"Really? He called my precinct telling me two female fugitives were hiding out for the night," the cop said.

We were at the end of the line, and if Helen dared to fish a gun from her bag, he would surely have shot her dead first. I put my hands up, careful not to dislodge the towel, the one item keeping me modest at the time.

"I told you it was them. Did you bring my reward?" Mike entered the living area near the kitchen. I was right. He had purposely stalled us to keep us here for the cops.

"Yes, I have your reward," the policeman said as he swung his arm around and shot Mike in the head. He put his gun away and looked back at our shocked faces. "We haven't got much time, girls. Follow me."

I took one last look at Mike and felt sorry for him.

"You'll learn to lose that guilt soon enough. Get some shoes on your feet, at least," he said.

Helen passed my backpack to me. I unzipped it, found my sandals, and quickly placed them on my feet, the towel falling off me in the process. I grabbed a skirt and top to wear.

"We don't have time. Get dressed in the chopper." The cop pulled my hand and dragged me outside.

"What the hell's going on?" Helen asked.

"You thought you were looking for us, but we found you thanks to the APB you managed to draw to yourselves. I was lucky to intercept the call before other officers could arrive here. Get moving."

The chopper was parked a hundred yards away in a bare field, the rotor blades slicing the air and looking majestic with its black paint and dark tinted windows. I had never seen such an object before, but in the life I was soon to lead, I would be seeing them a lot.

The cop ran ahead of us, Helen not far behind, and me trailing last in all my naked glory. The pilot watched us pile in the back, his face invisible through the dark helmet.

I quickly dressed before securing myself with the seatbelt. The cop smiled at us and pulled out two needles from a box sitting next to him. "Sorry, ladies, but I can't allow you to see the way to the compound."

He injected Helen first, who passed out. "What compound?" I asked although I knew the answer from a previous conversation with Helen, anyway.

He put the other needle in my arm, and the last thing I had heard before the world went black was, "The Praying Mantassassins compound."

Chapter 5

MY FIRST DAY at the compound was one of strangeness but provided so much information about my past. Everything Gary the cop and Helen told me changed everything.

First of all, I discovered my real parents were killed in a car accident when I was a baby, and I was adopted out to my mother's sister, who turned out to be Miss Lizzie from the commune. She had been seduced by the words of a smooth talking gardener, who along with four male friends of his had convinced several single female parents to escape the society with them.

Between them, they had enough money to pay for the land they set their commune on and to keep the local law enforcement inside to keep any outsiders from coming in. One of the first women to have been taken in was Helen's sister, so Helen spent a lot of time and money tracking down the place she went to after disappearing from their hometown. By the time Helen found the place, she had discovered through conversation that her sister had died while giving birth to one of the boys I had grown up with.

"Wow." I couldn't think of anything else to say to

him as they sat me down in a room and spilled out my life secrets.

Gary smiled. "It's a big thing to take in, Emily, to know so much of your life has been kept secret from you. But here you can become something new."

"You called me Emily. My name's Erica. Erica Steele according to you."

"We all take on different names here, and I think Emily suits you. Stay here with us and you get fed, have your own room, and get the best training at something you're already good at."

"Killing?"

"Yes. I think you could become one of our best assassins. You need to get some attitude," he said.

"I've got enough fucking attitude to make you choke on your boyfriend's cock," I said.

He stared at me and got to his feet, and I thought he would smack me in the mouth. "That's a good start, Emily, and yes, my boyfriend's cock is so big I nearly choke on it, but boy, does it pack a big load."

My jaw dropped open.

"A lot of us kind of dabble in sexual acts with both genders here. We're not judgemental about any of it. Hell, I'll probably do you at some stage if you play your cards right. Anyway, I'll take you on a tour of this place and introduce you to those who are here."

******

SEVERAL WEEKS PASSED, and each day, I found myself learning new skills in hand-to-hand combat, guns, and knives and swords too. I assumed the organisation had an unlimited budget for mannequins and clay targets, and Helen soon found she had great skills at shooting targets from a long distance. We were told that our situation was unique, with only two of us being taken in for our recruitment round, which got me to thinking they must have a hell of a lot of people working for them.

Talissa became my greatest mentor, following an explosive first encounter when she kicked my ass. She was super sexy too, just as Gary described her, and once this guy called Diablo arrived and created the famous communal showering block, I grew envious of her huge ass and tits. Diablo himself turned down my advances, knowing how young I was. And in turn, Talissa turned him down time and time again.

For my first assignment, I found myself teamed up with Helen, Talissa, and Diablo, posing as a young girl bought by a wealthy drug lord. Before we ventured off, Helen pulled me aside.

"Remember, no matter what happens, trust your gut. You can do this, girl." She embraced me for what would be the last time.

"My body is just an instrument for the job I have to do. If I have to fuck an old man to make this assignment a success, I'll do it, and if I have to be the one to slice his head off, I'll do that, too."

She looked at me, knowing the little girl she rescued from the paedophilic hippy elders was long gone. I liked the new me, the tough, take no shit and kick some ass me.

We all knew our parts, and after having to strip naked in a room full of henchmen as well as my fellow assassins, I was required to perform a blow job on one hell of a creepy prick. And then I was taken away to a bedroom with a man we were led to believe was the real target of our operation.

The man I thought to be Big Bill asked me to strip for him. I was ready to do so but had discovered a knife on a bedside table. I wondered if he intended to use it on me. He lay on the bed and pulled his trousers off.

"Come on. Get on board, love," he said, patting the bed.

I smiled at him, pulling my panties down from beneath my skirt. I climbed on top of the bed and pulled his undies down, rubbing him until he was hard, and then I straddled him.

"Oh, my God," he said as he slid inside me.

I bounced up and down, leaning forward until the bedside knife could be within my reach.

He closed his eyes, obviously enjoying what I was doing to him, and just as I felt him shudder from reaching the peak of his enjoyment, I swiped the knife and stabbed down hard and quick at his chest.

His face froze, and I stayed on with him inside, watching the life drain from him. It felt incredible, and I selfishly stayed in that position for a few more minutes, feeling as if his life's essence flowed into me with his death.

I knew this was the life for me and smiled as I slowly sawed off his head with the same knife I had put through his heart.

******

DIABLO PERISHED DURING the cocked up mission and Talissa ordered me to take some African bitch and a crying barmaid away in one of our transports to rendezvous with the chopper.

I didn't get to say goodbye to Helen. I found out she was shot dead by Talissa on the assumption she had ratted us out to the real Big Bill.

The word was that Talissa had been sent away to an undisclosed location—none of us knew where the place was. But I swore I would find her one day and take revenge, with or without the blessing of the Praying Mantassassins.

The woman who started out as my idol became my sworn enemy, but I took pleasure in my last conversation with her that I would get her one day.

CHAPTER 6

FOURTEEN YEARS HAD passed, and Gary's son Ed had long taken over the active recruitment role as well as being the Praying Mantassassin's eyes in the police force. He brought in some great women. Two of the best were his stepsister Hayley and a young but tough battler named Brittany.

Ed came to us with a mission, a weeklong assignment involving five of us women to really fuck a real estate agent over, but none of us was to do the killing. The details seemed peculiar, but a million dollars is a million dollars.

"Her name's Kate, a real estate agent who wants revenge on a work colleague for something that happened a long time in the past. Here's her picture and the amount she wants to pay us." Ed passed around two eight by ten enlargements of a less than attractive red-haired woman.

"She actually applied to be one of us. Can you believe it? I mean who would want to sleep with her for a fee," Ed continued. "But our target is to be left for her, who says she has something special in store for him. My opinion is she's a little bit mentally unbalanced but look at the zeros after that number five. That's what she wants to pay for a job done right, so that's what we'll do."

"I'm in," I said. Brittany and Hayley also added their interest, but the next piece of information got the hair on the back of my neck to stand up.

"There's something else. The target is married to someone who was an active member, so we'll be using this mission to bring her back in if she's still got the moves," Ed said.

I only knew of one Mantassassin in hiding.

Talissa.

I stuck around after the briefing had finished so I could have a quiet word with Ed. "That bitch killed Helen after a mission we were on went south, without a single bit of proof that Helen had ratted us out. If you bring her back, no one is safe."

"Hey, Emily, I'm not in charge of this facility, so I don't get to make the rules."

"But you could turn a blind eye while I put a bullet in her. We haven't needed her for this long, so what could she possibly contribute now? Please, Ed, trust me." I took a few steps closer to him and sat on the table.

"Emily, you're beautiful and everything and one of the best assassins who have ever served here, but if you plan on doing something to one of our own, you risk everything. So either get those ideas out of your head," he looked at where my skirt had hitched up from sitting, "or keep them to yourself." He took another look. "And please wear some undies for a change."

"You know how uncomfortable they make me, and you've seen me in the shower so many times you probably see my body more often than I do."

"Save that pussy for the target of the next mission."

"Another thing, Ed. Who's playing the part of your partner? Going by the details of the briefing, we seem to be a girl down."

"I have a new partner at work. She'll do fine. I don't entirely trust her, but we can take her out during the mission, make her look like the guilty person behind it all who met an untimely death by the hands of a great cop—being me."

I slid off the table and pulled the hem of my skirt down. I knew Ed only really had eyes for Hayley and Bjorn, but there was no harm in trying to score some sex to try to sway his opinion. If only he were more like other men.

I left the little room and made my way for one of the helipads. Even after so many years at the compound, I still didn't know where it was located. As usual, there were a couple of pilots standing by waiting to conduct their taxi service. I had a rented apartment I wanted to spend some time in before the mission to prepare myself for my next acting role—a temp real estate agent with a fake background.

******

WALKING INTO THE apartment, I found myself impressed with the facilities. Of importance was a computer I would need to use to communicate with the target named Terry under the guidance of our client Kate. I would only need to use the chat program once, and it was important he would hear my voice to throw his suspicions firmly in my direction.

It all seemed a little weird, but many missions had been that way. If any of the missions seemed bizarre, then what happened after I heard the knock on my front door made everything else seem normal in comparison.

Who the hell knew I would be at the apartment? I had my pistol at the ready and made my way taking short steps until I reached the door. Professional assassins knew you never look through a peephole. There was always the risk of being shot in the eye by someone who wanted to take you out.

I grasped the doorknob, flung the door open, and aimed my pistol with my other hand. Looking ahead, I felt like someone placed a full sized mirror on my doorstep. "What the fuck?" I asked.

"Erica, it's me," the woman smiled.

I knew the voice from long ago, it couldn't be. "Rebecca?" I asked.

"Yes. What do you think? Do you think I look like you?"

"Um... I don't know what to think. How much did all that surgery cost and why would you do such a thing?"

"Don't worry, Erica. I did this so we could make it work for us, start up our own killer for hire business, and be each other's alibi. I've been trained by the best, but when I heard through the grapevine where you've been since I left you and Helen that day, I came up with this great idea."

"You thought spending thousands to look like me was a great plan without discussing it with me first? I'm quite happy where I am and doing what I'm doing."

"But you don't have complete freedom. You don't even know where the compound is. At least where I'm from we come and go as we please. How about you just listen to me for a while, and if you don't like what I have to say, I'll drop the idea."

I smiled. "Okay, let's chat."

We sat and talked for hours, discussing where we each came from before life at the hippy commune and what we had done and who we had killed in our time working for our respective organisations. The more we talked about her idea, the more I liked the sound of it and how we could utilise that tactic to take out Talissa after the mission, deciding it would make for the better option.

We even searched online for information on the cop who Ed was bringing into the mission, Hannah Hall. While information on her was limited, we found she had a father who once had a vendetta for a mystery organisation. I read everything about him I could find, and then read it a couple more times, sitting and staring and thinking how we could use this.

"I've thought of it—how we could do this. I play my part as planned, and you find Hannah's father and hold him captive. We use him as leverage to get her to either kill or arrest Talissa after the mission, and if she's still alive, Hannah delivers her to me in exchange for her father. We just have to bait him to isolate him and take him. He's an ex-cop with forty years of experience and probably has a lot of friends."

"Is he still married?" Rebecca asked.

"Yes, but I'll see if I can get Hannah to spill the beans on whether he could be swayed," I said. I stepped away from the computer and looked her up and down. "You look great." I took a few steps towards her.

She closed the short distance between us and touched my face. "I should have come with you and Helen that day, but I let a boy come between us. I love you, Erica. I always have and I always will. I want us to finish what we started in that lake all those years ago."

I unbuttoned her shirt with one hand and slid my other hand up her thigh, finding that she too wasn't wearing underwear. Her hands returned my gesture. As weird as it seemed to be making out with someone who looked just like me, I was dripping wet with excitement as her finger invaded me. She rubbed me gently, finding my most sensitive area. In the moments leading up to our mutual orgasms, I decided yes, I would do one last mission for the Praying Mantassassins. Then I would retire and work with Rebecca.

EPILOGUE

REBECCA, AKA EBONY

WHEN I HEARD Erica had perished in the 5PM mission, I had cried for days. Our relationship had been a weird one. For so many years, we were friends in a hippy commune and then road buddies until she pulled a gun on her guy.

I should have gone with her and Helen instead of staying with the bikers. While they were nice guys, the brothers thought they had a right to use me when they felt horny. I could have said no on many occasions, but I feared they would send me on my way once I didn't put out for them whenever they requested some action.

It didn't end badly, though. I had an opportunity to slip away one night when a busload of swimwear models stopped at the same campsite, happily taking me on board and giving me a temporary gig showing off the best bikinis and one-piece sets on my trim body on the catwalks and beach exhibitions.

But one day, I found my true calling—killing. We were on a fashion parade along South Beach in Miami when a crazed gunman threatened to kill our manager for not taking his girlfriend into the modelling team. In a split second manoeuvre, I transformed myself from hostage to action hero, springing up from lying on the ground with my hands on my head to jumping on the guy's back and wrestling the rifle from his hands.

During the struggle, the gun fired and blew a hole where half of his internal organs had once been.

My journey paralleled Erica's, recruited by a corrupt cop and taken away to a hidden base to be trained to kill. We operated differently than the Praying Mantassassins. There was no sex before the killings, just a straight out murder of a target or targets as requested by the clients.

I was an official FFF, Foxy Femme Fatale, operating under the name Ebony. They were able to track down my history, and eventually, they were the source for my recent locating of Erica—or Emily, as she had become known. We had it all worked out. We would team up and work independently from any organisation. It would have been risky, but the money would have been huge.

However, after her failed mission, I decided I would set things right.

"Okay, ex-Sergeant Hall, your daughter failed to take out Talissa, and my sister is dead, so I have no reason to keep you alive. But I also have no personal reason to kill you, so I'm about to let you go on the condition you keep me updated on Talissa's whereabouts."

He sat hog-tied to a chair in the secret basement of a gymnasium. "Why should I do that for you?"

"Because I have no reason to hate you or your daughter, so I don't need to kill you. Why do you care about Talissa's well-being any more than my dead sister's or mine?

"You're all evil, every single one of you. You don't get to choose who dies for his or her sins because someone pays you. This isn't the time of the wild west."

I walked up to him and put the barrel of my gun to his temple. "I'm asking you one last time to do a simple task. You have a daughter. Think about her. Should she lose her daddy, even if you don't give a shit about your own life?"

He bowed his head, hiding his face from mine. "Okay, I'll do it. But you don't ever go after Hannah. Do you understand? If anything happens to her, you'll have the whole force on you in a heartbeat."

"I would expect nothing less." I cut the plastic ties securing him, keeping the pistol trained on him. Just one sudden movement would be the end of him. I caught his eye. If he was nervous, his body wasn't giving him away.

"I can tell you she is in the California Institution for Women and not expected to see the outside of the walls in her lifetime. You won't ever get to her."

He limped on ahead of me, and as he climbed the steps up from the basement to the main exercise area of the gymnasium, the sun appeared to almost blind him. If I still possessed an inkling of empathy like I did when Helen, Erica and I were together, I would have felt sorry for him. But I let him live, and for that, he should be grateful—and surprised given my history.

Those days of empathy had long passed, and the only thing I looked forward to was revenge. I took a long look at myself in one of the workout mirrors, reminding me of how Erica once looked. It was time to freshen up and prepare for the early morning exercise goers.

"Excuse me, young lady. When do you open?" A deep European voice almost made me jump and hit the ceiling.

I turned and faced the voice's owner, almost falling to my knees at the sight of his tight muscular body almost bursting the black shorts and white tank top he wore.

"Um...ah..."

He took a few steps and picked me up before I fell on the spot, his biceps bulging as he took my weight in his arms. "You look so much like Emily. Just as beautiful and as delicious as she was," he said. "I will help you do what you need to do. I will take your pain away, my sweet angel."

I smiled just before I drifted off and took a long nap.

BJORN

Chapter 1

Benny Hernandez aka Bjorn

I ALWAYS WAS a man of exquisite taste. From fine art to good wine and most of all, the female body. I have made love to over one thousand women, acquiring a great admiration for nature's most beautiful creation when, at the age of eleven, I saw the most heavenly example of God's sculpturing.

I was only a young boy, still two years from becoming a teenager when I was on vacation with my parents along the French Riviera when I saw her, bathing in the water in all her glory. The way the water droplets shone on her milky skin, and her face lit up as she smiled upon discovering my voyeuristic stares, it stirred up a feeling within me I had never experienced before. My penis stiffened as her soap-lathered hands ran down her breasts and to the hairy area between her legs, separating those lips of hers as she washed them. My father caught me watching her, and with a smile, he sat me down and told me all about men and women and where babies came from. I never did see that beautiful woman again, but when I reached the age of self-discovery, I used the vision of her stored in my memory banks from that special day.

Blessed with good looks, I never had trouble scoring with the girls through high school, followed by my college and adult life. My college degree led to nothing, which I believed to be the motivation behind taking it in the first place. When I was finished with studying, I drifted around my home city of Charleroi, Belgium, working in low paying jobs meeting many wonderful people and being a VIP guest at the party that was my life.

I did it all—smoking, alcohol, marijuana, cocaine and promiscuous sex with strangers.

It was fun—that is until one night a bit of unbridled recklessness led to two friends dying from an overdose.

I nearly lost my own life that night, too. Little did we know the coke we scored was laced with arsenic as if the dealer wanted to murder us all. When I recovered, and my anger subsided, I swore I would find the people responsible. I invested many hours into investigating the identity and whereabouts of the responsible duo, using my network of friends and contacts I had made over the years.

This path of intended vengeance brought me to America and to a chance meeting with the most influential man to enter my life. I tracked the dealers to a hotel in Las Vegas, travelling on an illegal passport created for me by a man who claimed to be an expert at manufacturing such things.

"Sir, do you have some identification?" the security officer asked.

I was playing on a roulette table and about fifty thousand dollars up, orbited by several voluptuous young women, each one seeming to try to out-do the others in the bathing of perfume prior to attending the gambling rooms. Their number and proximity grew with each successful spin of the wheel, but I had little care factor for the money itself. I wanted to garner enough attention to bring a certain two men out of hiding.

"Is there a problem?" I asked. I fished my passport from my pocket, satisfying his interest in me. He took a long look at me before nodding at me and walking away.

"Can I touch your chips," a blonde haired beauty asked. She stood barely tall enough to reach my chest, while her own only just managed to stay enclosed in the strapless dress she wore.

"Sure, beautiful lady," I said, holding the chips to her rosy lips.

She kissed them, and as I lowered them away from her, she blew gently on them like a cool breeze soothing a summer heat. I decided she would be my pick from the group to take to my room if the interest appeared to be mutual. The chips sat in place, and the spin of the wheel would either double my winnings or demolish my entire stack. The lady wore red, prompting me to place all my chips in the corresponding area.

"No further bets," the croupier announced. He flicked the little silver ball, and we all watched it as it sailed around the numbered wheel. My fate out of my control, I willed the ball to fall within a red coloured wedge when the time came for it to come to a stop.

The ball slowed as if selecting a pocket by choice. It bounced between a black, a red, a green and then back to number twelve, where it stayed to rest. The big-breasted woman hugged me as I jumped in the air, watching my stack of chips double as I declared my game over and stated my desire to collect my little round plastic chips and cash out.

"Congratulations, sir. Well played," said the

croupier, the obligatory smile on his face. Another employee put the chips on a tray, enabling them to be grouped and counted. I followed him to the cashier whereupon I received my winnings in cash.

"You've had a very successful night sir," the security guard from the roulette wheel said behind me.

"I had lady luck by my side," I said. The woman looked at me from near the table I played at and smiled.

"The manager would like to see you."

"I didn't do anything wrong, sir. There's no way I could cheat."

"I know. Just come with me. Bring your lady friend if you wish."

I waved her over. She complied, her little legs carrying her at a speed I didn't think she could reach given her height. Looking at her filled me with lust and with a hunger that only her body could satisfy.

"Hey, high roller, what's going on?" she asked.

"Please come with me," the security guard said.

"The manager wants to see me, said I can bring you along too," I said to her. Slot machine music filled our ears as we followed the security guard, people seated at said machines in a trance, the majority kissing money away in the process of pressing buttons and watching mini electronic screens roll past.

"You must have made an impression, winning a hundred grand like that," she said. I reached for her hand.

"Just like you have on me," I said.

We arrived at the base of a flight of carpeted stairs, the guard waving us to go on ahead to the room perched at the top of them. From my perspective, the room appeared as a dark tinted glass cube, and even as we approached the door, we couldn't see in.

"Aren't you a little concerned?" the woman asked.

"No, why should I be? I don't see how anyone could cheat at roulette," I said. I took a deep breath regardless and knocked on the door.

A sliding door disappeared into its recess, presenting a balding man flanked by two larger men. He grinned as we stepped in. "Sir, you had some pretty great luck tonight," he glanced at my companion, "on two different counts."

"Thank you, mister. You have a very fine establishment," I said.

"Which is why I'd like to offer you a free night's accommodation to check out our facilities, maybe have another splurge tomorrow."

"I feel unworthy, I just wanted to play tonight and go home."

"Your English, it sounds a little broken. I think home might be a long plane flight away. Where are you from? Germany?"

"Belgium. We make much better beer and chocolate than you do in America, but I like it here very much. Your women are very delectable."

He let out a big belly laugh, contagious to the other four of us in the room. "You know, I've always said that same thing about European women. We should swap notes perhaps."

The woman next to me rubbed my arm. I took a moment and answered the casino manager. "Okay, sir, I will happily stay a night."

"Excellent choice, young man. Please take this card to use for entry into room 1124." He took another look at my companion. "Have a very nice night."

******

"WOW, THIS IS nice," the lady said as I opened the

door. The king sized bed sat in the middle of a room almost the size of a basketball court. She kicked off her shoes, dragging her feet along the shagpile carpet in the direction of the floor to ceiling windows.

I followed her, hoping to get her out of more than just her shoes, and gazed at the majestic view of the Las Vegas nightlife from the top floor suite. City lights illuminated the scenery, a wash of brightly coloured hues with people weaving in and out at street level, filling our view as seen through the gigantic panels of glass.

"Your city is truly beautiful," I said. "As are you."

"Wow. Why don't we stop beating around the bush? You want me, and I want you. We have this one night together—let's make it count."

"So up front, it's sexy." I removed my jacket and kicked off my shoes.

She walked over to the bed, dwarfed by the size of our surroundings, but soon to be the centre of our joined universes. "I need you to unzip me."

Approaching her back, I grabbed the metal zipper, gliding it along the parallel lines of metal teeth where it finished just above her peachy arse. I released my grip from the zip, my hands trailing her skin to the low-lying strap of her bra. I've always been a fan of big boobs and unclasping her bra demonstrated the immense strength held within a tiny piece of clothing constructed by lace, wires, and elastic. As she turned and faced me, my eyes were drawn straight to the twins of perfection.

"You like them?"

I nodded as I began to gently knead her breasts. In turn, her hands moved to my tie and shirt, freeing them from my body. She pressed her chest against mine and started to kiss me. I grabbed her arse and lifted her off her feet, putting her at the same level as I was, before throwing her backward onto the bed.

"Oh, I like that," she said. She propped her back up by leaning on her elbows, slightly parting her legs, and giving me a smile saying to come and get her. I looked at those lace panties, and pulled them over her hips to her knees and finally off her ankles.

The sight of her exposed sex filled me with a hunger, only able to be satisfied by lowering my mouth to those inviting lips. "May I?" I asked

She smiled and nodded, and as I put my face between her legs, she wrapped them around my head making sure I wouldn't stop until she reached personal satisfaction. I've always loved going down on women. To me, it's a form of worshipping them as a holy entity. I learned from my teenage years how to do it well, thanks to a very vocal woman in her thirties instructing me exactly where to aim.

The lady began to moan, and with each flick of my tongue, she increased the volume and length of her vocal approval of my actions.

Fully emerged in the moment, I didn't hear the hotel room door open, but I heard it close. I went to turn, but my head was trapped between a pair of powerful thighs.

"Don't kill him," a male voice yelled out.

She released me. I saw the knife in her hand and wondered what the hell was going on. "But I'm getting paid to do it," she said.

I looked at her face. "Please don't."

"Hayley, we've been offered double the money to keep him alive," the security guard from earlier said.

She placed the blade on the bedside table. "Sorry."

"Can somebody tell me what the hell is going on?" I asked.

"Two men put out a contract on you a few days ago,

and I was here to cash in. Sorry, it's not personal," she said.

"Who were these men?" I asked.

"I never got their real names. The names they used didn't check out on the computer, but they paid us cash in advance for the job. It's a good thing I hadn't climaxed yet. You were to be dead as soon as I got there," Hayley said.

"Hayley, put some clothes on, please," the man said, and then turned to me. "They had accents like yours. I assumed you knew them from back home. One was tall with a moustache, the other short and fat."

"Ah, yes... I know them. They are the reason I'm over here in America. I plan to kill them." I headed for the door.

The man pulled out a gun. "Not so fast. We need to talk about what's going on."

I looked at the floor, then back to him. "They killed two of my good buddies and nearly me, as well."

"Oh, yes, the hapless need for revenge. You're not doing too well so far. They know you're here and have put a contract out on you, the needs of which were nearly met."

Hayley looked at me while dressing. "For what it's worth, that's one hell of a tongue you have, Bjorn." She smirked as my eyes widened recognising she knew my name. "Yes, we are aware of your name and know all about you, thanks to your two 'friends.'"

"So where are they then? I needed one hundred thousand dollars to buy a score, and I have the money to do that now. But thanks to you two, they are probably already gone."

The man held up a phone. "Oh, no they're not. I can get a hold of them anytime I want, and thanks to your counter offer you have in the form of tonight's winnings,

I can draw them out for you. By the way, the name's Ed."

******

I GLARED OVER the table at Hayley. "Bjorn, I'm sorry. I will make it up to you later," she said.

"And then stab me to death? No, thank you."

"She won't kill you unless someone is paying her to, and seeing as our payment has doubled, you should feel a little safer," Ed said. "So back to the plan. Your cash money will be packed into a briefcase. We'll disguise you so they don't recognise you as soon as you walk in the room. You will deliver the case to them, open it, and as you do, you'll reach in first, grab a pistol with each hand, and then blow them away. *Boom!*" Ed said.

"You want me to kill them?" I asked. I had plans to track them down and take revenge but never thought about how I would actually carry out a kill.

"No, I want you to have a three-way with them. Of course, I want you to fucking kill them."

"You Americans say this word fuck a lot. Does it help you express yourself better?" I asked.

"Sometimes, yes. Spend some time here, and you'll see how versatile it really is. Like maybe later you and I can fuck," Hayley said.

"I prefer the term make love," I said.

Hayley laughed at me. "Make love? We barely know each other. It isn't love—it's sex or fucking."

I let it slide. We needed to get back to the task. Hayley left the room to get the prosthetics required to disguise me as someone completely different.

"So, you like her?" Ed asked.

"She's beautiful, has the most lovely breasts, and a pretty little lady garden."

"You're an interesting man, Bjorn. Shows how little time I've spent with Europeans. You want to know something about her? She's my sister, and we have regular sex."

"That is disgusting."

"Well, technically, we're not related. She's my stepsister, so we say shit like we're siblings who fuck to shock people. Maybe we're a little mentally disturbed."

"We're all a little crazy, Ed. The world is a crazy place, and if you don't adjust accordingly, you either die or live like an invisible man. So I guess I'm crazy too."

"I think we're gonna get along well, Bjorn. You'll have to hang with us for a while after we've taken care of business. We can introduce you to a great many interesting things." He looked me up and down, sending a little shiver up my spine.

******

"OH MY GOD. I don't even recognise myself," I said, looking at the bearded be-speckled man in the mirror. I also gained many kilos and aged about twenty years.

"We'll have to avoid you speaking much. Once they hear that accent, you're in trouble, as well as us," Ed said.

"Why are you doing this for me?" I asked.

Hayley smiled. "We like you. You're a little different. You like to have fun and live free, and if you die, then we'll miss out on some fun with you. And I'd like to finish what we started earlier." She winked at me.

"Okay, let's do this," I said. I thought of my friends who perished back home at the hands of the scumbags who laced the coke, and how I would avenge them. My nerves kicked in, so I took a few deep breaths as my two companions exited with me out of the hotel room.

Hayley grabbed my hand, rubbing my arm with her other, trying to settle my nerves. By Las Vegas standards, the night was still young, the time being just after 11PM, and in a city that never sleeps, there seems to be no such thing as early or late. We followed Ed closely, walking down a carpeted corridor to an elevator, going all the way to the top floor.

"It appears as though the men who hired us are well financed. You must actually present a degree of threat to them. What the hell were you in Belgium?" Ed asked.

"I was just a wanderer, going from place to place picking up work wherever I could—drinking, taking drugs, and making love to lots of women. I learned English too, just in case I wanted to travel here."

"Now, when the time comes, you can't hesitate to shoot those guys. It will make a lot of noise and mess, and we have to leave as soon as the job's done. Now here's the case." Ed passed it to me as we reached the room. He tapped the door with his knuckles twice, loud enough for the room's occupants, but quiet enough not to draw much attention from people staying in adjoining rooms.

I took another long breath, waiting for someone to let us in. As the door opened an inch inward, I heard a familiar voice call us in, the smaller of the two men I was hunting. If I thought my room was impressive, this one made it look like a dog kennel in comparison.

We immediately saw a complication in our plan. The room was packed with party guests. Men in suits danced with scantily clad women to music making me want to stab myself in the head with a fork. I never liked rap music. I had always been a metal fan or maybe a bit of pop if I wanted to seduce a woman.

"Is there somewhere private we can do business?" Ed asked.

The man stared at him for a few seconds and then looked over at me. As his grey eyes hit me, the locked stare made me wonder if he could see through the fake facial hair and make-up and into the real me. I froze until Hayley poked me in the back.

"Follow me," the man said, leading us through the hazy room.

A woman laid on her stomach, her bare back containing parallel lines of a white powder, snorted up in a snap by one of the suited men. A spa bath near the sliding door leading to the balcony was packed with men and women, not a stitch of clothing to be seen on their bodies from the waist up. One of the women caught my gaze and rewarded me with a knowing smile.

"So, who the fuck is this guy?" The big guy in the bedroom said as his partner led us in. With his legs draped over the end of the bed, a female head covered with blonde hair bobbed up and down between his legs, not caring we were present.

"An associate who has the money. He wants to buy something," Ed said.

"I thought I would owe you two money for a job you were to do for us. I don't like this," the big guy said. "And who said I have never-ending supplies of what you want?"

Long have I heard the saying that all plans go to shit as soon as the battle starts, and this meeting soon travelled down the road of one of those situations. The smaller guy put a hand inside his suit jacket while I opened the briefcase, allowing the piles of money and guns to fall and hit the floor.

The big guy roared, pushing the girl away and not bothering to pull up his pants while he grabbed his own gun and swung it around in my direction. Ed and Hayley both dove to the floor in the direction of the spilled contents of the briefcase. Each of them scooped up a pistol, and in synchronised fluid motion, lined up a target each and fired.

The big man and the small man both fell. The blonde woman interrupted from orally satisfying the big man screamed and ran from the room, Ed and Hayley allowing her to flee.

I looked over at the men I came here to kill, noting the lack of movement in both of their bodies. It was supposed to be my kill, but I couldn't keep myself together to carry it out, and consequently, felt lucky to still be alive.

"Bjorn, grab one of their guns," Ed yelled. I had never seen a dead body before, not even those of my friends who died of a drug overdose. So seeing the bodies of those two men who met their demise from such a violent act sent my mind racing and my stomach lurching. I swallowed hard and slowed my breathing until I could move without fear of vomiting.

The big guy was the nearest of the two, so in a fumbled flurry, I rolled him over to retrieve the gun lying beneath his body, dislodged in the short-lived conflict. I made careful work not to touch his uncaged penis while in the process.

"They might have friends. Get ready to shoot anyone who comes through that door," Hayley said.

A few men in suits popped their faces in, looking at us and probably wondering who the hell we were. I aimed my gun at a random target among the group of men.

"We don't want any trouble," one of them called out. "We were just here to party and get laid."

"Well, leave then, and take those skanks with you," Ed said.

The men complied. Hayley stacked the piles of

money back into the briefcase and pushed ahead of me, "We need to go."

"Security will be on us in minutes," Ed said. He pulled a phone from his pocket and made a call. I kept my eyes on the people in the central part of the hotel room, looking for any hostile movements.

"Well, that didn't quite go as planned," I said. "Aren't you a security guard?"

"We should have left you behind in your room," Hayley said. "You could have got us all killed."

"I'm not a security guard. I was just posing as one to get closer to you. Maybe we should have settled for the fifty k job and let Hayley stab you," Ed said. "We need to get to the roof."

Making our way through the room, we were subjected to people climbing naked from the hot tub while other people were in various state of undress exiting the room to escape to the corridor on the other side. No one seemed interested in hanging around long enough to have to deal with security or the cops when they arrived.

We trailed behind the last of those to leave, making it to the corridor. Ed peeled away from the others, pointing to the stairs and then up. We only needed to ascend one floor, whereas everyone else would have probably been looking to take an elevator to the ground level. Ed held the door open for Hayley and me to go through and allowed it to self-close after he followed us.

The stairs were old concrete, but at least they didn't smell like those common to car parks and coated in the stench of animal urine.

I burst through the door at the top, exiting to the rooftop of the casino and looking over the brightly lit city. I would have loved to stay and just sit and watch the city go by in the cool, crisp air with a glass of wine, but the opportunity didn't exist for such.

"Our ride will be here soon. Bjorn, if you thought tonight was crazy, wait until you see what else we can deliver through our crazy lives," Hayley said. "Come with us, and I'll let you make love to me in the morning, any way you want it."

"Well, I'm not sticking around for the police to find us if I can help it. So this ride you speak off..." my voice trailed off as I looked up and saw a light heading our way along with the sound of helicopter blades chopping through the air accompanying it as it neared.

"Get used to choppers, Bjorn. Where we're going, you'll soon find we'll be using them a lot," Ed said. I smiled as the wonderful metal transport approached us, and it quickly came to rest on a bare space of concrete roof, using it as a makeshift helipad.

I stared wide-eyed at the magnificent beast, my trance broken as voices yelled at us from the top of the stairs, "Stop right there."

Hayley ran to the chopper first, and Ed waved me past as he fired wayward shots to keep the security guards at bay. I jumped in, sat next to Hayley, and watched Ed open the front door of the chopper to sit next to the pilot.

The pilot lifted us from the rooftop, taking us away from the zealous security personnel who wanted to prevent the departure of suspected killers. Once again, I soaked up the sights, and upon leaving the city limits, Ed passed me a takeaway coffee.

I accepted it and immediately sipped the warm liquid, savouring the fine blend as it flowed down my throat. My eyelids grew heavy, and I looked at the cup.

Ed looked at me. "Sorry, Bjorn. We're kind of strict about not letting people see the way to get to where we're going. See you in a few hours."

Hayley smiled at me. "It will be okay. Just relax." Her hand held mine, and the power of the sleeping agent that was slipped in my drink took effect, turning my world black.

CHAPTER 2

I AWOKE IN a bed in a room I had never laid eyes on before, my clothes stripped from me, but a sweet familiar face next to me. "Where am I, Hayley?"

"You're at your new home. We're going to train you to do some stuff for our organisation, which you'll be well paid for and in the company of great people."

I turned to kiss her, noting she was wearing pyjamas. She put a hand up.

"What?" I asked.

"Your breath could melt the paint off that chopper we flew in last night. You need a shower and a toothbrush."

"Where are my clothes?"

"Destroyed. You won't need them. We have everything you need and in your size."

I climbed out of bed, Hayley's eyes following my movements. I couldn't see any adjoining rooms able to lend themselves to serve as a bathroom of any kind.

"I've never had an uncircumcised man before. I can't wait to get my hands on it."

"It's a European thing. Where is this shower I can take?"

"Grab a towel from your cupboard and come for a walk. You'll love it."

******

AFTER WALKING FOR five minutes wearing nothing but a towel, Hayley pointed to a building. "This is our morning ritual."

I opened the door and saw a number of women and two men taking a shower in a communal situation, each of the women beautiful and sexy.

"I like this very much," I said, taking a glimpse of those before me without my eyes landing and leering on any of them in particular.

"Grab a spot and hang up your towel. Aren't you Europeans fairly liberal with this sort of thing anyway?" Ed asked. His naked form squarely in my view, he lathered soap all over his body. I couldn't help but feel a little envious of the size of his penis, looking away in an instant as the jealousy hit.

"Yes," I threw my towel over a metal rail. "It doesn't mean we walk around our cities naked, but yes, we're not so hung up on nudity as you are here."

"Does it look like we're worried?" a blonde asked. She smiled at me, and I mentally added her on my to-do list.

I felt someone tap me on the back. I spun around and saw Hayley standing within a foot of me completely naked, but something else was missing. "Where's your hair?" I asked.

"It's hanging up. I can be a blonde, brunette, and even a redhead. Of course, the carpet doesn't match the curtains in a lot of cases, but when a man is about to get some action, they're not about to express any concern." She looked me up and down. "So, let's finish what we started last night."

"In front of everyone else?" I asked.

"Hell yeah." She pressed her body against mine, "Well? Are you ready?"

******

AS SOON AS she was finished with me, Hayley grabbed her towel and left me in the shower next to Ed. I couldn't believe he stood there the whole time and watched me have sex with his stepsister and regular lover. Seeing the other women who occupied the room gave me the feeling that I would like my time at this place.

"Hope you enjoyed it, Bjorn. Experience has shown she'll only fuck a guy once, and then move on, with the exception of me, of course," Ed said.

I began to towel myself dry, aware of the fact Ed and I were the only people remaining. "Who is the dark skinned woman? She is exquisite."

"Her name is Nakato. No one knows much about her, and I can bet you that you won't get to first base with her. I can tell you she came from somewhere in Africa, but she won't say shit about her past."

"You've tried and failed then. I will try to succeed."

Ed laughed at me. "Listen here, you European stud, it's time to stop thinking about pussy and concentrate on the training you have to do."

******

I BELIEVED MYSELF to be in great shape until my first day at the compound proved to me otherwise. We started the day with a run, push-ups, more running, and boxing practice.

During my life, I had never needed much use of my fists, but with the training, I guessed I would soon become quite prolific in hand-to-hand combat.

"The boss wants to talk with you," the naughty looking blonde from the showers said.

"Good, I have a lot of questions for him." I followed her from the exercise yard to a small building where she pointed me to a desk.

"Take a seat. He'll be with you shortly." She walked away leaving me in the little building alone.

A male voice spoke through the intercom with a calmness I normally likened to a yoga instructor. "Good afternoon, Bjorn, and welcome to the compound of the Praying Mantassassins. We are taking a chance here, bringing you on board, but Ed tells me he can see potential in you. We require the services of what we call a cleaner. Basically, you will be responsible for cleaning up a scene if things have gone wrong or we need to cover something up. In return for this, you get to continue living here and are paid four-figure amounts for a job you're called out to handle. I understand you travelled here on a fake passport,"

"No, I'm here legally. I—"

"Don't ever try to bullshit me, Bjorn. One of my men or women won't hesitate to slit your throat if I ever catch you lying to me again. Now back to the passport issue, which, by the way, it was a statement and not a question. Ed is a cop, so he can spot these things and run checks whenever he likes.

"Anyway, back to what I was saying, if you do right by us, you'll be heavily rewarded in many ways. The rules for living here are quite relaxed, as long as you turn up for training, turn up when I call you, and that you don't ruin our recruitment process by informing any recruits on how we pick the one who'll go onto the next step from an intake. What we do and teach is brutal murder, but we all make a lot of money, and we want to keep it that way."

"I understand, boss."

"And please remember that you'll never meet me. It's not personal. It's just the need for secrecy is of the utmost importance. I no doubt have people who want me dead. We might be hard to find here, but we have an arrangement with the leader of this country to stay here and continue to do what we do to enable us to remain invisible to the US authorities.

"So please don't take it personal if we can't let you see the way here or if there are bits of information that you're not privy to—it's just the way it is. If the day comes when we're pissed off at you, it won't be a case of a group of people bitching behind your back. It will be a case of you being sliced up and your body dissolved in chemicals that will make it like you never existed."

I gulped as if I had a golf ball going down my throat.

"Bjorn, just toe the line, and you'll be just fine. Hope you enjoy life as one of us."

"Thank you, sir."

When I didn't hear the voice resume his speech, I guessed it was time to leave.

I walked outside and found a wooden bench seat to sit on.

I witnessed the sun making its departure for the day, leaving a bright patchwork of orange and red on scattered clouds before sinking from view and bringing with it the night sky.

"Something else to get used to here, Bjorn," the blonde woman stood next to me. "May I take a seat?"

"Sure."

"My name's Emily, and I need you to walk me back

to my room, take off all your clothes, and fuck me as hard as you did Hayley this morning."

I smiled and grabbed her hand, knowing I would indeed enjoy this place.

CHAPTER 3

A WEEK HAD passed when I got up one day for an early morning jog. A lap around the compound took about half an hour; such was the vastness of the place. I liked to catch as many sunrises and sunsets as I could, no matter what happened in my life. Those peaceful euphoric moments witnessing nature's start or end of a day always put my life in perspective and filled my inner bucket of happiness to capacity.

I always said the early hours of the morning were the best time of day, the crisp air hitting the exposed parts of my body, the sound of birds singing and the tranquillity of no other human being in my presence. This particular morning had been like the last few, slipping out of bed early away from the sleeping body of Emily, putting on a pair of shorts, and hitting the day head on. That was until Ed crossed paths with me.

"Nice day for a run. Mind if I join you?" Ed asked as he jogged in my direction.

I nodded. Running is one of those things I prefer to do in silence. If I have to talk while I'm jogging, I'm not going quickly enough.

"So, you like it here so far?" he asked.

I nodded again and hoped he wasn't intending to conduct a full interview while running.

I liked that the jogging paths were all natural, rather than footpaths made of concrete, and that the paths were worn down stretches of grasses and wildflowers.

"Sorry, I guess I'm so used to exercising that I can carry a conversation. Great to see you're getting in shape."

I never realised how unfit I had become in my wayward years until day one of my training. Ed must have been at the compound for years, his body ripped, perfect, and one I strived to achieve for myself. He kept quiet for the remainder of our run, which is how I liked it. We finished the run when we reached my room.

"Bjorn, I need to be straight with you. I'm a cop. That's how I find so many assignments for us and so many recruits. For the most part, I'm a competent policeman, I do my job well and make many busts and do everything I should be doing. But I have this side of me here, of hiring women to sleep with and kill men for whatever reason they pay us for."

"How have you managed to keep this side hidden from the police force all this time? Has anyone ever investigated you?"

"I have someone high up who takes care of things should the need ever arise. If someone has ever been onto me, they've done very well to not be noticed. Because if I catch them..."

As he motioned a slitting action around his throat, I imagined if anyone had been noticed investigating him, they wouldn't be around to build a case. "I just need to grab my towel and clothes," I said.

"Me too. I'll catch you in the shower block." He winked and jogged away.

I liked Ed. Sure he seemed like a cold-hearted pyscho in Las Vegas, but since arriving at the compound, he was friendly, helping me with everything I had a concern about, and assisting me to achieve a higher fitness level. Something made me wonder if there was something different about him.

******

I CLOSED MY eyes as I put my head under the water pouring from the high flow showerhead, washing away the sweat gained from my morning run. I didn't know how long I would have the block to myself, but I treasured every second of it.

The main door creaked as it opened, and a few seconds later, I saw Ed hanging up his towel on the towel rail adjacent to mine. There was room and enough showerheads for at least a dozen people to use the area, so when Ed chose to shower right next to me, I knew he was up to something.

"Do you mind?" he asked. He removed his shirt and shorts, his completely hair free body a few feet from me.

"Well, you're here now," I said and turned my back to him.

"Bjorn, please don't feel uncomfortable around me."

"It's the way you look at me, whether I'm fully dressed or going for a run, or even when..."

"Times like now when you're naked, and me as well. We were born naked, so why are people so hung up on nudity?"

"People liken being nude to having sex as if we can't be in our natural state without thinking of sex. But if I see a woman like Hayley or Emily or Nakato in their complete beautiful glory, I do think of having sex with them, so I guess society is right."

"We're just animals, Bjorn. Sure, we're human and considered the most intelligent of the animal kingdom, but we have animal urges, too. We all want to be on top of the food chain or the alpha male of the tribe, and we all want to release our sexual tension."

"Why do we humans have to be this way? Why can't we be strong enough not to give into addictions like sex, alcohol, drugs, and gambling? We know better, but we don't do better." I could feel Ed's presence closing in on me, stopping about a foot away, the distance hard to gauge with my back turned.

"Why do you think I like it here, Bjorn? Society's rules can't touch me here. I can be and do whatever and whoever I want."

I turned and faced him, looking him up and down. Whereas I had free growing hair on my body in the places it should be, he didn't have any apart from his head and armpits. He stood before me as like a sculpture, chiselled to Greek God standards with muscles toned to die for. I was skinny with a protruding belly from heavy drinking and bad eating.

"You too can be like this, Bjorn," he took a step closer.

We almost touched, my skin invaded with goose bumps as our eyes locked. "What is happening?

"We're doing what nature's guiding us to do, to give into our primal instincts."

"This doesn't mean I'm gay, does it?" I asked.

"No, it doesn't, but it does make you bisexual." His face moved towards mine, and I readied myself for his mouth. The rough stubble surrounding his mouth touched my own, like two sheets of sandpaper rubbing each other as our lips locked. I expected a male mouth to feel rough inside, but as our tongues touched and danced, I only thought of us as being two people sharing a lust for each other, not of the same gender.

His hand touched the side of my face, stopping for a few seconds before travelling higher to comb through my hair. He slid it along down the back of my neck to my back, pushing himself against me. Our groins touched, and I could feel the pressure of his cock growing hard and pressing into my pelvic region, my own doing the same back against him. I ran my hand along the side of his body, starting at his chest, nervously down to his hip.

"Your body is so tight and smooth," I said as I pulled away from his mouth.

"Your cock feels so nice against me."

"I don't know if I'm ready for this. I've always been about the pussy."

"And you still can be after this," he said. His hand moved to my front, finding my cock and gripping his fingers around it. "I've never touched an uncut one before. It's beautiful."

My own hand moved from his hip to his groin, cupping his waxed ball sack in one hand while my other made a desperate clutch for his stiff cock. I ran my hand up and down his length, much longer than my own.

"We can just jack each other off. We don't have to fuck," he said.

"I'm good with that." I pressed my mouth against his again, our hands working in unison on each other's rock-like excitement. His other hand moved to my arse, dividing the cheeks as his wet hand pushed along the crevice, and a finger found my opening.

I had lost control. My knees began to feel weak as my body's attention gathered in such a small region. My hand pumped him harder and quicker, my mind hoping he was at the same point I would be soon reaching.

I couldn't hold on any longer, his fist squeezing out

my load, pulsating and hitting his stomach each time. I used a hand to steady myself against the shower wall, looking down to see his cock spraying me in return.

He smiled and pulled away from me, "We need to shower."

"Um...yes..." I said between breaths. I looked away and grabbed a bar of soap to wash myself. My mind began to race about what I had just done and how I would be able to perform next time with a woman. Had I ruined everything I was in one heated moment? Or had I just discovered a world I never thought I would set foot in?

"Bjorn, you have nothing to be ashamed of. I know you enjoyed it, as did I."

"I'm not gay." I turned the shower off and grabbed my towel and clothes and ran out of the building to head for my room.

******

I SAT CURLED with my knees against my chest, thinking of my act with Ed. I couldn't feel bad for what I had done, but I had no idea how it would impact my life. I didn't turn up for training, and after three hours, someone finally came to check up on me.

Someone knocked on my door. I ignored it, and a minute later, the knocking resumed. Could it be Ed trying to coax me to come out and join the others?

"Bjorn, I know you're in there," Emily's voice yelled.

I tried to shut it out. She knocked again and called out.

"Bjorn, you can't stay in there forever. Please, let me in."

I looked up. "Leave me alone."

"Bjorn, please. You need to talk to me."

She was right. I couldn't keep whatever feelings I had bottled up. "Coming," I yelled.

I spun my body, putting my feet to the floor and realising all I wore was the towel. I covered the few steps in a longer time than normal for such a short distance and let Emily in.

"Bjorn, you've done nothing wrong."

"I'm not gay, Emily. But I enjoyed what I did with Ed and am not sure how to deal with it."

She was wearing just a sports top and a skirt. "Bjorn, you don't have to deal with it. Why do you think you and Ed did what you did? It's because we have instincts, and if we can just act on them rather than block our desires. We can be truly happy."

"Have you...?"

"Yes, I've licked more pussy than ice-cream, and I'm a dessert addict. I love being with women, but I still love being with men." She pulled her sports top over her head, exposing those perfect breasts of hers before unfastening her skirt.

"Do you ever wear underwear?" I asked.

"I did for a few years, but I don't like the constriction. Drop the towel, Bjorn, and fuck me like you did last night."

I discarded the towel, feeling my groin stir at the sight of her fully exposed body. I smiled. Everything was still working, and Emily and I had our best sex together ever.

CHAPTER 4

A FEW YEARS had passed, many women had come through the compound in groups, and with each intake, only one could come through to become a fully-fledged Mantassassin. Ed and I were the only men there most of the time, apart from this one crazy man called Jack.

Nakato remained my only unrealised objective to engage with intimately. It was like each day she subjected me to seeing her body in all of its glorious, natural state, only to keep me from getting inside. So when I heard Jack had managed to score with her, I knew she would stay out of my reach.

So the night Jack went to extract Brittany from her date that turned into a bloodbath, his non-return didn't concern me. What did piss me off was he shooting her.

"I'm okay, Bjorn. It's just a flesh wound. I was just lucky I managed to move out of his way," she told me when I visited her at the compound's infirmary the following night.

"If I ever find him..."

"Please don't hate him for it. He never really belonged here. And look at me. I'll be back at work in no time."

"Well, stay safe, baby girl. I have to go on assignment." I kissed her on the forehead, and she waved me away.

I checked the time. I only had a few minutes to meet my 7PM deadline at Helipad Four. Everything Nakato and I needed would be waiting for us in the helicopter.

"Leaving without saying goodbye?" Ed stepped onto the path.

"I wouldn't dream of it," I gave him a big kiss and squeezed his arse. I felt a weight off my shoulders when I accepted my existence as a bisexual.

"When you get back, I'll be away on a big mission. There's a lot of preparation for this one, but the money will be huge." His expression turned serious. "You be careful, Bjorn. I love you."

I grinned at him and nodded. The only person I ever expressed love for was my mother. Everyone else was about sex and or friendship.

Nakato already took a seat in the back of the chopper, strapped in and waiting for our deployment. We nodded at each other. She wasn't a woman of many words, so finding conversation was never an easy task with her.

Even with the number of years we had been part of the organisation, we were still blindfolded for much of the trip, adding to the awkwardness of the silence between us.

The task for the mission was for us to go in and take out a sugar cane farmer. His wife disgruntled with his womanising habits, she wanted him to pay the ultimate price. Nakato would be his newest temptation, and as usual, she would fuck him and kill him, and I would be in the next room ready to help her get back to the chopper and away again. We didn't expect much in the way of security, but I would be concealing a pistol just in case.

I hadn't been involved in many killings, the first time I shot a man I found it didn't freak me out anywhere near as much as I feared it would, but I still had trouble removing the imprint of the victim's face from my mind.

Every kill since then, however, had been a piece of cake.

I nodded off to sleep during the chopper ride. The first night would be a quiet one, checking into our assigned hotel in Brasilia for the night before making our way to the extensive sugar cane farm, our assigned driver taking us there.

"We are sharing a room tonight. You keep your hands to yourself, or we'll have trouble," Nakato said.

"Why are you always busting my chops? I've never done anything but ask for sex, and every time you say no, I accept it and move on."

"Yeah, because some other girl is always willing to lie on their back and spread their legs for you. Tonight there won't be another option for you but your hand."

She looked away from me. I couldn't argue with her. I never went a night without sex unless I didn't want any, which was rare. "So, why Jack? He has a head like an Easter Island statue, but you slept with him."

"He may not be pretty like you, but he knows how to treat a woman... outside of the bedroom as well as inside. Jack's twice the man you are."

I clenched my fists. I couldn't stand the mere mention of that traitor's name, let alone being compared to him. I doubted I would ever see him again, but if I did, he wouldn't be getting away.

"You keep thinking he's a traitor, but don't you think if he wanted to kill Brittany, you would not have had that conversation with her today? He meant to injure her, not kill her."

"He left us. He didn't even ask."

"You miss him. You are not happy that he let Ed have sex with him and wouldn't touch you."

I tightened my fists again. "I would never fuck that guy. Ed is an exception to my 'pussy only' rule."

"The worst lie to tell is the one you tell yourself."

"You know, I think I like it much better when you don't talk to me." I closed my eyes again and allowed slumber to fully envelop me.

******

I AWOKE AS the chopper landed, and wondered how the hell we were given clearance to land in Brazil. But it wasn't my concern.

"You get a good sleep?" Nakato asked.

"I must have slept for hours," I said as I opened my eyes.

"You haven't worked it out yet, have you? You think you know where the Praying Mantassassin base is, but you have no idea. We're just here to catch another flight. See that sign?" she pointed at the airfield.

"New Mexico," I said.

"Yes, we have a plane to catch. We've barely started our journey."

Great, I would have to endure more time engaged in uncomfortable silence with Nakato. I hoped the plane was of a size enabling me enough space to sprawl out and not forced to sit right next to her.

A man in a suit opened the chopper door for us and signalled for us to follow. The sun made its descent a fair time earlier, so the man's guidance and lighting of the plane nearby helped us to get to our destination.

"Welcome to New Mexico. Sorry your stay will be short," the man said to us.

"Can I ask who you are?" I asked.

"You can call me Mr Gun. Piss me off and you'll find out why."

I decided to quit with the questions at that point and just make my way quietly to the plane.

I felt like another lengthy sleep and began to regret the assignment already. I would have to share a private plane with an African femme fatale, who didn't like me, and a well-suited man who didn't like questions.

A short stack of stairs awaited us, and the three of us climbed to get inside the little plane.

As I stepped inside, I decided I would buy a plane just like it one day. There were four sets of seats able to recline into bed type formations, a round table in the middle with an ice chest and bottled drinks inside, as well as shagpile carpet throughout.

"Get comfortable, it's going to be a long flight," Mr Gun said.

******

I DON'T REMEMBER much of the flight. I drank the contents of a glass bottled rum and cola and fell asleep while watching the movie playing. Mr Gun tapped me on the shoulder a few minutes before our descent, so I sat upright and strapped myself in. My partner for the assignment looked like she hadn't slept at all, which worried me.

"Are you going to be okay?" I asked her.

"Back when I was a girl, I was lucky to sleep four hours a day after getting food and water for my family. I was the oldest child, so I had the responsibility to take care of the younger brothers and sisters. These days, I get everything handed to me, so yes, I am going to be okay."

"There's been a change in plans. You'll be driven directly to the plantation where you will carry out your mission today. It seems the farmer's daughter has decided to take an unplanned visit, so Bjorn, it will be your job to keep her... occupied. She's a real daddy's girl," Mr Gun said.

"He's just a farmer. Why couldn't someone just get sent in to shoot him in the head?" I asked.

"The wife wants him to die doing the very thing he loves, cheating on her. You two are being paid big dollars for this, so just fucking do it. Anyway, I have to disappear. Your cab will be here soon. Here's a stash of local currency. If you need any more than this, then they're ripping you off. And here's the address. Read it and remember it."

"How do we get back?" Nakato asked.

"A cab will arrive in six hours' time to collect the two of you. Your names are Mariel Jones and Darrell Davids. Start using them now when you address each other."

He turned away and left, and just like I had viewed numerous times in the movies, he crossed the road and vanished from our view as soon as a bus drove past. The Brasilia airport's traffic was crazy, and I wondered if there were any road laws in this country.

We located the waiting area for cabs, and being the early hours of the morning, we had no trouble promptly getting into one. I relayed the required address to the taxi driver, who, in turn, informed us it would take half an hour to arrive at our destination. Nakato sat back and closed her eyes while I sifted through the bag of stuff we were supplied with for the mission.

I had two pistols and a semi-automatic rifle to pack

into a backpack. A fake lining served my purpose well to keep the weapons hidden from prying eyes. Outside the lining, the backpack was stacked with books on the American civil war, a topic much loved by the plantation owner who apparently thought himself an aficionado.

I plucked one of the books from the pack. I briefly studied American history in high school and found the idea of a nation fighting itself a curious one. A near silent ride allowed me to indulge myself in some quiet reading, a passion I hadn't taken part in much since leaving my home country.

******

THE DRIVEWAY LEADING to the house served as a clearway between two halves of a sugar cane jungle, the sight of the towering tubular plants a hypnotic sea of green. A group of men waved the cab to a stop adjacent to a shed. None of them appeared to be armed, so the chance of a threat to us leaving on completion of the mission didn't seem obvious.

I handed over a pile of money to the cab driver, who agreed to meet us back at the same place in five and a half hours and was polite enough not to ask any questions. Nakato and I stepped out of the cab and surveyed our surroundings.

One of the men walked our way, a mouth full of teeth communicating with us in a language I didn't know. Nakato spoke back to him in the same dialect, laughing and pointing at me.

"What are you two talking about?" I asked.

"I told him I'm a book salesman, a line Mr Rooney's using to bring us into the house without his daughter suspecting anything. Oh, and I told him you're here as my personal security guard, which is why I laughed."

I nodded, and we walked in single file to the entrance of the house. A pair of concrete columns supported a ceiling above them almost twice my height.

The target of our mission greeted us at the door. "Good morning. You must be the book woman I've heard so much about." The young woman to his right peered straight at me, and I thanked my lucky stars that my job on the mission was to entertain such a beautiful object.

Nakato smiled back at the man. "Yes, my company told me you are a civil war buff. I have a whole bundle of books you might like to take a look at," she said.

"Please, come inside and get comfortable," the man said to Nakato. "And you," he said pointing at me, "I would prefer if you waited outside the house. I have no intention of doing anything to harm your business partner here."

"Well, what would you like me to do then?" I asked.

The young lady looked me up and down. "Interesting accent you have there," she said. She smirked at me. "Would you like a tour of the plantation while your assistant talks books with my father?"

It seemed too easy. "Sure. I've always had a thing for sugar."

"Easy there, boy," Mr Rooney said. "Please, lady, let's get this started." His gaze met Nakato's eyes.

She snatched the bag from my grasp, pulled out the five books and then handed it back. "It would be my pleasure."

I watched her walk inside the house, and the young lady grabbed my arm and marched me away from the house. "So, tell me where you come from."

"Belgium, I moved to the United States a few years ago as a lost man, and now I get to do what I love, bringing books to people all over the world."

"My father is quite the collector. He loves anything that is a first edition. Those books you brought for him, they must be worth a few thousand dollars for you two to come all this way."

I had no real idea about books, apart from the fact I never hit them as hard as I should have in college. "My company says they were written not long after the war, and first edition copies are hard to come by."

"Don't you think it's strange he asked your partner to come into the house and not you?"

"She is very beautiful. Maybe he would be more likely to listen to her than me."

"I know my father. I'll make a bet he doesn't care about the books. Sure, he'll buy them, but he's really buying the services of your African friend."

"Why are you telling me this. You've only just met me."

"I know about my father's infidelities, but I don't blame him. My mother is a bitch. She's made him work for so many years, and he has no joy in his life except for the occasional female company he purchases." She made a detour into the midst of a cane field. "Are you coming?"

I nodded and chased her as she started running between rows of the sweet smelling plants. Her skirt jumped up and about as she ran, and I tried to do the polite thing of not looking, but my eyes caught a glimpse of a peachy looking ass barely covered with a thong.

She changed direction, ducking to the right, and I put my arm up to stop the leaves hitting me in the face as my pace quickened. I could hear her steps but lost sight of her. Her giggling gave me a hint on which direction she had run, but I stopped to try to listen for the exact direction.

A breeze blew through the fields, leaves rustling,

but my hearing was unable to isolate any other sounds. I could neither see nor hear a sign of her. What the hell was she up to?

"Here I am," she said as she jumped in front of me, a couple of her blouse buttons unfastened. "I've got something for you," she teased, turning her back on me.

"I can't wait," I said. I took a few steps towards her.

"Stop right there, mister," she said. She turned and pulled something from her blouse pocket. "Do you feel like a smoke?"

"Um, what would your father say?" I said, looking at the joint in her fingers.

"If he knew half the things I did, he'd cut me from his will." She put it in her mouth and lit it up, taking a long toke.

Emily and I quite often shared a joint after sex, and my nostrils took in the scent of that sweet smell.

I accepted the joint from the Brazilian woman, taking a long drag and feeling the smoke soaking into my lungs. I coughed—my instant reaction to the pot, a blend more potent than what I regularly smoked at the compound.

The thick cloud inside me took an almost instant effect on my mind.

"It's good, isn't it? My father has no idea I've been growing it all these years." She accepted the joint back from me and inhaled again. "My mother keeps telling me I need to work out what I want to do with my life, and I tell her I don't want to end up a bitter old bitch as she is."

"You speak English very well," I said.

"I was sent to the best school from the age when I could first walk. I could speak four languages by the time I started high school, but I never imagined I would be speaking English to a European." She took another drag from the joint. She coughed a little, a smile growing on her face. "I'm so sorry. It should be your turn."

I accepted it back from her, taking another puff and feeling light on my feet. "This is really good," I said.

"I know. Please finish it. I've had enough," she said and took a seat on the ground.

Part of me wondered how wise it was to smoke to the point of losing control. I knew I could handle the effects, but if Nakato found herself in trouble, would I be quick enough to react? I couldn't raise any suspicion on a straightforward mission, so I did as she asked.

"Can I ask you a question?" she asked, patting the ground next to her.

I took the hint, picking a piece of earth to sit on, situated only a foot away from her. "Sure, shoot."

"When you saw me for the first time, did you see someone you wanted to have sex with? Or did you see someone who you think you could have a long conversation with and get to know?"

"Wow, you don't mince words, do you?" I asked.

"Life is too short to talk so fucking long without saying anything. Please, just answer me."

I looked her up and down, the length of her tanned legs enhanced as the skirt rode up her thighs where her body made contact with the ground.

"When I first looked at you, I saw a beautiful woman who I mentally undressed, then ran my hand up one leg while holding the side of your face with the other, kissing those red lips. You then pressed your body against mine, your jiggling perky breasts rubbing against me while you pushed my hand between your legs, letting me cup your hungry pussy in my hand, and allowing a finger to find itself inside you, preparing you for my hungry cock."

"Wow. Your honesty astounds me, and while you're

obviously a walking erection, I thank you for being true in what you say. But we've only just met. I don't know if I should let you enjoy my body for your own selfish pleasure."

I laughed. "Hey, I give back as much pleasure as I receive. Give me a chance, and you'll see that I am very proficient at providing pleasure."

She stared at me. I stared back, not knowing what I should say next. "You're a funny man," she said, bursting into a fit of laughter.

I joined in, and I noticed her unfastening each button on her shirt while giggling and then sliding it down her shoulders and arms. "Oops," she said.

I decided I would copy her, looking into her chocolate coloured eyes as I removed my shirt. She got onto her knees and rubbed her hand over my waxed chest.

"I work out a lot," I said.

"You have a very good body, nice tight abs and such a smooth chest. I think I want you to give my body this pleasure you've promised. And you better make sure you deliver the goods."

I had no doubt I could. We both stripped ourselves of all our clothes and proceeded to make slow, passionate love for the next hour.

******

WE MUST HAVE both fallen asleep. I woke up with her curled into my chest and checked my watch. "Oh shit," I said under my breath, seeing I only had a half hour to get back to the house to meet the cab.

The woman woke and smiled as our eyes locked. "Oh, Bjorn, you are a most amazing lover."

"And so are you," I said and kissed her lips. There is

much to be said for being one with nature. I could happily have stayed with her for a long time, but a mission deadline is not to be trifled with.

"Can we do it again? Before we return to the house I want you inside me again," she grabbed me between the legs. "You have a very beautiful penis. I want to take a photo of it."

She patted through her discarded clothes, obviously looking for her camera phone. I watched her and decided that Brazilian women have the best-looking bodies in the world. The worst part of the whole thing was that her father would most probably have been dead by this time, and my partner was responsible.

A gunshot echoed through the air, followed by another. The next thing I knew, my phone started to ring inside my backpack. I grabbed it and answered it, hearing Nakato's panicked voice on the other end.

"I'll be there as soon as I can," I said to her. She managed to tell me she killed Mr Rooney, but a group of armed men had stormed the house.

"What's going on?" the girl asked. "I heard a gunshot, and you sounded worried on the phone."

"It's okay. We just have to meet our ride home soon. Don't worry about it."

"You're lying to me," she threw the phone at my head.

I just managed to put an arm up to block the projectile, and she rolled over to my backpack and upended it, spilling all the contents, including the three guns.

I dove over her, grabbed a pistol, and pointed it at her. "Please don't do anything silly."

"Oh, Bjorn, what is going on?" a tear ran down her cheek. "Why have you got these guns?"

"My partner was hired by your mother, who is sick

of your father sleeping with other women."

"Hired to do what?" she asked.

Another gunshot echoed throughout the plantation. "I'm sorry. It was just supposed to be a quick job. You weren't even supposed to be here."

"Oh no," she sobbed and grabbed something to cover herself. "I hate you, Bjorn."

"I don't blame you. I have to go." I grabbed the guns and put two of them back in the bag, keeping a pistol on the ground next to me while I dressed. The girl sat down crying and hiding from me the best she could.

I looked at her, and said nothing and began to walk away.

"I will tell the police everything. My father was a good man, and your friend killed him, didn't she?"

"Yes, she did."

She allowed the garment she was holding up to fall to the ground and began to press some buttons on her phone. I pointed the gun at her again. "I can't let you do that. Please, put the phone down."

"You'll shoot me in cold blood? Well, come on then, you big man, shoot me." She held the phone to her ear, waiting for someone to talk to.

"Please, I don't want to kill you."

"Hello, my name is..." her words died as I pulled the trigger, firing a shot into her forehead from less than a few feet away. Her body flung backward from the impact, eyes staring out with no life behind them.

"Oh fuck!" I said.

I had just murdered one of the most beautiful creatures on the planet—and for what? I gave her one last look, wishing I could undo this awful act, and then slung my rifle over my shoulder and picked up the other pistol with my left hand. I had to get my mind back to Nakato and help her out of her bind.

I kept off the main track, choosing to cut straight through the cane plants in the direction of the house. Another gunshot rang out, followed by another a few seconds later. I prayed that Nakato was still okay and cursed myself for getting so carried away with Rooney's daughter and losing consciousness like I did.

I held one arm up, keeping the flapping cane plants from hitting me in the face as I ran. The house much closer, I soon slowed my pace, looking out for any potential shooters who may have been sent my way. I thought I heard a noise, so I stopped on the spot.

The rustling continued, and I knew it wasn't the wind, the sound being too loud for nature to be the cause. I crouched, one gun aimed from my side, the other dead ahead, waiting for any hostile actions. Sweat poured from my brow, stinging my eye as I saw a flutter of movement from my peripheral vision. Red and blue checked clothing stood out through the field. I steadied my aim and fired once.

I heard a groan and the sound of a heavy weight crunching cane plants as the body fell. I took a few steps and recognised the dead man as the one who stood by as we arrived at the property. Continuing my journey to the house, I heard a feminine scream.

I threw all caution to the wind, heading for the clearway between the two halves of the plantation with both pistols pointing out in front of me. I heard another gunshot, the bullet hitting cane plants to my left and slicing through. I fired several shots from both pistols in the direction of the entry of the house, hitting a target as it stuck halfway from the open doorway.

"Stop right there," I heard a male voice boom out. "We have your partner, and we will kill her if you don't end hostilities now."

I stopped in my tracks, keeping my eyes peeled for

any movement ahead. Was the man bluffing? "Let her go. Your boss is dead," I yelled.

"No, she's not," a female voice called back.

"Mrs Rooney?"

"I'm coming out, but if you shoot at me, your black girlfriend will get a bullet in the head," the lady yelled back.

"Okay," I said back. What the hell had happened in there?

A woman looking to be around the same age as Rooney made her way out of the house. She smiled as she set eyes on me. "Wow, professional killers are very cute these days." She took many steps, stopped a foot away, and touched my face. "Now, should I have you killed or have you in my bed?"

"We came here to do what you asked of us. Now let us go."

"It doesn't quite work like that, young man. I can't have my dead husband lying around and have to try to explain it to the police. Now, what have you done to my daughter?"

"She's out on the field."

"And why didn't she come back with you?"

I gulped. "She's sleeping. I wore her out."

"Wow, maybe I should take you to my bed. Mr Rooney and I sleep in separate rooms, so you don't have to worry about his dead pompous body being in sight. But you better make it quick. The police are on their way."

"What about my partner? Where is she?"

Mrs Rooney turned to the house. "Bring her out, please. She's alive, but covered in Mr Rooney's blood, so we have to keep her restrained so the police can test the blood on her."

"You're a bitch and a double crosser. I might just

shoot you where you stand."

"And if you do," she chuckled. "Your girlfriend dies."

I glared at her, keeping my pistols locked on her as she smirked back. I saw Nakato exit the house, naked and chained up, blood splattered over her body and her eye all puffed up and bruised. I couldn't believe they managed to catch her.

"Let her go and take me instead. After all, I killed your girl," I said.

"No, you didn't. You don't have it in you to kill a young woman."

"Shoot her, Bjorn," Nakato said. "I'm dead anyway, but you can get away."

Two men built much bulkier than I was stood on either side of her, guns raised at her ready to fire at a second's notice. If I raised my hands to aim, they could end Nakato's life before I could even get off a wayward shot.

"No, we can make an arrangement. You let her go and take me. I'm the one who deserves to be punished. Nakato killed the man she was paid to kill, but I killed an innocent young woman after fucking her brains out."

The mother lost her smile. "You're not joking about this, are you?"

"No. I took my gun and shot her in the head while she was still lying on the ground naked. I even got her high before we had sex. She was powerless."

Mrs Rooney shook with rage. "Kill him!"

The two men flanking Nakato moved their aim towards me. I watched their weapons rise as I lifted my own and fired a shot from each. Nakato opened her mouth as the bullets flew, each one hitting a target, and putting the two men down.

Nakato ran towards Mrs Rooney, grabbing hold of

one of her chains and swinging it through the air.

I could see rage flowing from her body as she smacked her target in the side of the head with the metal chain, knocking her to the ground.

"You fucking bitch. You stupid fucking bitch," Nakato said, wrapping the chain around the fallen woman's neck, tightening it and pulling as hard as she could. Mrs Rooney kicked her heels into the ground as her face turned blue while her life came to a painful end.

I went over and pulled the dead woman's pants down while Nakato undid the shirt. "Not my colour, but they will do," she said while putting the two garments on.

I handed her one of my pistols and patted my pockets looking for my phone, realising I must have left it in the field near the woman I had killed. We had five minutes until the cab was due to arrive.

"Were you really willing to take my place?" Nakato asked.

"Of course I would, in a heartbeat."

Nakato put her arms around me and kissed me full on the lips. When the kissing ceased, we held the embrace for a few minutes until our cab arrived. She drew away and looked in my eyes. "Thank you, Bjorn."

"My pleasure," I said. I went to add something else when she pressed her lips against mine again and kissed me deeper than the first time. As muscular as she was, her mouth felt soft inside, her tongue gentle as it twisted inside our mouths with my own.

"You kiss okay," she said, and as the cab came to a stop, we released each other and separated, each heading to a different door. "Tonight we fuck like we should have a long time ago."

I smiled back at her and wondered if it was something we should do, given how long I built an image inside my head on how much I wanted her.

"Looks like there's been a wild party here, we better get the hell out," the driver said, and put his foot to the floor.

Chapter 5

BEFORE SHE SET out on the failed 5PM mission, Emily handed me a sealed envelope, which was only to be opened in the event of her death. I liked her very much, as well as Ed and Hayley, who also lost their lives in what should have been a straightforward assignment.

Nakato always said they should have never brought another police officer into the operation, and she should have posed as Ed's partner, but the client Kate wouldn't have things that way. And then the Praying Mantassassin organisation was in disarray. The reputation we had took a bad hit, and we needed someone to step into Ed's spot.

I was requested to enter the communications building and spoke to the boss, who told me I could be the new Ed. He believed in my skills as a killer and said I had the type of charisma a recruiter should have, but we would be missing the police connection unless Gary, Ed's father, could find a way back in.

I accepted and carried the burden of having to step up. I sat alone in my room and stared at the envelope, aware I had to open it and read what the now deceased writer wanted me to see.

Dear Bjorn. I could start by saying if you're reading this, then blah blah blah, but I won't. Every mission carries a risk, and with this one paying so much, I want to be sure someone knows my big secret. I have a childhood friend who has undertaken surgery to look just like me, so if you can, please make contact with her at my gym. You should recruit her, and organise her to take ownership of all my properties and assets, and live as if she were me. You are one sexy motherfucker, Bjorn. Fantastic in bed, but most of all, you have a great heart. Please don't cry for me. I have done a lot of wrong in my life, so death is my rightful sentence for the life I led. Please destroy this letter once you've read it. No one but you can know I have feelings.

Lots of love,

Emily xxxx

Well, I had to break one part of her wishes. The tears came and wouldn't stop for several minutes. I tore up the letter and threw it in the bin and set fire to it, and smoked a big fat joint, falling asleep soon afterwards.

******

I WAITED NEARLY an hour for her to wake, her face bathed in beauty as she slept. After she had awakened and we both drank a strong cup of coffee, I told her about Emily's letter and the request she penned before her death.

"So what's your answer, Ebony?" I asked the woman who easily passed as Emily in the physical sense. The conversation had been long and the tears plenty. I didn't know this woman, but if her personality was anything like Emily's, I had no doubt she would carry on her good friend's legacy.

"I'm in." She leaned in and gave me a big kiss.

"I will find a way to bust Talissa out of jail and let you hunt her down and kill her. And we will find her husband Terry and their children..."

"Please, Bjorn. No child killing. If you need help making inroads to Talissa in prison, I have a couple of biker friends who could find someone on the inside. We can do this, just you and me."

I smiled. Her face reminded me of Emily, and I knew I would be making love to her by the end of the day. I had gone places in the PM organisation. I would make many contacts and help Ebony get her revenge.

Life was good.

EPILOGUE

FIVE YEARS LATER

"SO, ARE THEY all accounted for?" the man asked the woman sitting opposite from him at the table.

"Three of them are in prison, but I have someone on the inside to pull target five out. I'll see to it personally that target ten is picked up on a transfer, but target one will be the biggest problem. There's only so much even I can do."

The man sighed. So much preparation had gone into the mission, but if he couldn't get target one to come to the party, they risked everything.

"The postcards are ready to be sent, the venue is ready, and I have the team assembled. This is happening."

"So why go to all this trouble?"

"I like games."

"You could just send me out to take them out one by one, and the risk will be zero. Think about it, at least."

The man pulled out a pistol. "I'm in charge here and don't you forget it. You're lucky to even be alive, let alone given such an opportunity to participate in an active role."

"I'm sorry. I forgot my manners."

"It's natural. But you'll get to have your fun once the dice are cast and able to personally take out some of my eleven prized marks."

Other Books By Chris Heinicke

5PM

REAL ESTATE AGENT, Terry Cooper, has it all—a beautiful, loving wife, a young son and daughter, and a successful career which provides them with a wealthy lifestyle.

However, things change when his best friend and workmate introduces him to an animated chat room.

A woman he meets in the online world manages to find him in the real world, which leads to a whirlwind of disturbing internet chats, infidelities, and murder.

Can Terry get himself out of this mess before he loses his soul and life? Or is he too far gone to bring normal back to his life?

11PM

A Sneak Peek

CHAPTER ONE
JUNEAU, ALASKA

TERRY STARED AT the postcard, reading it once, twice, and then a few more times. Were his eyes lying to him? Could he still be in his bed dreaming this crazy stuff? No. This was the mailbox at the end of his path leading from his house, he emptied the contents of said mailbox, and this postcard really was sitting in his hands.

On the front of the postcard, a Caucasian male held a guitar in a pose almost looking like he was making love to it. To his left, an African-American played a harmonica into a microphone on a stand. But the back of it put Terry's mind in a spin. The message giving him goose bumps each time he read it—

Miss me, Terry?
Love, BluesGirl88 xxx

He turned his head in each direction, searching for any signs of someone possibly hiding amongst the throngs of trees surrounding much of his property. The driveway ran to the east side of the house, cutting a clear way through the forest allowing people access to come and go by road. To come from any other direction would require trekking through thick forests.

His eyes followed the driveway as far as his visual range extended, but from where he stood, he couldn't locate any movement in that direction either. Taking yet another look at the postcard, a chill ran down his spine as his mind absorbed the name of the sender—BluesGirl, a chat handle for a woman who had caused him much trouble and changed the course of his life forever. Barely surviving the real life encounter with the woman behind the name Bluesgirl88, Terry didn't dare peek at the chat program known as 3DDreamchat ever again after those crazy times.

"Yeah, right," he said aloud, dismissing the card as being sent as a prank from someone he knew, albeit, an extremely sick prank. He bundled up the postcard with the rest of the day's mail, to show it to his long-time partner, Hannah, when she arrived home from work later in the day.

But he couldn't deny the presence of a nervousness creeping inside him, travelling up through the extremities of his body, and an unnerving chill felt on top of the freezing bitterness of the snow blanketing the ground.

He took a few steps towards the house, the best place to seek refuge from the biting winter air.

Terry thought about giving Hannah a call about the strange postcard once he reached the inside of his residence. The unmistakable clapping sound of a bullet slicing its way through the air stopped him in his tracks. Frozen on the spot, he glanced sideways as bullets rained down near him, burying themselves into the snow, and splashing specks of the white powdery substance coating the ground. He needed to make a decision where to run and doubted he would be fast enough to outrun the lethal lead storm hunting him down.

A single shot thundered over the pelting of the bullets, silencing the gunfire but causing a person to scream out loud before the screamer's body thudded to the ground. Terry scanned the area and saw snow dust rise up in a thin cloud from where the body had fallen.

He decided running to the house to be the best course of action, and as if the ground lay booby-trapped, the shooting resumed. "Oh fuck," he yelled, taking a couple of steps backwards from the last location where bullets had pelted down. He stole a quick upwards glance, an attempt to spot any sign of movement in the trees around him.

A second loud boom echoed through the dense forest, resulting in another scream and downward crash. With the shooting at a halt again, he placed one snow buried foot in front of him ready to make a mad dash for his house. As he pulled his rear foot out to overtake the other, further shooting erupted, making its way closer to him again. He backed away in the opposite direction from which he wished to take, and almost wet his pants as a couple of bullets hit the ground between his feet and spat snow in the air at the point of impact.

Once again, the shooting subsided, and Terry yelled at the top of his lungs, "Okay, you've made your point. If you're going to kill me then just do it."

A third single shot reverberated through the air, followed by the falling of a body, its downward journey to the ground interrupted courtesy of the roof of Terry's house. The head of the body covered with a balaclava, Terry had no idea if the corpse belonged to a male or female.

Bursting through the foliage and onto the driveway, a tall, lean figure approached him with a rifle pointed his way. Unable to see another way out of his predicament, he put his hands up, waiting for the next thing to happen.

Step by step, the figure's physical features became more apparent. Looking at the hips and small protrusions from the chest, Terry guessed the body belonged to a female. She wore dark jeans, a hooded parka, and a pair of sunglasses covering most of her upper face. He stood like a statue, not daring to make any sudden movement to give the woman a reason to shoot him. The armed visitor stopped a few feet from him, and as she removed her eyewear, Terry took a few seconds until his realisation of the identity of the person in front of him smacked him in the face.

"Brittany?" he asked.

"Hi there, Terry, how's my favourite womanising real estate agent doing these days?"

"Holy shit. You were in jail, death row even. How the hell did you get out?"

"Long story. We'll save it for another drinking session perhaps. The question you should be asking me is what am I doing here? At your house? And who were those bad guys? But if you really want to know, can we please get the hell out of this damn freezer box environment and in front of your fireplace, perhaps?"

"Brittany, you were going to kill my kids, and my mother, and me. Apart from the gun you have pointed at me, what the hell reason would I have to let you in my house?"

"There's something big going on, Terry, and it's something bigger than you and your family and me and those dead C-grade snipers painting the snow and your roof red with blood. This shit is bigger than the Praying

Mantassassins even. Please, for the love of puppies, let me in the goddamn house or else I'll shoot you in the nuts."

******

"SERGEANT HALL, THIS came directly to the station," the young female constable handed her superior a postcard.

"Strange they didn't send it to my house instead of the station," Hannah said. "Thanks. Oh, could I bother you for another coffee, Officer Kempson?"

"Sure," she said, happy to be asked to do anything her idol requested. She almost floated out of the office high on enthusiasm.

Hannah looked down at the postcard on her desk. Gracing the front of it were two musicians on a stage, a caption near the bottom of it read 'Greetings from the House of Blues, Las Vegas, Nevada.'

"Who the hell do I know who's visiting that place?" she asked out loud and flipped it over. She almost fell back on her chair when she read the handwritten note on the back—

Confess your sins,
Regards
Dancergirl.

"No way. This has to be some sort of sick joke." She flipped it back over, studying the two musicians before turning it over and reading the message again.

She placed the card in the top drawer of her desk. Apart from the reference to a chat handle she knew to be used by a corrupt police officer a few years back, the card made very little sense.

"Your coffee, Sergeant," Kempson said, making sure not to spill a single drop of the precious beverage Hannah craved most in the morning hours.

"Stevie, did this postcard arrive by regular mail to the station?" Hannah gripped the card in question by a corner.

"Yes. I guess they mustn't know your home address."

"There's no imprint on it, see? Any mail going through the system receives a rubber stamp, but this card is blank." She stood and looked through her office window, across the flat surface, and onto the quiet street, attempting to spot anyone or anything who might raise her suspicion. Not one person stood out, seeming normal for modern day terrorists and criminals who spent hours learning how to blend in.

"Can you please do me a favour? I'm expecting calls from people, so if you could watch the office and take any calls for me, I'll make sure you'll be noticed by those single malt drinking types up high in the Alaskan police authority. So, do we have a deal?"

Stevie extended her hand, waiting for Hannah to make a move, who then soon accepted the younger woman's gesture and pointed to a seat next to her.

"Deal."

"And if you hear of anything you feel I need to know, please call me without a second thought."

Hannah smiled, stood up, and exited the office, forgoing the coffee Stevie had made for her. She turned the necessary corridors to make her way to the front of the station, seeking anyone or anything out the front of the building looking out of place. As she scanned the area, a van left its park, revealing a tall and near bald man across the other side of the road. The man turned his head, locking his sights on her and sending a shiver up her spine. He turned away and disappeared using a bus as cover while it drove past.

She left the office through the glass automatic double doors, checking for traffic and jogging to the other side to pursue the man who raised her interest. She drew her pistol from her holster in preparation for any trouble he might present.

Spotting movement from the corner of her eye, Hannah followed it with her aim and picked up the pace. Running through a residential area, she hoped not to have to fire any shots should the man turn out to be hostile. She lost trace of the movement and took long, steady steps through the alleyway slicing through the two halves of the land providing low-cost housing. She passed by a tree on the corner of a block, taking a long look at it before passing it by, only to hear a voice behind her.

"Looking for me?" he asked.

Spinning on her feet, Hannah's forearm soon ended up in the clutches of the man she had chased to this point, the weapon in her hand wrestled out of her control. She threw a punch at him, only to find her fist caught in the grasp of the menacing figure's other hand.

"I'm not here to hurt you, Hannah," he said.

"You're assaulting an officer of the law. You better let me go."

"My name is Griffon, Jack Griffon. You first contacted me some time ago on my blog, and now I'm here to warn you of a threat we need to take care of."

"Did you send the postcard?"

"No. I received one just like it, though. You left some loose ends a few years back, and now they seem intent on taking out a big name target in just two days. I need you to sit down and listen to what I have to say. I ask that you hear me out before passing judgement."

"I could take you into the station. We can have all the time you need to chat, lots of coffee, and I know you won't try anything deadly."

"If I were going to try something deadly on you, we wouldn't be having this conversation now, miss. If you don't mind, I'd prefer somewhere more public like a café, and I'll even buy the coffee."

"Wait, you said I contacted you on a blog?"

"Yes. You know me as DS, and I believe I gave you some very top secret information which helped you make a break in a case against the Praying Mantassassins."

Hannah's eyes lit up. "I know a great place, and yes, I will take you up on that offer for a free coffee."

******

BRITTANY AND TERRY sat in lounge chairs that faced each other, sipping coffee by the wood fire. She no longer wore her parka, revealing her new look to the man she once had a part in trying to take down. Her hair was shaved on one side of her head, the remainder flicked over and back to its natural brown colour. Wearing a singlet top, Terry admired the collection of ink she had gained over the years since he had last seen her, some of the tattoos coloured, some plain, and mostly covering her arms and shoulders and the visible parts of her back.

"Terry, I simply can't apologise enough for what happened. It was just business, and now I feel privileged to still be breathing. You and Hannah are in danger. You will soon realise this when you visit the internet address printed on the back of that postcard you got in the mail today."

"But you held a gun to my little girl's head. That's

not something I can just forgive and forget." He stood up and walked over to poke a log in the fireplace."

"I've done a lot of thinking in that time, and I really want to be a better person. I hid in that tree for three days waiting for those guys to make a move on your house, living on snack bars and melted snow. I killed them, and if I hadn't, you would be dead."

"How do I know you weren't with them, double crossing them at the last minute to make your case and gain my trust?"

"I don't think I'll ever gain your trust again, Terry, and that's okay because I don't blame you. But I busted out of prison on a bit of information I came across in that shithole, something I wasn't supposed to hear, and it could have got me killed if I had stayed there."

"Quite ironic for someone on death row."

"You need to listen to me. No doubt you've heard of Robert Bannister, the presidential candidate who's gaining a gigantic following. Well, he's attending a function in Las Vegas in two days' time, and someone intends to end his campaign trail right there and then for good if you know what I mean. I had to reach out and find people I could trust and at least one person who would believe me. Well, one of the first places I went to after I broke out was an internet café, and I discovered Jack's blog. I found that person I needed to believe me and to help me find you and Hannah."

"So you put a postcard in my mailbox? Scared the shit out of me and expected me to believe this far-fetched idea you have about someone going after Bannister? Well played, but I'm not buying it."

"You don't have the internet here, do you? Or a cell phone?"

"No, and that's why we like it here. I know you have a gun and everything, but I need to ask you to leave."

"Okay, Terry." Brittany pointed the gun at him. "I tried to be nice, but get in the fucking car now and drive us to town."

******

HANNAH SAT ACROSS the table from the man with a tough as nails appearance, Jack Griffon, but she guessed inside the tough exterior, a big soft heart existed. She knew the military types since way back when she was just a little girl.

"I did a lot of bad things to get into that organisation, Griffon. I can't even think about what I did without feeling dirty."

Jack took a long gulp of his latte. In his experience, the independent café owners made some of the best coffee he had ever tried. "But you found Terry, and YOU saved him. I did some bad things too back when I worked for them. I trained girls to kill people. I helped to create monsters. I lost all respect for women and myself and had sex with anything that drew breath. I even got together with—" he cut himself off.

Hannah reached out to him and touched his hand, "Then we have some things in common. Your blog got my attention, and I bet you thought no one would listen to you. People love to read conspiracy theories, but who actually does anything about something they read? I saw what you wrote, and went through some cold cases, found some things relating to what you wrote, but I couldn't find someone to back me until Morrison came through. Now he's in the FBI, holding quite a high rank too, and I wouldn't mind betting it was because he took the credit for the 5PM case."

Jack released Hannah's hand. "I'm in awe of how you got through that ordeal against five of them."

"I had some help from Terry's sister Janet. The woman she killed was the one who hired the team."

"I guess you couldn't let the press get hold of that one. Anyway, take a longer look at that card, near your name and address."

Hannah did as he suggested. Beneath the handwritten entries, she saw a typed website address, www.HOB/2/.com. "It's probably just the venue's website address."

"Now, come on, Hannah. Where's the detective in you? Everything serves a purpose. Don't just neglect the big clue in front of you."

She turned her eyes in the direction of the computers in the corner of the room where patrons could pay two dollars for fifteen minutes.

"I got this too," Jack said, pulling two one-dollar bills from his wallet.

"Thank you." She accepted the money and walked over to the counter to purchase her internet time. "Are you coming?" she asked Jack.

He shook his head. Hannah shrugged and took a seat in front of one of the available computers. As soon as she clicked the mouse, the countdown started. Her fingers tapped clumsily at the keys, typing never having been one of her strengths. As she entered the address and pressed the return key, the page went to a black screen, and a few seconds later, a video loaded.

"Come to the House of Blues for fine dining, great music, and the best time you'll ever have in Las Vegas," the smiling middle-aged man said, standing in front of a desk with 'House of Blues' in bold black lettering painted on it. The video cut to a face speaking through a black balaclava, through a voice masker. "Greetings, Hannah. I know all about you, everything you've done, the people you love, and exactly where you live. You have until 5PM, November the fifth to check into the House of Blues, Las Vegas, or else I'll kill everyone's favourite presidential hopeful, Mr Robert Bannister."

The unknown masked speaker disappeared, and a slideshow of surveillance photos commenced. First was her father, in a series of pictures taken of him standing outside his home. Next was the priest at the church she attended as a child, photos snapped of him unaware as he prepared his pulpit for a Sunday service. And lastly, her partner, Terry, sitting in his office at the house they shared with the children.

The video cut back to the masked presenter. "I can get to anyone, at anytime, at any place. So please ensure you meet our appointment." The screen went blank at the end of the video.

She stared at the screen, taking in all she had seen in the harrowing minute the video had lasted. What could the masked person in the video truly be capable of if they were able to capture so many photos with unaware subjects? A psychological whirlpool ravaged its way through her mind. She placed her palms on the desk the computer sat upon and looked down at her lap.

"I got a similar video," Jack said behind her, "not that I saw yours, but I'm guessing you saw a masked person talking in a tone sounding like the lovechild of Darth Vader and a thrash metal singer, followed by a series of photographs of people you care about."

Hannah lifted her head and spun on her chair, "I swear if you know—"

"Please trust me, I don't."

Hannah's attention switched to two people entering the café, doing a double take as she saw Terry walking with a tall woman he had opened the door for. Forever the gentleman, but as her eyes studied the stranger, she almost gasped out loud. She lifted herself from her seat and headed in the direction of the woman, drawing her pistol from its holster.

"Karla Young, also known as Brittany, aren't you supposed to be on death row?" she said.

"Hannah, it's been a long time, but I'm not here for any reason other than to save your boyfriend from the certain death he almost suffered at you house. I bet you got a postcard and then typed in the internet address?"

"You know a fair bit about this. Jack, do you know this girl?"

"Yes, we actually travelled here together. We had to make sure Brittany had found Terry before the bad guys did. She's been hiding in a tree, watching your place with a buddy who I hope she left in Terry's car. And I had to make sure you didn't find her and shoot her in the head or something. She got a postcard in jail and had to get the hell out. We go back a long way, Brittany and me, and so when she found me on my blog and told me she was on the run, I went and picked her up."

"And who the hell are you?" Terry asked Jack.

"I used to be a drill sergeant, teaching young men and women how to fight and get in shape. I helped Brittany become a killer, and then one night, I shot her and left that job for good."

"It was his blog that got me onto the Praying Mantassassins, so I guess you can say he brought you and me together, Terry," Hannah said. She lowered her pistol and put it back where it belonged.

"Wow, here he is in the flesh—DS himself," Terry said. He gave Hannah a kiss and whispered in her ear, "I think she's legit. She shot three men dead outside our house."

"You need to watch the video, and then you'll know how serious this is," Hannah said. "I should have a few minutes left on the computer on the right."

He nodded back at her. "Thanks," and he walked over to the computer Hannah had used. He watched the introduction from the presenter, then the masked person and the picture slideshow commenced. He saw pictures of his mother, his sister Janet, Hannah ordering lunch at a takeaway drive through, and finally, each of his four children playing in their respective schoolyards.

Terry took a minute to recover. He walked back to sit with the other three, the colour washed from his face. "I'm going to need something stronger than coffee."

THE MAN IN BLACK

HAVE YOU EVER thought it strange that Earth is the only planet with human life forms? But what if that wasn't entirely true?

Imagine the presence of parallel universes—each one having its own planet of humans, but existing in a different era of Earth's own history.

Mr. Black, an avenger with questionable motives, travels through time and dimensions, executing criminals, gangsters, and those who try to stand in his way, in addition to individuals on his own personal hit list.

What drives him to kill? Is anyone safe from his wrath? And can he be stopped before he travels to the next universe on his list?

Acknowledgments

FIRST, MY WRITING journey wouldn't be where it is without the love and support of my family. Special thanks to my wife, Glenda, for being there from near the start of my writing endeavours, and to my three beautiful children, Ethan, Krystal, and Siobhan.

My parents, Noel and Barbara Heinicke, have always been supportive, encouraging me to chase my dreams and keeping me grounded to stay responsible in the process. My sister, Rachel Foster and her husband, Troy have always cheered me along, and for that, I thank them, too.

My writing wouldn't be what it is without the hard work of my editor, Rogena Mitchell-Jones. Not only is she great at her work, but a great friend in helping me get over my self-doubts.

Rebecca Berto from Berto Designs has come through with yet another great cover. Thanks so much again to her for her eye-catching design.

The cover to 7PM is also the work of Mark Holzigal's photography, and the cover model his wife Nicole. Thank you both for providing such a great photo.

Thanks to my beta readers, Kate Annabel, Tracey Hayer-Roberts, and Kathryn Booker. Your input and the time you took to read a yet to be published work is much appreciated. Special mention to Kate Reedwood for going above and beyond for her work on the later volumes and helping me to think more about the characters' motivations.

Over my years on Facebook, I've met many fellow writers at different stages of their writing careers. A network of support and friendship has helped me learn not only about the craft of writing but marketing and networking as well. With each book, the list increases, but those who have been there and who have never hesitated in giving advice or helping to promote my work, and I promise to return the favour where possible. Special thanks to Laura Hunter, Lili Saint Germain, Jacinta Maree, Melissa Crowe, Stephen Ormsby, Kim Stevens, Hayley Coates, Earl Chessher, Desley Polmear, Lea Kirk, Samantha A. Cole, and Baer Charlton, just to name a few. Anyone I've forgotten, I'm very sorry.

I would also like to take this opportunity to thank a local bookstore owner for not only stocking my books but also for allowing me to use his store to launch my book releases. Thanks to Andy Gasson from Magpie Books for his generosity and friendship.

And most of all, where would a writer be without their fans and readers? Thanks to everyone who has supported me, given me feedback, and read my books. Thanks for the words of encouragement and spreading the word about my books. With your help, I know someday I'll be a full-time writer and able to devote time to releasing more books. Special mention to those I call my cheerleaders, Christine Dupre,Kerry Radford, Rose-Marie Haddow, Bianca Lloyd, Tracy Grover, Leesa Barrell, Cooper DMSelector as well as a huge number of my work colleagues with one, in particular, Barb Mawby, following this whole series.

About the Author

CHRIS HEINICKE WAS born in the town of Port Pire, South Australia in 1971. Growing up in a family who moved a lot, Chris was able to see a lot of Australia as a child and teenager, meeting a broad range of people and living in four of six of the country's states and the Northern Territory. Although working as a baker, writing has been a passion for some time, starting in high school and reigniting again in 2006. Since then, he has worked on the first part of a science fiction series. The Man In Black, released in 2015, and a short story, which culminated in a 2014 NaNoWriMo project called 5PM.

Apart from writing, Chris enjoys travelling, reading, and watching movies, as well as all things geeky. He resides in the New South Wales beachside town of Coffs Harbour with his wife and three children and is currently working on projects connected with 5PM and The Man In Black.